PARTY'S OVER

All at once the sound level dropped to a hush. The silence was broken by Jeffrey's voice at the front door. "What are you doing here?"

"Why, darling, you know I adore parties."

Amanda stood at the front door, stately, slender, frighteningly erect and composed. She was absolutely breathtaking. But her eyes were hard, cold, crystalline, hate-filled.

Suddenly their gazes locked. Victoria felt scorched and withered by a gust of hatred of incredible ferocity. Then a mocking smile widened the corners of Amanda's mouth...

The Ex

JERAMIE HYATT

AVON
PUBLISHERS OF BARD, CAMELOT, DISCUS AND FLARE BOOKS

THE EX is an original publication of Avon Books. This work has never appeared before in book form. This work is a novel. Any similarity to actual persons or events is purely coincidental.

AVON BOOKS
A division of
The Hearst Corporation
1790 Broadway
New York, New York 10019

First Avon Printing, July, 1984

AVON TRADEMARK REG. U. S. PAT. OFF. AND IN OTHER COUNTRIES, MARCA REGISTRADA, HECHO EN U. S. A.

Printed in the U. S. A.

WFH 10 9 8 7 6 5 4 3 2 1

Für mein bess'res Ich

Prologue

IT IS THE KIND of lovely afternoon only the city can create—the air clear, the sun warm on the sidewalk, the breeze cool. It is sweater weather, with a hint of the pinch of winter to come, the kind of day that lures office workers from their desks to lunch on frankfurters purchased from carts, the kind of day that brings secretaries outside to sit on concrete benches and turn their faces to the kindness of the sun. Even executives, hurrying from boardrooms to luncheons, breathe deeply and remark on the invigorating weather.

It is a perfect day, just the day for a long stroll around the neighborhood, for looking in shop windows and pausing to examine the items displayed there. Victoria Keating, seven months pregnant, is doing just that. Her doctor has said that walking is the best exercise, long walks, in fact, so she is circling the blocks directly across town from her apartment, gazing at the items in the windows she passes, dreaming about the baby and how she will wear the new fashions once her figure has returned to normal. She sighs and inspects a display of mannequins dressed in suede skirts, culottes, vests, and shirts; the suedes are buttery-looking and beautifully colored, tans, blues, soft greens, mauves. She could never afford them but she appreciates their beauty.

She is on Madison Avenue, where one shop after another displays European names and fashions. She knows this stretch of the street very well, since she has worked only a few blocks away for five years. In that time, she has seen many older shops close as the rents escalated. They were replaced by fancy boutiques, specialty food stores, Italian shoe shops. She cannot afford to shop here, but she loves to look.

She passes La Cuisinière, glancing at the copper pots and porcelain bowls and platters displayed in the window, then moves downtown, toward Yves St. Laurent. She knows the order of the shops by heart, knows that the following block will have the Madison Avenue Bookshop, George Kovacs, Pratesi for linens and towels, the Surrey Liquor Shop. She moves confidently past, familiar with the neighborhood, wishing she could afford to shop in many of the stores. She crosses Sixty-ninth Street and begins one last block before turning back and there, where she is accustomed to seeing Veneziano—no, it is next to Veneziano, but what is it doing there? She sees a black awning protruding over the sidewalk . . . a canopy, supported by four metal posts. She stops to see if anyone else has noticed this change, but the pedestrians continue their cool progress up and down the avenue. She stares. There is no name on the canopy and, oddly enough, the canvas is black. She walks to the door of the strange shop, but it is closed. She reaches out and turns the knob, but it is locked. There is no sign to indicate the shop's name. She moves to the plate-glass window. It is draped with black curtains. A placard rests against the glass, supported by a small ledge near the bottom of the window. She has to stoop down very low to look. It seems to be a menu; of course, that would make sense—a new restaurant, one that hasn't yet had its name emblazoned on its awning. She bends over awkwardly and tries to read the small print on the placard. She reads only one word, "Rosemary's," when someone taps her on the shoulder. Thinking it is perhaps the owner of the new establishment who is pleased by her interest, or perhaps another passerby as curious as she about the place, she fixes a smile in place as she slowly raises herself up, smooths her hands over her protruding belly, and begins to turn around, saying, "I really didn't get a chance to read the—" when she catches a glimpse of something glinting in that bright afternoon sun, something bright and metallic. Then it registers—*a knife blade*, this is a knife *that is going to hurt me*—down comes the glittering blade in an arc, moving both fast and slow, and the blade is plunged into Victoria's protruding belly.

She screams. Her mouth is open and she can hear

8

the scream echoing in her own head but there is no sound. She is trapped in a kind of ether. Everything is moving very slowly...everything is thick...no sound comes out of her mouth.

Then, as if a short circuit in an electrical wire is finally repaired, the scream connects, the sound comes on, and she sits up. She is completely drenched with sweat. She is awake now, but she is not safe.

Chapter One

THERE'S NOTHING QUITE LIKE dumping blueberry yogurt on a man's shoe to get the love of your life off on the right foot. Only in this case it was the left foot.

As so often happens, the event which was to send Victoria's life into its wild new orbit started on a totally prosaic note. Her friend Gail had called to say she had come down with a devastating strain of flu and needed a few things from the grocery. Could Victoria bring them up to her apartment and keep her company after school?

That was perfectly fine with Vicky, although there were three hundred things she needed to do, such as correct a batch of English tests, pick up her shoes at the repair shop, wash her hair, call her parents to wish them a happy anniversary, shop for a new cotton suit to wear to school, go to the library to see if the new Margaret Atwood had come in, and visit the new health and racquet club in her neighborhood to check out the facilities, membership fees, and social potential; and then there were the things she would have preferred to do on such a glorious spring afternoon, like dash over to the Metropolitan Museum to catch the exhibition of Persian miniatures before it closed, or even just sit down on a bench to people-watch and take some notes for the stories she wrote in her spare time.

It wasn't as if Gail were an invalid shut-in languishing in a cold-water flat, exactly. She was a lawyer who lived in a Park Avenue co-op in the heart of the Gristede's luxury supermarket district, and had not one but two boyfriends who gladly would have done her bidding. Nor was it as if Gail and Vicky were such tight friends. They knew each other from college, and from time to time they got together for a drink and a little gossip. Nor, certainly, was it that Gristede's didn't deliver. But whenever Gail got sick, she absolutely *had* to have Vicky come over and nurse her. No one else would do. Sometimes Vicky was flattered by Gail's request, but this time she felt imposed upon.

Watching her storming up and down the aisles of the Gristede's on Madison Avenue and Eighty-fifth Street, then, the casual observer would have found it hard to conclude that she was performing an act of charity. She tossed cans into the cart so hard they rang and flung cardboard cartons about with fury. She broadly interpreted every instruction, so that "any kind of coffee" became an incredibly expensive Hawaiian Kona and "a wedge of cheese" became a quadrant of imported Brie that could vie with silver on the commodity exchange. And "pick up something for yourself" sent Vicky to the deli counter for half a pound of sliced Westphalian ham that would have made a serious dent in a private school teacher's salary if it were not to be reimbursed.

She felt a profound kinship with bag ladies as she trudged over to Park Avenue and south toward Seventy-ninth Street. In addition to two grocery bags weighted with a sixty-four-ounce bottle of apple juice and a six-pack of diet soda, Vicky carried her attaché case under her left arm and her purse, with a shoulder strap that had broken three months ago, under her right. As she approached Gail's apartment building, a prewar beige brick building faced with rose-colored marble, a red-cheeked Irish doorman in braided black uniform cast a gimlet eye on her until he realized she was turning in to the lobby. Then he snatched the bags out of her hands, cleared her admittance with Gail on the intercom, and carried the bags to the elevator, where he set them down heavily on the marble floor. She thought she heard a bottle crack.

Just as she had pushed the elevator button a tall, athletic-looking man in an expensive linen suit turned the corner. He was carrying an attaché case of soft suede; it put to shame her own tattered leatherette case which she'd parked next to her groceries while waiting for the elevator to arrive. He clutched a thick collection

11

of mail and glared at it with such preoccupation he almost bowled her over. He muttered, "Excuse me," and shuffled through the envelopes, most of which had glassine windows. He raised his eyes, studied her, then returned to his bills. He tore open several at random (she noticed his fingers, long and graceful, nails professionally buffed and coated with clear lacquer) and studied their contents, uttering expressions of displeasure. "Jeez!" "Shit!" "Oh Christ, not again!"

Vicky tapped her foot impatiently, waiting for the elevator. Out of the corner of her eye she noticed something moving on the floor. She looked down and saw with horror a puddle of juice beneath one shopping bag, a stream of which was extending in amoeba fashion toward the gentleman's elegantly shod feet. She tapped him on the shoulder. He looked faintly annoyed, as if perversely resenting being interrupted in the torturous examination of his bills. His eyes were limpid, gray or green, and intelligent but self-important and businesslike. "Excuse me, sir, but your foot? It's about to be engulfed."

He looked down and sidestepped the brachiating puddle.

"Apple juice," she explained sheepishly.

"Wouldn't it be easier to buy it in bottles instead of having them pour it into your shopping bag?" His mouth remained solemn, but his eyes flashed momentarily, belying his seriousness.

"Bottle broke," she explained unnecessarily, feeling extremely dumb. She knelt to remove the groceries from the sopping, disintegrating paper bag and to transfer them to the other.

"Careful, there's broken glass in there." He delicately reached into the wet bag and fished out the remaining items, stuffing them into the last nooks and crevices of the good bag. He stepped back and admired his handiwork. "I graduated from the A&P checkout counter, class of fifty-four."

But Vicky was too embarrassed to smile at his little joke, and she hastily snatched up the heavily laden bag. That's when the container of yogurt tipped out and fell to the floor, bursting open and hurling a blob of purple yogurt onto his shoe. Although it happened in an instant, it had that dreamy slow-motion quality that seems to characterize significant events in life. Years later, she could still remember the white cup with the purple-blue lid somersaulting out of the bag like a space satellite tumbling through the sky. She could read the brand name written in script and see the spray of blueberries beneath it, the print that said "net wt. 8 oz. (227 g)," and, on the back, the nutrition information per serving and the Percentage of U.S. Recommended Daily Allowance and the list of Protein and Vitamin A and Thiamine and Riboflavin.

The man stared down at his feet. "A baby kangaroo died that that shoe might live," he said. The odd thing was how little anger there was in his voice. He was being almost good-natured about it, or at least fatalistic. He seemed to care less about his shoe than he did about her mortification, which was so intense she thought her cheeks would burst into flame. "Of course," he added, reaching into the pocket of his suit jacket, "if these things have to happen, one could wish for plain or vanilla, or at least coffee yogurt to match the leather, don't you agree?"

"Oh, God, I'm so, so sorry," she moaned, putting the bags down and opening her purse. She fumbled for some tissues and knelt down to wipe his shoe.

He reached down under her arm and pulled her sharply to her feet. "Hey, no, don't do that!" He snatched the tissues out of her hand and knelt down himself. "I pay two bucks to have my shoes shined." He put his mail on a little table beside the elevator and proceeded to wipe off his shoe. The elevator arrived and several people stepped over the gobbets of yogurt floating in a pool of apple juice.

Victoria glanced at the mail fanned out on the table like a poker hand. As she'd guessed, it was almost all bills: the gray of Bloomingdale's, the purple of Bonwit's, the aqua of Tiffany's, a rainbow of charges requiring, no doubt, a pot of gold to pay for them. They were addressed to Mrs. Jeffrey Keating, she observed.

Jeffrey Keating covered the mess with the remaining tissues and shouted, "Andy!"

"Yes, Mr. Keating?" the doorman answered.

13

"We've had a little accident here. Get the porter to mop it up."

"Sure thing, Mr. Keating."

The elevator door had closed, but it opened immediately when Keating touched the button. "Here, I'll help you," he said, tucking his attaché case under one arm and sliding the grocery bag into the elevator. "Floor?"

"Um, twelve."

He tapped twelve, then fourteen. He knitted his brows. "You don't live here."

"No, I'm just visiting a sick friend."

"Ah. I hope your friend wasn't counting on blueberry yogurt and apple juice."

They looked down at his left shoe. The polish had warded off any serious damage. When Vicky looked up again she noticed with a start that he was studying her face. The mask of good humor he had donned after the accident had fallen for an instant to reveal a face intense and troubled, even grave. He was studying her, but not in the sense of some interested male looking over an attractive female. He seemed to be searching her face for something, something he needed badly, though he could not articulate just what it was. It was not a rude stare, but its directness unsettled her. She lifted her eyes to the row of lighted numbers over the elevator door. She felt she'd spent an hour with him and was surprised to find that the elevator had only passed the sixth floor. When she turned her eyes back to his face, he had donned the mask again, and indeed he seemed to have reddened slightly with embarrassment.

"I hope it isn't catching," he said.

"Catching?"

"What your friend is sick from."

"Oh no, she's just got the flu."

"Ah, *she*," he said with a strange note of relief.

The elevator stopped at twelve and Vicky stooped to pick up her package. But he had grabbed them and stepped out of the elevator. "Where to, lady?"

"Oh, thank you. Twelve-J, to the left."

He followed her down the corridor and set the bag down in front of the door to 12-J. She had a definite

14

feeling that he was clinging to the moment, reluctant to disengage from her. She raised her hand to the doorbell but lowered it when she realized he was not going to turn away. "Well," she said, "thank you. And I'm sorry again about your shoe. It doesn't seem to have been fatal, though."

"No, not fatal." He seemed rooted and kept looking at her with the same intensity as he'd done in the elevator. Then, realizing he was staring, he blinked and reassumed his casual manner. He thrust out the palm of his hand. "Just waiting for a tip."

Vicky smiled, then placed her hand over his and gave it a hard shake. "Here's a tip, Mr. Keating: go back to Mrs. Keating."

He seemed almost flustered. "How did you know my name?"

She tapped his bills with her fingernail. "And the doorman shouted your name, remember?"

"Right." He stood another moment, milking it. "You're absolutely right. I must go back to Mrs. Keating. I hope your friend is better." He pivoted and trudged back down the corridor. As she pushed Gail's bell, she watched his receding figure. He seemed to have lost a little bounce, like a balloon left overnight in a child's room.

Gail Harrison, less than resplendent in chenille robe and fuzzy slippers, stood pathetically at the kitchen door watching Victoria put the groceries away. Ordinarily attractive, well-groomed, independent, and self-possessed, she reverted completely to infancy whenever she came down with something and invariably turned to Vicky for mothering. Vicky always resolved to have an excuse handy the next time Gail called, but somehow Gail seemed to catch her unprepared, and Vicky was a poor liar.

"It's *so* dice of you to do this for be," Gail intoned, dabbing at red-rimmed eyes.

Vicky stood before an open cupboard, trying to figure out how her friend organized her shelves. "Where does the mustard go?"

"Id the door of the refrigerator."

Vicky looked at her. "Why? The jar is unopened."

15

Gail shrugged. "By buther did it that way, ad by buther's buther. Who ab I to break with traditiod? Who were you talkig to id the hall?"

"This man I met in the lobby. He helped me with my packages. Jeffrey Keating?"

Gail raised an eyebrow. "Are you od a first-dabe basis yet?"

Vicky shot her friend a dirty look. "No, I still call hib Bister Keatig."

"Ohh, do't bake fud of be. How'd you like it if I bade fud of you whed you were at death's door?" She picked up a kettle and filled it with water. "Baybe sub steab would clear by dose." She placed the kettle on the stove and turned on the flame. "So? How'd you get Jeffrey Keatig to carry your packages to by door?"

Vicky told her what had happened in the lobby. Then, "Tell me about him."

Through the pall of flu, Gail beamed. "Why, Victoria Lewis, you have udclead thoughts! Daughty! Daughty!"

"Oh, for God's sake! I ask about a man and I have unclean thoughts!"

"Why dot? *I* have unclead thoughts about hib. He's very hadsub."

"That's easy to see. But he also looked, well, a little lost."

Gail tilted her head. "You really thik so? He's the last bad I'd call lost. He's the origidal bad who has everythig."

"And pays for everything, too. You should see his bills."

"He showed you his bills?"

"I just saw the envelopes. A great big stack of them."

"Well, it *is* the edd of the budth."

Vicky stared at her uncomprehendingly. "Edd of the budth?"

Gail stared back, frustration written on her face. "Edd of the budth, edd of the budth. What do you call the last day of April?"

"Ah, the edd of the budth."

"Right. Everybody gets a lot of bills at the edd of the budth."

"Not like these. He got more bills in one mail than I get in one year."

"If you saw his wife, you'd udderstad why."

"A real clotheshorse, huh?"

"Oh, buch, buch bore. Studdig, studdig wubbid."

Vicky burst into laughter. "Wait a minute, folks, until I read the subtitles. You said, 'Much, much more. Stunning, stunning woman.'"

"I'll get you for this, Vicky Lewis." Gail padded to the linen closet in her foyer and returned with a beach towel, which she threw over her head to form a tent. She leaned over the spout of the boiling kettle and inhaled the steam.

"So, she runs up a lot of bills?" Vicky asked to her friend's back.

"He can afford it."

"Rich, huh?"

"Seems to be. Has his own P.R. agency. Big co-op upstairs, bought two apartments and broke through. Beautifully decorated. I think Amanda did it herself."

"The wife."

"Un-huh. I was up there once for a co-op meeting. Notice I said 'meeting,' not 'beatig.' I think the steam is working. Anyway, it's right out of *Architectural Digest*. *Plus* a house in the Hamptons."

"Children?"

"One, a little girl. Also right out of *Architectural Digest*. A Romney portrait come to life. Spit 'n' image of her mother. Titian hair, porcelain skin, crystal eyes, the whole bit. Anyway, that's Jeffrey Keating. Believe me, he's not hurting."

"I'm not so sure."

Gail furrowed her brow. "What did he say? Just how long did this elevator ride take?"

"It's just something I saw in his eyes."

Gail's brow furrowed another wrinkle. "Vicky, are you interested in this man?"

Vicky waved her hands. "For God's sake, I spent six minutes with him! Can't I ask questions without your putting the wrong interpretation on everything? He's married, Gail. From what you tell me, he's *very* married. And you know where I stand with married men."

"'Never again' were your precise words, I believe."

"No, my precise words were, 'Never, ever, *ever* again,'" said Vicky, face darkening.

17

Gail shrank back, intimidated by the power of Vicky's emotion. Then Gail shrugged. "It's mandatory for single girls in New York to get fucked over by a married man at least once. You can look it up—article six, section three of the New York City Single Girl's Code."

"I'm not ready to laugh about it," Vicky said. "Maybe ten years from now, but not now." Even as she spoke she felt the searing pain of those months of torture. It all came back as if it had happened moments ago. Once more she was lounging in Steve's bed, her body tingling with the love they had made a half hour ago. Steve had run downstairs to get cigarettes, and the phone rang. He had told her never to pick up his phone—business reasons. But it rang so insistently, she thought maybe it was Steve calling from downstairs to say, "I'm nuts about you, I'm coming right up, don't move." He did crazy things like that.

After about twelve rings she picked it up. "Hello?"

"Is Steve there?" It was a woman's voice, a nice voice but congested as if the woman had been crying.

"He just went out for a second. Who's calling?"

"His wife. Who's this?"

"His . . . wife?"

"Who *is* this?" And then, in the background, a tiny little voice, and the woman cupping the phone and saying, "Hush, Bethie, I'm trying to get hold of Daddy now."

That's when Vicky learned that Steve had a wife. And a child. And that's when Steve's wife learned that he had a girl friend living in their Manhattan pied-à-terre.

What had been a heavenly dream turned into a nightmare in those seconds, but one from which she could not wake up, one which in fact got worse and worse as Steve tried to cover his betrayal with lies, excuses, promises, doubletalk, and more betrayals. Then came the climactic scene where he had gotten drunk and struck her, and she'd stormed out of his apartment . . .

She blinked and realized that Gail had been talking to her, giving her a pep talk about getting over bad love affairs. ". . . otherwise," her voice dispelled the fog in Vicky's brain, "you'll be afraid to take chances for the rest of your life."

"You're right," Vicky said automatically. "But I'll never be as naive as I was then."

"I should hope not. But at least tell me this: *would* you be interested in Jeffrey Keating if he weren't married?"

"Well," Vicky answered after a moment of solemn pondering, "as you say, he's very hadsub."

That closed the case on Jeffrey Keating, or at least Vicky thought it did. Then came the incident in May.

It happened on a Friday, assembly day at the Colby School for Girls where she taught. Fridays were half days at most New York City private schools, a tradition created to enable parents to get away early for their weekends in the Hamptons or Bucks County. As little work got accomplished Friday mornings, school headmasters and mistresses wrote the day off by scheduling assemblies.

The program for that Friday was the lower school's adaptation of *Peter and the Wolf,* followed by a musical presented by the upper school. Assemblies were conducted in the basement auditorium.

A little before ten, Vicky led her ninth grade homeroom class down the spiral staircase of the old Creighton mansion, which had been converted into a school some forty years earlier. The stairs resounded and the halls thundered with the shouts of hundreds of children and parents funneling toward the basement stairs.

As Vicky approached the first floor landing, she casually surveyed the crowd of parents. She never failed to be awed by the collective affluence of these handsome, beautiful, confident, coiffed and manicured men and women. She did not envy them particularly, and indeed when she got to know them individually they seemed as vulnerable and fallible as anyone else. But en masse they were formidable, radiant, and not a little intimidating.

She was just reflecting along those lines when her eyes were drawn to a splendid profusion of red hair that magnetized attention like a splash of burnished gold in a dark portrait. The color was unique, copper tinged

19

with auburn that converted the sun streaming through the fanlight of the portal into something more akin to energy than color. Vicky's eyes moved quickly downward to see if the rest of the woman was worthy of those tresses. She was. Tall, slim, stately; her face was exquisitely molded with high cheekbones and noble nose. It was hard to see her eyes from Vicky's angle on the staircase, but she thought she glimpsed a slate-gray or green, the color of a winter sea. Her full and sensuous mouth was slightly pursed in exasperation, apparently because the crowd was moving too slowly to suit her. She wore a white knit dress with a light linen jacket. Her figure was perfect. Altogether the impression was one of imperial hauteur, and Vicky did not begrudge it to her, saying to herself that if she had even half of that woman's attributes, she'd carry herself no less regally.

It was natural for Vicky to wonder what manner of consort would attend such a creature, and her eyes moved to the figure beside the magnificent red-haired woman. The answer brought her up so sharply she caused a chain reaction collision all the way up the stairs. Jeffrey Keating was the manner of consort who attended such a creature.

So this was Amanda Keating, the "studdig, studdig wubbid" that Gail Harrison had rhapsodized over!

Jeffrey Keating looked dapper in a navy summerweight blazer, from the breast pocket of which a flamboyant yellow handkerchief blossomed. From his neck dangled a 35-millimeter camera in black leather case. The principal emotion on his face was pride in the spectacular beauty whose arm was linked in his. It was comical the way several men maneuvered their wives through the crowd in order to obtain a fuller view of Amanda Keating. One man, obviously a casual acquaintance, said something to her, and Vicky surmised that what he said was not entirely proper. Amanda threw her head back and laughed lustily.

Jeffrey Keating must have been accustomed to such exchanges, for he did not change his expression but merely gazed around the lofty foyer, absorbed in his own thoughts. It was then that his eyes came to rest on Victoria's face. He tilted his head and frowned faintly as he tried to place her. Suddenly recognition filled his eyes, and he raised his hand in a friendly wave. At that moment his wife, spying a gap in the crowd, surged through it, and Jeffrey lurched after her like a vaudeville comic being yanked off the stage. Jeffrey cast one last look at Vicky over his shoulder. Within moments they had blended into the throng descending to the auditorium.

What were they doing here? The answer came to Vicky at once, and after shepherding her class to their appropriate section she picked up the mimeographed program that had been left on her chair. She ran her finger down it until she found what she had been looking for. The part of the bird in *Peter and the Wolf* was to be played by Daria Keating. Of course! The Keatings' daughter was a Colby student.

Daria. Vicky rolled the name around her mouth. A mellifluous name. A delicate name. A pampered name. She searched her memory for a recollection of the child, and once red hair was programmed into the equation it was easy to figure out who Daria Keating was. There was only one head of hair like it in the school. Sure enough, when she fluttered out on stage, Daria confirmed Vicky's speculation. Gail had once again hit the mark squarely: titian hair, porcelain skin, crystal eyes— a Romney portrait come to life. Vicky watched her performance with enchantment.

The role of the bird, Daria's part, was not exactly substantial. Dressed in tutu and cap to which some pasteboard feathers had been appended, Daria flapped around the stage tweeting, chased by Lisa Bantree in the role of the cat. At that moment a flashbulb popped and Vicky, remembering the camera around Jeffrey Keating's neck, traced the blue flash to him. He was kneeling in the aisle close to the stage. He took another shot of his daughter perched in a tree just beyond the cat's frustrated claws. Then he did something unexpected. Instead of returning to his seat, he leaned over and said something to his wife, then walked up the aisle toward the exit. He looked left and right, peering into the darkness as if seeking someone. Vicky had the unsettling feeling that he was looking for her. This time he did not catch sight of her.

21

He did not return, and she figured he'd had to rush off to work, as many parents often did during assemblies. To work was not where he had gone, however, as Vicky learned the following Monday.

On that day, late in the morning, Vicky had to visit the headmistress's office to pick up some permission forms for an upcoming outing. Mrs. Dolittle, a stiff gray-coiffed woman who ran the school with no-nonsense firmness, was examining some ledgers when Vicky came in. As she opened the file drawer containing the forms, Mrs. Dolittle called out to her, "Did Mr. Keating get in touch with you?"

Vicky stiffened. "I beg your pardon?"

"Jeffrey Keating—did he contact you? He was up here Friday morning asking about you. During assembly."

Vicky swallowed hard and felt her neck and cheeks warming with embarrassment. "Uh, no, he didn't. Why would he?"

"He said he thought you were the daughter of an old war buddy of his father's."

Vicky almost laughed. It was among the most preposterous stories she'd ever heard. Vicky was twenty-six. Her father was fifty; he could not have been more than five or six when World War II broke out. She could imagine Jeffrey Keating grasping at whatever impromptu excuse that came to mind for inquiring about her. Did the suspicious look in Mrs. Dolittle's eye suggest that the headmistress didn't buy Keating's story either? "He went through *The Colbian*," Mrs. Dolittle said, referring to the school yearbook.

Vicky caught her breath. "He must be mistaken. At any rate, Mr. Keating didn't get in touch with me. I'm sorry if he took up your time."

"He pays for my time," Mrs. Dolittle said with a glimmer of humor in her eyes. Vicky tucked the permission forms under her arm and departed as quickly as she could.

In the corridor she leaned against a wall, slightly stunned. Jeffrey Keating had not only been looking for her, he'd been looking her up. And what's more, he *had* gotten in touch with her. For, late Friday afternoon and again on Sunday evening, her phone had rung. She'd picked it up but after a pause the caller had hung up without speaking.

She now knew who it had been.

She received no more anonymous calls that week; in fact, she received no more at all. But for weeks afterward she thought about the man who had made them, and tried to construct a profile of him based on their one encounter, her glimpse of him at school, and his subsequent strange behavior.

From Gail's description, he was very married. That was easy to see. Any man with a wife of such surpassing beauty would have to be very married to her indeed, particularly if he had enough money to keep her happy. Now, from the bills he'd displayed that day, and his agonizings over them, it was clear that if Jeffrey didn't *have* enough money to keep his wife happy, he at least *spent* enough to do so. Or could you ever spend enough on someone to keep her happy?

For the answer to that question, Vicky had only the flimsy evidence of his troubled look in the elevator, a look that spoke of some unfulfilled longing, some vague restlessness and dissatisfaction. Did he look at everybody that way, or was there something special about her that promised an answer? She certainly had not "come on" to him, as her students liked to say. She'd been so embarrassed in the elevator she'd scarcely looked at him at all.

After the elevator incident he must, she figured, have put the matter aside. But Friday, when he saw her on the staircase, that interest must have been aroused in him again, this time to such a degree that he'd gone to the trouble—the risk!—of inquiring about her. War buddies, for God's sake!

In the weeks that followed, she sometimes found herself standing before a mirror and gazing at herself through what she imagined might be Jeffrey Keating's searching eyes. What was he seeking, and what in Vicky's face suggested she had what he needed? The mirror told her only that anyone looking at her face would find honesty. She was attractive enough, with shoulder-length dark hair and a well-proportioned oval face. But there was no guile in her dark eyes, no promise of anything more than warmth and sincerity. Was that it?

23

Was that what Jeffrey Keating needed so urgently he would take partial leave of his senses?

The anonymous phone calls were the real mystery. Why did he call? And, having called, why did he not speak? The contradictions pointed to a man in quiet but possibly profound conflict. It was as if he needed desperately to speak to her, yet feared that once he did so he might be committing himself to some treacherous course, forging the first of a chain of events that would lead God knew where.

That would explain why he called no more. Had he now concluded how pointless it was to start something he would not be able to finish? Inevitably, as time passed, he would put her out of his mind as he had done the first time. She could imagine him becoming caught up in summer plans, the house in the Hamptons, a trip to Europe, camp for Daria. He had regained his senses, and so must Vicky. Just as inevitably, he faded from *her* mind.

School ended the first week in June, and she plunged into summertime as if catapulted. She had accepted a position as group counselor in a music and art day camp in Westchester where she'd worked the previous summer, and before camp commenced in July there were a thousand things she wanted to cram in, for it was her only truly free time during the entire year. She shopped for clothes, visited art galleries, rearranged her furniture, visited with girlfriends, spent a weekend on Fire Island, read eight or nine books and wrote a couple of short stories. After camp began, she had no more free time. The work was stimulating but taxing because of her heavy responsibilities. In addition, it rained a lot the first two weeks, requiring her to organize many indoor activities. Every evening she returned home exhausted, flopping into bed and falling asleep by ten-thirty after reading two or three pages of a book.

The weather turned clear the third week in July, and things eased up at camp. Vicky, tanned and fit, felt herself swelling with ambition and energy and began venturing out a little later in the evenings.

One of her projects was to go to Sloane's furniture clearance center on the East Side to look at some convertible sofas to replace the frayed, saggy couch that had followed her like an aging pet since college days. It made sense that for the price of a couch she could get something convertible into a bed when friends or family visited her in New York. And so on a muggy Thursday evening she boarded the Eighty-sixth Street crosstown bus and got off at Lexington Avenue, then walked over to Eighty-fourth Street to survey Sloane's selection. She narrowed the choices to three and decided to return with a friend to help her make the final choice.

Absorbed in the profound quandary of fabric color versus price, she was only dimly aware as she crossed at the corner of Lexington and Eighty-fifth Street that someone was following her, calling her name. At last the voice penetrated, a male voice she recognized from someplace in the past. "Victoria? Victoria?"

When she reached the curb she turned around.

It was Jeffrey Keating.

On the two previous occasions she'd seen him he'd been modishly dressed in suit or slacks and blazer. This evening he was wearing tight white duck pants, an open neck checked sports shirt that revealed a muscular chest, and tennis sneakers; it required an act of intense concentration to link this man to the one she had encountered earlier. He carried a plastic shopping bag filled with a few groceries. He was darkly tanned, and his hair seemed a little blonder than she'd remembered, probably because it had been bleached by the sun of the Hamptons. A faint patina of perspiration glistened on his forehead. In the glare of the avenue's streetlights and store windows, his expression was unguarded; a grin crinkled the fan of little lines around the corners of his eyes. He caught up with her, panting slightly.

Victoria felt a surge of gladness completely at odds with the urgings of her better judgment. This was a potentially dangerous situation, given the signs of interest in her that Jeffrey Keating had shown. In the moments that passed before he spoke, she resolved to discourage any ideas he might have about developing that interest.

"Victoria Lewis, right?"

"That's me."

"I thought so. I just caught a glimpse of you as I was

25

coming out of the superette, but when you didn't answer after I called your name..."

Victoria gazed at him but said nothing, waiting to see what he said next.

"Jeffrey Keating, remember? The yogurt-on-the-shoe man?"

"Of course," said Vicky, struggling to maintain a frosty tone. He seemed so genuinely happy to see her, she almost felt it would be wrong to dampen his enthusiasm. "Our fathers fought in the war together, right?"

"Oh God." He grimaced.

"I was a little unclear as to which war. Was that World War II, Korea, or Vietnam?"

He squared his shoulders pugnaciously. "I'm not going to apologize for what I did."

"I didn't ask for an apology. You'll notice I didn't even ask for an explanation." She took a few steps toward Eighty-sixth Street but he blocked her path.

"But I do owe you an explanation. You see..." He hesitated, opened his mouth a second time, then shut it dejectedly. His shoulders slumped. "I don't think I have a good explanation."

"I don't think you do, either," Vicky said.

"I hope I didn't get you into any trouble."

"I'll tell you the answer to that only if you'll tell me if that was you who called me that weekend."

He lowered his eyes and nodded. "It would take hours to explore the intricacies of my motivations. So how about having a drink with me?"

"No. And good night, Mr. Keating." Vicky dodged around the obstacle of his body and continued purposefully up Lexington Avenue toward her bus stop. Jeffrey walked briskly beside her, imploring.

"Please? Just a quick one? What's your rush? Do you have to get home to someone? I can't leave things this way. Please, Victoria, I have to talk to you. I won't hurt you. I'll check my guns at the door."

Vicky stopped and planted her feet. "Look, I'll be as blunt with you as I can. I don't want anything to do with married men."

"I'll get a divorce," he said. It was supposed to be a joke but he almost reeled with the shock of having ut-

26

tered it. "Jesus, did you hear what I just said?" He said it as much to himself as to her.

"I've heard that particular line before, Mr. Keating, and that's why I don't want anything to do with married men."

His eyes had suddenly glazed and he appeared to have withdrawn deep into himself. "Yes. Of course. It was crazy of me. I'm sorry. I won't bother you anymore." He seemed to be in a dream.

Vicky found herself rooted to the sidewalk, incapable of letting him go. "You seem a solid family man, Mr. Keating. What you want from me I can't imagine."

"I can see that."

She ordered her muscles to move but the hurt in his eyes was like a magnet. The power to resist her own curiosity was draining from her with each passing moment. She looked at his grocery bag. "Aren't you expected home?"

"Huh? Oh, these? These are for me. I'm by myself. My family's out of town."

"Summer bachelor, eh?"

"Hardly. Something came up with my business. I had to return to the city."

Vicky nodded. "I couldn't imagine you'd choose Manhattan sidewalks over Hampton beaches."

"Yes, I..." He brought himself up short and looked intensely at her. "How do you know about my house in the Hamptons?"

Vicky flushed. "Uh, I just assumed..."

"No you didn't. You asked someone about me."

"No."

"Yes," he gloated. "You've been inquiring about me the same as I've been inquiring about you."

Vicky swallowed hard. His face was a portrait of triumph. Then she thrust her chin up combatively. "I'm not going to apologize for what I did." Her imitation of him was perfect. He laughed.

"Will you change your mind about that drink?"

She fought one last skirmish with herself, then yielded silently. He clasped her arm and guided her to Third Avenue and Eighty-third Street, Martell's. They took a table outside near the railing, and for a minute, before the waiter arrived, Jeffrey sat staring at her euphorically. Disconcerted and embarrassed by his directness, she said, "I hope you don't have any groceries that will spoil in this heat."

He opened the bag and looked in it. "Stouffer's Escalloped Chicken with Noodles. I give it an hour to melt." He raised his eyes. "How long will it take you to melt?"

"I'm a much bigger chicken," Vicky said.

The waiter came and Jeffrey issued the drink order with the easy confidence of a man comfortable with command. Vicky said white wine, he scotch and soda, and he was very specific about the twist of lemon and not too much ice. There was an uneasy hiatus in their conversation. They sat in their chairs avoiding each other's eyes, watching the people strolling by on Third Avenue, the taxis and cars speeding by, the other couples drinking, eating, chatting, smoking. It had been dark for some time but the sky was still lit by the city's lights projected against a low cloud cover. The still air was damp and hot; there was a strong smell of auto exhaust trapped near the ground.

When the drinks came, Jeffrey saluted her with his. She did not return the gesture. She simply sipped her wine in silence and looked at him over the rim of her glass. "I'm waiting," she said at last.

"I know you are. I'm just having a hard time putting it into words. You see, when I saw you in my building...there was something about you...oh, shit." He tilted his glass and gulped twice. Then he brightened as he apparently found a handle. "A friend of mine once said to me, 'Falling in love is sometimes a matter of who's standing next to you when you're seized by a great idea.'"

Vicky pondered it and said, "I'm sure your friend was a man. That's not how women fall in love." She lapsed into silence, reflecting again on the epigram. "Have you been seized by a great idea?"

"I think so," he said. "Yes, I think I have. But I'm not sure what it is, and I'm afraid to think about it. It's too scary. But I know one thing. There's something about you that's attracted me as nothing else has. It was instantaneous."

"Love at first yogurt," she laughed, but the laugh

28

sounded hollow to her. His solemnity was making her extremely nervous. She said, "Do you really expect me to believe that?"

"I would give anything to make you believe I have not spoken to a woman this way, not even thought about one this way, in my entire ten years of marriage. Tell me what I have to do. You want me to cut off an ear? Waiter, a steak knife, please?"

There was no waiter within earshot, but it made her laugh, and she relaxed a little. His sincerity was touching, and she realized that she did want to believe him. Could she? Should she? The wine seemed to warm her emotions, and she could feel her resistance softening, like asphalt on a hot summer day. "You know," she said, "I went back to visit my friend Gail in your building a couple of times after that day. But I never did see you."

"You looked for me?" He half raised himself out of his seat. "Tell me you looked for me. Tell me you just eeny-teeny this much looked for me," he begged, holding thumb and index finger a quarter of an inch separated.

She laughed again, holding her thumb and index finger up. "Eeny-teeny."

"You liked me, right? *Like* at first sight."

"I don't know if I would say that."

"Oh God. Waiter, make that a ceremonial sword. I'm going to kill myself."

"I mean, I guess I was interested in you. But I don't know you."

"At least you know I'm not a homicidal maniac, right?"

"Not a homicidal one, no."

He laughed heartily. "Why am I a maniac? Just because I fell in love with you like that?" He snapped his fingers. "It only means that I'm more susceptible than you."

"Oh, I'm very susceptible, Jeffrey. Just a little better at protecting myself than you seem to be."

"You called me Jeffrey."

"Of course I called you Jeffrey. That's your name, isn't it?"

"You could have called me Mr. Keating. But you

called me Jeffrey. Proving beyond a shadow of a doubt that you're in love with me too. Waiter, cancel the sword, bring me champagne instead."

A waiter happened to be standing just behind him. "Champagne?"

Jeffrey gagged. "No, I was just...yes, champagne. Champagne, goddammit. Piper-Heidsieck."

The waiter's eyebrows arched.

"And two straws," Jeffrey added.

"You *are* a maniac," Vicky said, gasping at his impulsiveness. Then she caught herself and pulled back. How easy it was to find this man charming! "But you're also married. And I told you, I have a policy about married men."

"Maybe I can sell you a better policy," Jeffrey replied. And he began to talk about himself, about his marriage, a stumbling, raw, sometimes impassioned monologue that was too fresh to have been rehearsed like a "line" handed out to potential seducees. She felt she was watching the birth of a painful realization. He seemed to be enunciating many things for the very first time. She began to have a glimmer of what he'd meant by being seized by a great idea.

He said he saw his life as a kind of pyramid. At the pinnacle was his public relations firm, created with his sweat and time and capital and good name. It had been touch-and-go at the start, but he'd landed an airline account and now people were saying his shop, though small, was hot.

Then came the co-op. He'd had the foresight to buy out the old lady next door. She'd moved, and he'd broken through her walls to create a huge apartment that was now worth what? Seven hundred thousand? Eight? And the two original apartments had cost him less than seventy-five total, because the tenants had bought the building practically at distress price from an owner whose business was in trouble.

And of course he had Daria. With her red ringlets, her heart-melting eyes, her saucy mouth, a miniature of her mother. A knockout kid. A special kid, too, charming and delightful and sometimes astonishingly precocious.

He had friends, too, lots of them, witty couples he

could phone and invite to dinner, people who made amusing, lively company when he threw parties, a crowd that went out as a group to restaurants, theaters, discos, movies, eating at the latest places—Joanna's, The Odeon, Mr. Chow's. Of course, it made little difference to Jeffrey where he ate, but it was important to Amanda, so Jeffrey always deferred to her.

And that brought him to Amanda.

On the subject of Amanda, Jeffrey waxed eloquent. He could not praise highly enough her beauty, her charm, her wit, her good taste and sense of style. She was the chatelaine of his castle, and in all matters domestic he deferred to her. It was the second time Jeffrey spoke of deferring to Amanda, but it was not to be the last, and as he went on—and on—extolling Amanda, Vicky began to see a picture emerging of a man who did a great deal of deferring to his wife, who indeed seemed to defer to her in—everything.

It had not always been thus, he said. In fact, at the outset things were quite the opposite, with Amanda paying Jeffrey not merely deference but homage. She had been awed by his charm and breeding, his ease in the company of the rich, the powerful, the cultured. Public relations was Jeffrey's natural element, whereas Amanda, raised in poor circumstances, had had to struggle for every scrap of refinement. That she had achieved so much of it was her glory, particularly because no seams showed. When you told her she had class she virtually glowed with the secret of how dearly she had paid for it.

She had come to work for Jeffrey as his secretary, and when he began taking her out she genuinely could not understand what he saw in her. What he saw in her was a vivacious, high-spirited girl with a depth of feeling he had not experienced in other women he had gone with. But she had so little self-confidence that she refused to take him seriously. When he finally convinced her by asking her to marry him, she was so overwhelmed with gratitude she cried.

During those first years she could not do enough for him. She spent her meager savings lavishing gifts on him, making him elaborate dinners, furnishing him with considerate little comforts he never thought to get

31

for himself: a new watchband, a frame for his parents' picture, a silver money clip to replace the oversized paper clip he used. She had even taken out a bank loan to pay for a surprise birthday party she threw for him. She doted on Jeffrey, and in return he spared nothing to make her happy.

It took years for Amanda to believe she was worthy of Jeffrey and all he did for her. Had it stopped there, the marriage would have turned out quite differently. At precisely what point Amanda began to feel she had it all coming to her, at what point she started taking Jeffrey's largesse for granted, at what point she began taking advantage of him, it was hard to pinpoint. But certainly, around the time Daria was born, Jeffrey woke to the realization that Amanda had become a taker. Oh, he had spoiled and pampered her, no doubt, but it was by no means all his doing. What became manifest was Amanda's determination to be repaid for all the deprivation she had endured as a child. Her gratitude for all Jeffrey bestowed on her gave way, little by little, to an attitude that, at the very least, this was what she deserved. Her greatest skill was in manipulating Jeffrey into believing that he deserved these things too.

Take the summer house, for instance. Every year Amanda had complained about summer in the city until finally Jeffrey relented and rented a place out in the Hamptons. Amanda then felt it would be nice to have a house out there all year round and began pressing him to buy one so that she could decorate to her own taste. Again he deferred, yielding first to her blandishments, then to the gratification of owning the house itself. Jeffrey had come to love that house enormously, just as Amanda had promised he would. Oh sure, it cost him a pile, but hell, you couldn't keep up a life-style like the one he had with Amanda without spending a pile, right? Every additional improvement in that lifestyle demanded its own support system: the birth of the baby meant they had to get a nanny; the new kitchen meant they had to get a cook; the house in the Hamptons meant they needed a maid for the country in addition to the one they had for the city. After fighting Amanda on each improvement, Jeffrey ultimately gave in; though it cost him a bundle, in the end Jeffrey got to like the nanny and the cook and the second maid, just as Amanda had promised he would. Why, if it weren't for Amanda's ambition, taste, style, they'd still be in the one-bedroom on the air shaft off Second Avenue.

The more Jeffrey spoke in praise of Amanda, the less convincing he became, and at last Vicky was able to focus on what it was that would make this man, who in her friend Gail's phrase had everything, gravitate to a woman who had so little.

Jeffrey must have realized it himself, for in the middle of cataloging all the bounties Amanda had bestowed on him, he stopped midsentence and stared with disturbing intensity at Vicky. "I sometimes think," he pronounced, "that I'm bewitched."

Vicky grasped it immediately, but listened in fascination as he described himself as a man around whom a woman had woven a golden net, alternating threads of gratitude and deprivation, reward and punishment, promise and threat, until he was bound all but inextricably, helpless to thwart her least desires—trapped. The arrival of five hundred dollars' worth of Tiffany notepaper with her name linked to his seemed to paralyze his will, though the very night before they had fought over this extravagance with appalling viciousness. "She can unman me with a wrinkle of her nose," he said hopelessly.

"She sounds," Vicky said after a few moments' reflection, "more like a bitch than a witch."

"No," Jeffrey said flatly, leaving no room for argument. "I've known bitches. Amanda is too big for that category."

"Couldn't it be that you're just, well, weak?"

His face colored darkly, and Vicky shrank back. She had come close to angering him. "I'm not weak, goddammit. I fight her every inch of the way, but what can I do? Whenever I say no to her, she says, 'You can't tell me you hate all this.' And she's right. I love it, love it all. But the burden, Vicky. It's become so heavy! That pyramid I described to you—the co-op, the house in the Hamptons, the friends, the kid, the cook, the nanny, the maids, the wife? It's like I'm carrying that pyramid point down on my head. And I've begun to think I'm

33

going to collapse under its weight. I've always thought of it as a monument to my successes. But lately I've been thinking of it as a monument to my mistakes."

He slumped in his chair, the picture of dejection. Vicky was so moved she wanted to reach out and touch his face with her hand.

He looked at her, fingering his glass. The champagne had gone completely flat. "I'm sorry. I don't know where all that came from."

"It sounds like it came from the heart."

"I've depressed you. I've depressed myself. And I don't know anything about you."

"There's so little to know, compared to you."

"Compared to me? Why would you want to do that?"

She shrugged and spoke. She told him how much she enjoyed teaching, but how she loved most of all to write stories. She hadn't tried to sell them or anything, but she was confident she would one day. She was also taking courses toward her master's degree so she could teach at a university. Marriage? Children? Perhaps one day, but there had never been any really promising prospects.

"Except one," Jeffrey ventured, "and he was married already."

Vicky straightened sharply. "How did you know?"

"Your phobia about married men," he said. "It's obvious you really got burned."

She waved her hand. "If you really want to get depressed someday, I'll tell you that story. But..." She looked at her watch. "I have to go. Reveille in my apartment is six-thirty A.M. I'm a counselor at a day camp."

"Go?" Jeffrey cried. "You can't go."

"Why not?"

"It's...it's not part of my fantasy, that's why."

She looked at him steadily, seriously, fearlessly. "What *is* your fantasy?"

He leaned over. "Don't you know? Are you going to make me say it?"

She hunched her shoulders. "No, you don't have to say it. But Jeffrey, it's *your* fantasy. I'm not sure it's mine."

"What's yours? Tell me."

"Mine has a future." She reached out and covered

34

his wrist with her hand. "Jeffrey, I do like you. It was like at first sight, just as you said. And this evening...well, nothing has happened to make me feel differently. In fact—" She cut herself off; that thought was too dangerous to express. "But where is it going to go? Give me this much hope"—she made the gesture with thumb and index finger that had already become something intimately their own—"and I'll go home with you. Because I'm as needy as you are. But I'm not self-destructive. I haven't been in love much, but I've been in love hard." She finished this speech with a heavy expulsion of air from her lungs and took a big gulp of the remaining champagne. It was dead and sour.

Jeffrey hung his head. "I'm not sure I can give you the kind of assurances you're looking for. I can only tell you that if I thought this was the last time I'd ever see you, I don't think I could live with my sorrow."

They exchanged a look that seemed to last an hour. She searched his eyes for some kind of pledge, some kind of guarantee. He struggled to project one. His eyes seemed to say, I will find a way. It was the most suspenseful moment, she felt, of her entire life. Then she nodded and rose from the table. He tossed a lot of money down, as if fearful of jeopardizing the moment by waiting for the check. They walked silently out into the uncertain night. He took her hand and she looked up at him. "Aren't you afraid of being seen three blocks from your home?"

He laughed. "You've got to be kidding. Everyone I know is in the Hamptons in July!"

He got her into his building by allowing her to go first, pretending she was going to see her friend Gail. He stepped into the elevator behind her. They were alone. The door closed. He pressed fourteen. Then he stepped close to her and touched her cheek with his fingertips. His fingers were soft and gentle, his nails gleaming with clear lacquer. He lifted her chin and lowered his face to hers. His lips were tender and warm. She breathed in the aroma of cologne faintly mingled with perspiration. She felt almost dizzy with excitement.

The door slid open at fourteen and they walked rapidly down the corridor. Vicky held her breath, hoping no neighbor would see them. The hall was empty.

He opened the double locks and pushed the door open. She entered in front of him. He turned on a foyer light and led her through a vestibule. It was painted a vivid Chinese red and the walls were hung with hunting prints. They entered the living room, where he turned on more lights. He left her standing there a moment while he went into the kitchen to deposit his grocery bag, which had begun leaking, undoubtedly the frozen escalloped chicken melting.

She looked around, and it was hard to catch her breath. Gail had said it was something out of *Architectural Digest,* and Gail had been right once again. The walls were covered with white lacquered paper, the windows with chic vertical blinds. Burgundy upholstery covered a curved sectional that commanded one end of the room. Facing it across a lacquered coffee table were several plump, low-slung armchairs. On the table were silk flowers in a huge round crystal vase. At the other end of the room from the conversational area, set off by the splendid inlaid mahogany table, was a grouping of smaller French Provincial chairs placed near a grand piano. The floors were covered with Oriental rugs, the walls with bold modern art that would have overwhelmed a more modest room. She found herself drawn to one picture in particular. Oddly, it was not modern at all. It was a nineteenth-century American oil painting by a painter she had never heard of. It was a Constable-like scene of bucolic tranquillity and was absolutely breathtaking.

"Amazing," Jeffrey said behind her. "You went straight to the thing I love most in this apartment. Do you want to see the rest of the place?"

"Where did you get it? The painting, I mean."

"Amanda bought it for me." He snorted. "Actually, she buys gifts for me with the best intentions, but I always end up paying for them. She has no money of her own, except the few bucks she makes in an art gallery where she works a few days a week."

He took her through the dining room, with its round glass table and Chinese Chippendale chairs, and through the kitchen, which Amanda had just redone the previous year. It was beautifully functional, with a Spanish tile floor, miles of white cabinets and cupboards, polished copper pots and pans and kettles suspended from hooks over a professional-sized oven of spotless chrome. "On the old refrigerator we used to put Daria's drawings up with magnets, but that's not allowed now," he said wistfully. "Spoils the decor, doncha know."

He showed her Daria's room, yellow and white with flowered wallpaper, matching curtains, bedspread, and thick grass-green rug. Toys and games spilled out of colorful bins and overflowed from shelves, and a collection of stuffed animals that must have numbered a hundred crowded a special étagère near her bed.

Then they came to a study, beautifully paneled and lined with books, one cabinet reserved for those bound in leather or vellum. An antique desk was scattered with Jeffrey's work, and a leather love seat was strewn with papers. It was here, obviously, that Jeffrey felt he had a corner of his own. She scanned the shelves, nodding. She touched one book and removed it respectfully. "Joseph Conrad," she said. "This is a nice edition."

"I bought the set for myself years ago," he said proudly. "I love Joseph Conrad. I've read *Lord Jim* six times. Ask me anything. The name of the ship? *Patna.* The name of the old chief? Doramin. His son's name...?"

"You don't look like someone who loves books," she said.

"I don't? What do I look like?"

"You look"—she bit her lip, looking for the right word—"like a consumer."

He blinked, stung. "You make it sound like a fatal disease."

"It can be," Vicky said.

"Yes," he said. "Yes, it can."

They talked about books, small talk aimed not so much to inform as to dispel the nervousness that was beginning to grip them. In the silence, the enormity of what they were about to do manifested itself more and more, almost palpably, like a constrictor winding them ever tighter in its coils.

"Amanda reads best-sellers in paperback," he told her. "She flattens them until she breaks the spines with an awful crack. Then they fall apart and she throws

37

them away when she's finished. Once she was reading *Valley of the Dolls* and it came apart in sections. She discarded each section as it came off in her hands."

Vicky smiled politely. "I don't know if I want to talk about your wife right now."

"Yes, you're right. I'm sorry."

She had begun trembling. "Jeffrey?" She stepped close to him. "Be good to me, please?"

"Just give me the chance," he said, lowering his face to hers. They stood a long moment, lips barely grazing, inhaling each other's aroma. Then they broke apart and he led her to the bedroom. She had been more than a little curious about the bedroom but decided that this was the wrong time to look, to think. She wanted to forget that he belonged to another woman, forget that they were about to make love in that woman's bed, in her home.

She stood before Jeffrey with her arms at her sides and head bowed, like a supplicant. Her shaking had gotten worse, causing her limbs to quiver as if she were freezing. He had not touched her and she was already aroused beyond belief.

He undressed her silently, murmuring and gasping as her clothes slid off her body. She stood naked before him and he stepped away, the better to see her. "Oh God, you're so beautiful I could cry," he gasped.

He was out of his clothes quickly, and when he saw her shivering he embraced her. His body was radiant, like a stone that retains heat hours after the sun goes down. "Take a deep breath, hold it, and let it go slowly," he said. "It'll help you relax." She did as he'd suggested and felt her limbs lightening. The twitching ceased, but she was still intensely aroused, and she became aware of him growing hard against her. Though afraid of being too aggressive, she could not resist reaching down to hold him. He was smooth and beautiful but not excessively large, and when she enfolded him he moaned.

She lay down on the bed, knees parted, hands outstretched, beckoning to him. It was his marriage bed. The sheets smelled faintly of Amanda's perfume. The bedclothes, the table lamps, the pictures on the walls, all bespoke Amanda, and she could almost feel her presence in the room, arch and disapproving. She concentrated on purging Amanda from her mind, focusing instead on the image of male beauty poised above her. He knelt down and touched the mound beneath her belly with his lips. A fire erupted in her secret places and she squirmed under the pressure of his mouth. Then he entered her with his fingers. She arched her pelvis to accept them. They both satisfied her desire and whipped it to greater frenzy. God, how she wanted this man inside her!

He rose, stepped between her thighs, and lowered himself onto her, into her. Her arms and legs enfolded him, her mouth took his tongue in, and she felt herself penetrated to the core with pleasure. She was not a lustful person, but the act of having Jeffrey was one of intense lust, and she heard herself groaning with the ecstasy of orgasm only moments after it all began. He came a minute later, in long, sleek sweeps and gusts of frenzy.

He said, "I've loved you from the first moment," and she started to cry. He kissed away her tears but they kept mounting in her eyes and rolling down her cheeks. She could not explain why she was weeping, but he seemed to understand and refrained from asking foolish questions. It did not take great sensitivity to know what was tormenting her. Her desire, her curiosity, her intense attraction to him had been satisfied. It could all end with this night and that would be that, and perhaps that was for the best. She had never had a one-night stand with anybody and had always reacted with shock when a girlfriend told her about them. But tonight she understood that such things had their place. It would be so easy to end it now, a perfect experience, satisfying from start to finish. And what would she be giving up? The complications of an affair with Jeffrey unwound before her mind's eye in an almost endless skein. Almost but not totally; she knew how these things ended. She had stood at the collapse of one of them, and she had wanted to die.

And yet, she wanted more of him, wanted to get to know him so much better than this. She felt he was a wonderful man who, little by little, had permitted the best part of himself to be taken over and now must have realized he hadn't far to go before he became utterly

39

enslaved. What he saw in Vicky was an opportunity for rescue from that dreaded prospect. The question was, was that reason enough to go back on her promise never again to get involved with someone who could hurt her?

She almost felt the questions were too large, that she should not try to answer them but just let things go along unguided by her hand and see what happened, perhaps leave it to Jeffrey to make the decision for her. But no, that was not in her nature. Though not a decisive person, she wasn't, certainly, so passive as to toss her life out to the tides. She knew this was *the* critical moment: she stood at a fork in the road and the next step she took would cast her future as surely as if a judge had decreed it. In the delicious torpor after their lovemaking she could actually hear the two halves of herself debating. She cheered first one advocate, then the other. Her body went heavy and darkness stole over her. She could hear her own rhythmic breathing and felt her head bobbing gently on Jeffrey's chest, like a cockleshell boat on a pond.

She heard his voice, muffled, as though through a snowstorm. "Are you awake?"

She was disoriented for a moment. Had it been a minute or an hour ago? Her cheek was hot and wet where it lay on his breast. "Jeffrey," she murmured, burying her lips in his flesh.

"I said, I want to spend these next few days with you. Will you see me?"

In the evanescent moment that she had dozed off, her heart had made its determination. The answer sprang to her lips without hesitation, and with the strong directness of certainty: "Oh, yes. Yes, yes."

Chapter Two

VICTORIA HAD NEVER thought of herself as beautiful, but she knew what her good points were. She had an excellent figure, with well turned legs, a slim waist and flat stomach, and high small breasts. The first man she'd ever been seriously involved with had told her the French believe that a breast should be no larger than a champagne glass. If so, hers qualified as perfect.

Her brunette hair was straight, glossy, and soft. From her viewpoint, the best thing about it was that it didn't require constant washing, but many people, men and women, had complimented her on her beautiful hair. Others had said her eyes were her most striking feature, dark and expressive. Steve had called them doe-like. Perhaps they were, but they were also slightly farsighted. When she read she needed glasses, but she hated wearing them and often sat in restaurants squinting at menus rather than don her horn-rims.

Her ears were flat—her brother had gotten the elephant ears that were a trait of the Lewis clan. Her nose was a nose, her mouth was a mouth, that was about the best that could be said. She gave herself "attractive" on the beauty scale. When she got it all together for a big evening of dining and dancing, however, she was ready to admit to "lovely." But that's as far as she was willing to go.

She didn't do much to stay in shape. She did like to walk and in fact walked everywhere she could. But she watched joggers with little interest and did not do sit-ups when she arose in the morning. She was considered slender, but she did not work at it.

Jeffrey Keating, however, made her feel as if she did. He admired her body and bestowed lavish praise upon all of her parts: her tight belly, her exquisite breasts, her hips and small waist. She listened, enraptured with what he was saying but also slightly dubious, thinking that he was simply starved for sex or love or, worse, he was an extravagant liar. Still, she wanted to believe him and after several nights together, she started to enjoy his image of her as a beautiful woman. "Woman" was not a word she had used about herself. She was, after all, only twenty-six years old. But Jeffrey made her feel womanly. When they were in bed together he courted her body passionately; when they were not, he courted her mind. He was gracious and attentive, unlike anyone else she'd ever known.

She liked feeling womanly. In fact, she loved it. She could have stayed in bed with him for a week, listening to him describe her shoulders and breasts and skin and the shape of her mouth and eyes. His words made her want him all the more and liberated her to say things she had never dared utter; it was an exciting, sensuous experience. She started to feel confident, though she was sleeping in another woman's bed, in another woman's bedroom, with another woman's husband.

She had not seen any photos of his wife, Amanda, during their first days together in his apartment. He had stayed in the city three more nights and on the fourth and last one, her curiosity got the better of her. She prowled through the apartment while Jeffrey lay in bed sleeping lightly. She checked the photos in every frame; almost all were of Jeffrey's daughter or family members posed in various combinations. Two older people hugging Jeffrey and his child were probably his parents. They looked kind. She stared at the bookshelves, wondering where the family albums were.

Suddenly the light flipped on. Jeffrey stood in the doorway. "Looking for something to read?" he asked. She hugged her arms over her breasts. "Just looking. I can't seem to keep away from books. It's an obsession, I guess."

He smiled. Then he said, "Is that all?"

"I want to see her picture," Victoria said finally.

"Why? Does it serve any purpose?"

She thought for a moment. "Yes," she said. "It will help me understand things better."

"Fair enough," he said. He turned and left the room, then came back with a framed photo in his hand. "She doesn't look like most pictures of herself. She destroys the ones she doesn't feel she looks good in. This is from a few years ago." He handed it to Victoria. It was a photo of mother and child, dressed in identical sundresses. Amanda was even more gorgeous than Vicky remembered. Voluptuous was the word that sprang to her mind. Thick auburn hair, pouting lips, beautiful bosom, the cleavage showing at the top of the snug-fitting bodice, which then flared to the knee, revealing a well-formed calf. And the eyes were diamond-bright eyes. This woman was as beautiful as a movie star. Victoria expressed that sentiment.

Jeffrey shrugged. "It's hard to think of her looks alone anymore." He stared at the photo, then turned it facedown and left it lying on a shelf. "I don't want to see her face. I want to see yours."

"But why me?" asked Victoria. "The first available face? Someone standing next to you when you were seized by a great idea, you said."

"The only face," said Jeffrey. "I have been looking for your eyes for my entire life. You can't leave now."

"I'm not leaving," she said. "You are. Back to Long Island."

He looked down, shrugging. "Maybe I won't go."

"You have to." Here it was, the scenario she had dreaded. I can't because of my wife. I can't because of my child. She put her hands over her ears.

He pulled her hands away. "I want to be with you."

Victoria sobbed. "Why would you give up *her?*" she asked, pointing at Amanda's photograph.

"You don't know what it's like," he said. "You have no idea how lonely I've been."

She looked around the beautiful apartment, the family photographs, and tried to imagine. She shook her head.

"My daughter compensates to some extent, but she is so much like her mother that sometimes I feel the judgment of both descending on me."

Victoria said nothing.

"I know what you're thinking. I'm throwing myself in your lap. Well, maybe I am. But you are the most wonderful thing that's happened to me and I don't intend to lose you. Don't leave me, Victoria," he said. They went back to bed and he wrapped his arms around her and, after a while, fell asleep. As he slept, an enormous overwhelming tenderness and passion swept over her.

He went back to the Hamptons and for the last weeks of the summer she heard from him only a few times; two or three times by telephone and a few by mail—short, hurried letters written in bursts of pain. Victoria missed him terribly. There were times during those weeks when all she could see was his face, all she could feel were his hands all over her body, all she could hear was his voice telling her things she'd never heard before. Then she knew she wanted to be with him forever.

Her friends found her distant and unemotional when inside she was seething with emotion. She knew that when he returned to the city something was going to happen, but she was afraid to contemplate what. She was alternately resolved not to see him and terrified that she'd never see him again.

The night before Labor Day, Jeffrey called her. As soon as she heard his voice she knew something momentous had happened. "I've told Amanda."

A cold hand clutched at Victoria's heart. "Told her what?"

"That I can't live with her anymore. That I need a separation."

"My God." Victoria stood dumbly for a moment, trying to absorb the news.

"I don't think you thought I was serious," Jeffrey said.

"I know now. What did she say?"

He laughed hollowly. "She asked who the summer romance was with. I told you, Amanda knows everything."

"What did you say?"

"I denied it, of course. I mean, denied there was someone else."

"Is it?"

"Is it what?"

"A summer romance?"

"Tomorrow is Labor Day. The summer is officially

44

over. I want to go on seeing you. I want to be your man for all seasons."

"Where will you go? What will you do?"

"I think we'd better talk."

"My God," Victoria repeated.

The next few days were as upsetting as any she could remember. Jeffrey had thought nothing through—legal formalities, his daughter's welfare, living accommodations, none of it. Nor had he thought his emotions through. There was no doubt he was deeply unhappy with his wife, but whether his unhappiness could be alleviated by leaving her, leaving his beloved daughter, taking up with someone new, he didn't know, hadn't really addressed himself to. As she raised these questions for him he wavered, weighing the price of this violent change and questioning whether he was truly willing to pay it. Jeffrey's vacillations only aggravated Victoria's doubts. She knew that some of what Jeffrey felt for her was genuine, but she also recognized that his love may largely have been a matter of contrast. How could any new love not gain in comparison to a woman with whom one has lived intimately for so many years? Jeffrey intensely needed romance, needed the perfection represented by a passionate young woman who made no demands on him and gave selflessly of her body and soul. But what would happen the first time she made a demand on him, as must inevitably occur—not because she was a tyrant but merely because she was a human with normal needs? He would feel disillusioned, betrayed. She had read once that over ninety percent of the first affairs conducted by men and women who leave their spouses do not last. Now she understood why. Jeffrey's expectations of her would be impossibly high.

She told him so. And told him that for this reason, she didn't think they should see each other.

Which led to another round of desperate phone calls, treacherously risky trysts, and emotional fluctuations that left them exquisitely elated and abysmally depressed in turns. It all boiled down to two things. First, did she love this man enough to want to spend her life with him? The answer was yes, yes, yes. Reservations? Of course she had reservations. But she was prepared

45

to fight, accept, compromise, do whatever had to be done to make it work.

More serious, indeed potentially fatal, was the second matter: did Jeffrey love her—truly love her and not idolize some projected image of his own fantasies? At long, tortured last, she presented him with her ultimatum. "You must search your heart, Jeffrey, and you have to know, not just guess or think or hope—*know*. Know the way I know about you." He had opened his mouth to protest but she put a finger over his lips. "Don't answer yet. Get away and think. Think as you've never thought before."

And he did. For ten days she did not hear from him. The tension mounted, and how she got through that period was a miracle of self-control. She kept herself busy to the point of exhaustion, taking in movie after movie, museum and gallery exhibits, even traveling up to the Bronx by herself to see a Yankee game. She worked intensively with her children at school, volunteered for any after-school activity she could find, including street corner monitor, helping the younger children cross the street to waiting buses.

A thousand times she reached for the phone, a thousand times withdrew her hand. Hope and despair charged each other like warring armies, each capturing the no-man's land of her heart for an hour, then relinquishing the ground to the other. The suspense began to take its toll; her eyes grew puffy and blue from sleeplessness; she lost five pounds; she became irritable and moody, barking at her students. She was approaching the crisis point.

And that's when he came to her.

It was a warm, still, springlike evening. She had made a futile pass at the refrigerator, staring at its contents apathetically, reaching for a Coke, then changing her mind and closing the door. She was surveying a pile of test papers for grading when her building intercom buzzed. "You got a Mr. Keating down here," the doorman announced.

Her heart trip-hammered. "Send him up." She stared at the intercom for a moment, paralyzed with conflicting feelings. Should she greet him with joy or anger? She was deeply hurt by his silence, a silence suggesting doubts and reservations. But was that really what she felt at this moment? She had only to look into the bath-room mirror, to see her eyes glistening with tears of gladness, to know what the answer was. Quickly she ran a brush through her hair, touched the mouth of her L'Air du Temps cologne bottle to her wrists, and composed her face. Suddenly fear stabbed her. Suppose he was coming to tell her it was all over? Suppose his wife had—? The doorbell severed the thought. She took a deep breath and walked to the door, frowning at the disarray of her normally tidy apartment. She had let things go to seed the last week or so.

She opened the door. Jeffrey stood before her, grinning. He carried two suitcases and a shopping bag from Henri Bendel. In his teeth was clamped a posy of flowers, the stems dripping water onto his shirt.

Victoria's jaw dropped and she stared at him, trying to comprehend. He made a muffled sound and she removed the flowers from his mouth. "I've left her," he said.

She stood dumbly for a few seconds, trying to absorb the information, but nothing registered.

"If you've gotten married in the last few days, I'm in very big trouble," he said, grinning again.

"Oh Jeffrey," she cried, throwing herself into his arms. He dropped his suitcases and took her into his powerful embrace. She shuddered and began to sob. He held her tightly and let the wave of emotion subside.

She picked up one of his valises and lugged it into the apartment. He carried the other and the shopping bag, kicking the door closed behind him. Then he took her in his arms again and kissed her, pulling her body hard to his until their every contour was matched. All of her doubts and trepidations drained from her, leaving her only with the certainty that she was in love with this man and wanted to spend the rest of her life with him.

And it now appeared she was going to. "I have a million questions," she said.

"I have only one. You will have me, won't you?"

"Oh, Jeffrey, yes."

"I was so worried," he said, slumping with relief. He looked around, noticing his surroundings for the first time.

"This is it, I'm afraid," she said. "You could put my whole apartment in your living room."

"We'll manage," he said. He clutched her hand as she led him around the place. He'd never come up before, afraid of disturbing her privacy, he'd said, but she knew he'd also been worried about being seen.

The apartment had a tiny foyer, with a scatter rug in the center that always slipped if you walked too fast on it. Beyond the foyer was the living room, long and narrow with three windows giving on to a courtyard. The room had a long couch covered in a blue flowered print and heaped with small throw pillows and cushions, several with needlepoint coverings that she had made during what she called her crafts period. There was a bentwood rocker from the Columbus Avenue Bazaar, a wicker armchair with cushions covered in blue cotton, and a glass and chrome coffee table on which stood a potted ivy. African violets lined the window ledge, and several well-tended plants hung from the ceiling. Along the wall opposite the couch were open bookshelves sagging under the weight of several hundred books—well-worn college texts, paperbacks, and some hardbound books in brand-new, bright jackets. Along the front edge of the shelves were small pottery vases with bits of baby's breath and dried straw flowers, and a collection of framed family photos, a college diploma, and a small Eskimo soapstone carving of a figure in a parka seated on a rock. Near the entrance to the kitchen were posters from European art museums, framed in stainless steel and glass. One said "Uffizi—Firenze," and showed a reproduction of the Simone Martini *Annunciation*. Another was a Leonardo sketch from the National Gallery in London. A third, from a Metropolitan Museum exhibit, was a picture of a leering African mask.

The kitchen, off the living room, was bright and colorful with a small window beneath which stood a high table and two stools painted red. There were pretty enamel pots and pans hanging from an overhead rack, baskets lining the tops of the cabinets, spice racks, cheerful plastic canisters in rainbow colors, and ceramic pitchers filled with utensils. The impression was of an area well used and well loved. A funny-looking clock that was designed to resemble a plate of spaghetti and meatballs kept sluggish time over the sink next to a rack of worn-looking knives. Another plant, a coleus, hung over the table.

Directly off the foyer, at a right angle to the entrance to the living room, was the bedroom. It was small and square; the double bed occupied most of the space. The bed had no headboard and was covered with a crocheted afghan, each square made with a different color of yarn. On one side of the bed was a small wicker chest on which sat a pile of books and a reading lamp. On the wall opposite the bed was a high, old chest of drawers looking faintly Salvation Army, with an old-fashioned doily covering its top. Beyond the bureau, the door to the bathroom was half open. The apartment building was old and the floors were made of worn oak parquet; they squeaked and creaked when walked on. Pieces of carpet, obviously remnants, covered parts of the floor of both bedroom and living room. There was no dining room. For more formal dining there was only a gateleg table in the living room beneath the overhang of the bookshelves. There were two closets in the apartment, a large walk-in in the bedroom and a much smaller one in the foyer. As Jeffrey completed his tour he smiled at Victoria. "It's nice and cozy," he said. Then he went on. "As soon as we're better organized we'll find a bigger place. I need a study."

Victoria didn't even have a desk; she did her writing at the table in the kitchen, perched on a high stool, and often did her schoolwork lying on the bed. She wished her apartment pleased him more. She wanted him to love it.

She helped him unpack and cleared out two drawers in her bureau for his things. His clothes were beautiful—cashmeres, expensive shirts, silk ties, all with fancy labels and designer names. She did not have designer things; they were too expensive on a schoolteacher's salary, as well as too ostentatious. After Jeffrey's suitcases were emptied and placed on the floor of her overcrowded coat closet, he opened the Bendel's bag and produced—an espresso machine!

"Amanda never liked espresso," he said. "I'll put it in the kitchen."

49

Victoria sat on her bed and surveyed what he had brought with him: some shirts, sweaters, a suit or two, a couple of sports jackets, belts, socks, underwear, toilet articles. Out of that enormous apartment with all those lovely, wonderful things in it, all he thought of bringing was an espresso maker? What had Amanda said? Take your espresso machine and get out?

Jeffrey came back into the room and embraced Victoria. She had to bite back the thousand questions that flooded her mind. "I desperately need a shower, then we'll talk."

"I'll make some drinks," Victoria said, and while the water ran busily in the bathroom, she tidied up the bedroom, putting away her briefcase and the test papers she had been working on before he arrived. School could wait.

She went into the kitchen and fixed a tray with a bottle of red wine, a dish of salted peanuts, some black olives, a small wedge of cheddar cheese, and a few Carr's water biscuits, the last of a tin a friend had brought as a gift for a dinner party last spring. She took it into the bedroom and lay back against the pillows, waiting for Jeffrey to emerge from the bathroom. When he did, she burst out laughing. He was wearing her bathrobe. He looked ridiculous. "I forgot mine," he said, then threw off her robe and climbed, naked, onto the bed next to her.

They opened the wine, poured it, and touched glasses. They sipped a little, then touched lips. Victoria studied him, unbelieving. A few minutes earlier she had been desolate, despairing. Now there was this...this naked man on the bed beside her, a man she loved desperately, and he had come to stay. Stay not just the night or the weekend but...

"Forever," he said, raising his glass in a toast. They lay quietly awhile, absorbing the enormity of it. Then he spoke. "We hadn't talked about it, Amanda and I, since the evening I'd told her I wanted a separation. She was giving me room to think it over. In fact, she was nicer to me than she's been in a long time. That helped me decide to leave her."

Victoria looked at him. "I don't understand."

"She was on her best behavior. I didn't buy it. I had

50

this feeling that if I decided to remain with her she'd throw off the mask and pounce on me with all fours. She'd eat me alive."

"Goodness, all this jungle imagery!"

"You can laugh, but you don't know what a...predator she is. She isn't happy unless she can dominate. If I'd changed my mind she'd have taken it as a sign of weakness. She despises weakness."

"It isn't weak to love somebody, to want to live with them."

"Tell me about it. But that's Amanda. She wanted my soul. And you know what? I came close to giving it to her."

"What exactly happened?"

"Well, I spoke to a few people. Renee, my marketing director and my friend—you'll meet her, she's a very together lady. And Herb, my lawyer. They gave me a lot of good advice—Renee spiritually, Herb legally. This isn't going to be a picnic, but I must do it."

"I'm so glad to be with you," she said, reaching out to caress his chest.

He took her hand and pulled her closer, setting the plates and glasses on her night table. "I came home and opened the bills. There was her loan, higher than ever. She buys, I pay off her loan. And I remembered she'd bought me that picture with it, the one you loved? And I said, 'Don't you think you should at least pay for the picture? After all, it was a gift.'"

"What did she say?"

"She said, 'I don't have the money.' I said, 'I'd rather have a one-dollar gift from you that you pay for with your own money than a five-thousand-dollar one that you pay for with mine.' She said that was ridiculous. And that's when I saw the whole course of my life with her, stretching out to old age, to the grave, my begging her for a one-dollar morsel of love, her bestowing expensive objects on me that cost her nothing. The words just came into my mouth reflexively. I said, 'I'm leaving you.' Just like that. 'I'm leaving you.' And I went into the bedroom and started packing. It was so clear, so simple. She didn't understand, and she never will."

"What happened then?"

"She followed me into the bedroom. She was...calmly

51

blazing is the only way I can put it. I've seen her throw incredible tantrums. This wasn't one of them. It was worse. She just stood there watching me pack and said..."

Jeffrey paused, a shadow passing over his face.

"What did she say?"

"She said...I would regret it."

Victoria scrutinized his eyes, which blinked and dropped. She tilted her head. "I don't believe you." Anxiety squeezed her heart.

"The exact wording isn't important," he replied. "Let's just say it was a curse."

"I know all the four-letter words," Victoria said.

"It wasn't that kind of curse."

Victoria pulled up sharply. She looked into his eyes again and saw fear, a dark cloud over a gray, turbulent sea. She decided against pressing the question for the moment. "What about your daughter?"

"After I finished packing I went into Daria's room. I shouldn't have. It was..." The tears welled over his eyelids and streamed down his cheeks. She put her arms around him and held him tightly, shushing him gently. "I'm sorry," he said at last. "Her innocence..."

"You'll see lots of her. I'll make it nice for her. You won't lose her. I'll never give you cause to feel the cost was too high." She held his head against her breast until his breathing became soft and regular. Then she said, "Jeffrey, undress me and come into me. I've missed you so terribly. I need to feel you inside me."

He removed her clothes and she pulled him to her. She had never been so aggressive with a man before, but neither had she felt such a deep stirring ever before. He hardened quickly and slid between her thighs, filling her with a physical joy she had never experienced. She held him tightly until their fright drained and they could focus intently, exclusively, on one another.

They made love for hours, exploring each other's wants and satisfactions with an urgency that belied their realization that they would have a lifetime of exploration together. It seemed as if they didn't believe it, didn't believe it wouldn't be taken away from them momentarily. Even after they lay totally spent, the gray of dawn filtering through the dark of night, that uneas-

52

iness hovered in the atmosphere like a wisp of acrid smoke.

They fell asleep at last, tangled in each other's arms and legs, but Victoria awoke with a start, realizing she was due at school in three minutes. She debated with herself for one of those minutes, then, gazing at Jeffrey, decided to treat herself. She phoned in sick.

She sat down on the edge of the bed and watched him sleep. A warm happiness suffused her body, as after a glass of red wine. He slept contentedly; his even features reposed without the tension that had marred them ever so slightly when she'd slept with him at his apartment. She wanted to wake him, make love with him again. But there would be time for that—hard to believe, but there would be all the time in the world. Best to let him sleep, for when he awoke there would be problems to solve that would test him, test their love. From all Victoria knew of Jeffrey's wife, the days ahead were going to prove difficult. But she felt that they could face anything together.

He awoke a little after eleven and called out to her. She was in the kitchen and quickly poured a cup of coffee from the electric pot on the counter. She carried it into the bedroom and found him up on his elbows, disorientation in his eyes, his brow damp.

He avidly drank the coffee and brightened. "Bad dream," he said as his features relaxed. Then he looked at her, eyes aglow again. "God, you're real. I'm really here. This is going to take some getting used to." He set the cup and saucer down on the night table and drew her into his embrace. Then he said, "We have to talk business. What's your rent here?"

She told him. His lip curled; it was obviously more than he'd thought. "I'll give you a check every month as a contribution to rent and household expenses. When my lawyer has worked out the terms of my separation agreement with her, I'll know what my monthly nut is going to be and we can adjust my contribution. I hope eventually to pay for everything."

"Oh, that's all right."

He put his finger over her lips. "Now: lawyer talk. My lawyer—his name is Herb Glass if he ever calls here—is going to be contacting Amanda and telling her to get a lawyer. When she has one, Herb is going to negotiate a separation agreement. It's a kind of contract that spells out what my alimony and child support obligations are going to be, what my visitation rights to Daria are, stuff like that. The terms will be incorporated into the divorce decree when that eventually comes through. According to New York State law, I can file for divorce one year from the signing of the separation agreement, and divorce is automatic."

Victoria took the information in with a sense of detachment. It was hard to equate New York State law with the beautiful man who sat on her bed expounding it, who had lain between her thighs last night, sending volcanoes of ecstasy through her body with the avid strokes of his hard penis. She eyed that instument, now soft and without sexual connotation, and felt a temptation to take it into her mouth, something she had never done with another man.

"Pay attention," Jeffrey said.

"Yes, sir."

"For the time being I'm not going to tell Amanda where I'm living. It would complicate my negotiations with her. I'm going to tell her I'm in some seedy hotel off the Theater District. She'll never ask to see it; she doesn't usually venture below Fifty-seventh Street."

"What about phones?"

"Good thinking. Herb suggested I have my own phone installed here."

"Why?"

"He said legally she has to be able to reach me, otherwise she can claim abandonment. So I'm going to have a hot line put in, just for Amanda. You don't have to answer it. In fact, you mustn't."

"But can't she find the address where the phone is located?"

"It'll be unlisted." He read something in her eyes, and squeezed her hand. "I know all this sounds a little cold-blooded, but it's important for me to have an advantage. Amanda normal is formidable; Amanda scorned is..." He groped for a word, then realized he was upsetting Victoria. "Let's just say I don't want to provoke her more than I have to."

"You told me she does suspect there's somebody else."

"Yes."

Victoria bit her lip. "Should I be worried?"

"Worried? About what?"

"About my safety. Is she that...formidable?"

"She's not going to hire a hit man, if that's what you mean. Just be alert and keep your foul-weather gear near at hand." He studied her. "What's that look in your eyes?"

"You're scared of her, aren't you?"

He blinked. "Her anger is fundamental, like a natural force. It's taken me ten years to realize I can't tame it, can't placate it. But I do respect it, and that's what I advise you to do."

"What did you mean when you told me she'd—how did you put it?—said a curse? What exactly did she say?"

He twisted his face and made claws with his fingers. In a witchy voice, he quoted, "'Eye of newt and toe of frog, Wool of bat and tongue of dog...'"

"Be serious."

"I've been serious enough for one morning. Let's have lunch and make love."

"Except for the lunch part, it sounds like a wonderful idea," she replied, throwing herself into his arms.

Later they had lunch.

The second phone was installed at the end of the week. It went in the living room. Jeffrey told Amanda he had moved from a hotel off Broadway to a small sublet in the East Village, and gave her the number of the phone in the living room.

The problems began immediately. As soon as Amanda knew where to reach Jeffrey, she phoned him incessantly. The phone rang hourly, and Jeffrey spent hours talking to the woman. It forced Victoria to remain in the bedroom, where she pretended not to listen. But she compulsively positioned herself near the bedroom door and opened it a crack, putting her ear to the opening, straining to hear what Jeffrey was saying and to reconstruct the other end of the conversation. Sometimes the discussions grew heated, at other times subdued. It was easy to perceive how difficult the woman must be;

Jeffrey talked to her like a wrangler dealing with a high-strung horse that refused to be mounted.

Victoria took her own phone in the bedroom off the hook while Jeffrey talked to his wife so that Amanda would not hear it ringing and grow suspicious. She appreciated the need for circumspection; if the negotiations were blown by Amanda's discovery that Jeffrey was involved with another woman—the ugly phrase "keeping a mistress" sometimes insinuated itself into Victoria's mind—it could be ruinous for Jeffrey.

Circumspect or not, it was hard for Victoria to believe that this couple was heading for the divorce court, not with all those soul-searching dialogues going on. But Jeffrey remained obdurate and firm in his dealings with Amanda, always returning to the position that the damage Amanda had done to him could not be repaired, and he was not going to be reconciled with her. He was particularly admirable in his handling of Amanda's appeals in the name of their daughter, for this was the hardest part of the separation for him. But he stressed that it was not his child that he'd left but his wife, and that he would demonstrate this to Daria as soon as his visitation rights were worked out.

After these marathon conversations he would come into their bedroom looking ashen and weary. Victoria would wrap him in her arms until he relaxed. Then they would eat or make love, after which they'd talk long into the night, reviewing the developments.

One evening, the phone business reached a crescendo, and even Jeffrey grew weary of what was becoming a futile dialogue that was better held between lawyers than between estranged husband and wife. They were about to sit down to dinner, and when Victoria wailed as the phone sounded, Jeffrey marched to the instrument in the living room and yanked the jack.

They sat down to a simple dinner—a salad of endive and watercress, swordfish steaks, tiny peas, and wild rice. Jeffrey had more extravagant tastes than Victoria, but was content to satisfy them at business lunches. Victoria liked natural foods, stir-fried vegetables, plain broiled fish, salads, roast chicken, not much red meat, not much by way of sauces. She loved to cook, however, particularly for this appreciative man who declared

56

everything she made fantastic. So she indulged him, though she knew the expense would drain her food budget even with his contribution to it.

As they were finishing their salads, Victoria's phone in the bedroom rang. She got up, eyes rolling into her head. "Probably one of my friends. They must think I've been abducted by terrorists." As she went inside she thought about the excuse she would give about her whereabouts of late. She picked up the phone.

"Hello, Victoria." The female voice was honeyed, mellifluous. She did not recognize it but she knew who it must be even as she asked. "This is Amanda Keating, dear. Jeffrey's wife? Mother of his daughter?" Victoria listened, stunned, transfixed, incapable of the simple muscular movement that would pull the phone away from her ear. "This *is* Victoria Lewis, isn't it? My husband's mistress? Since Jeffrey isn't answering his phone, I thought I'd try yours."

At last she was able to function, but only enough to put the phone back in its cradle, and this she did quietly, as if fearful of giving offense. She stared at the wall for a moment, then the dread swept across her body like an icy squall, and she started to cry and shake uncontrollably, calling to Jeffrey. He rushed in, gulping food. "It's her, it's Amanda, she knows, she knows everything!"

He held her tightly. "That couldn't be."

As if in response, Victoria's phone began to ring again. He picked it up and listened. His neck muscles tightened and his jaw clenched. He listened for a long time. Then he said, "This is Jeffrey. You're never to call this number again, do you understand?" He slammed the phone down and pulled the jack. Vicky huddled on the edge of the bed, still trembling.

"How did she find out?" Vicky asked.

"I don't know. I told you, she has a way of finding everything out."

"Her voice...it was like silk. Like a snake's. I mean, if snakes could talk....Oh, Jeffrey," she wailed, "she called me your mistress." Vicky began to sob again. He pressed her head to his chest, stroking her hair and reassuring her, but it was close to a half hour before she could catch a shuddering deep breath and talk calmly again. "I feel violated," she said. "I want to bathe or something."

"I'd better call my lawyer."

"What are we going to do?"

He shrugged. "It had to come out sooner or later. What difference does it make?"

Victoria eyed him, perceiving he was more shaken than he admitted. "You said it could affect the negotiations."

"My lawyer said that these days the courts aren't very tough on adultery. I doubt...what's the matter?"

Victoria had slumped again, her chest heaving as if she were on the verge of crying again. "Mistress. Adultery. They're like curse words when I hear them said aloud. They don't have anything to do with the way I feel about you. Yet that's what the language calls it. It's vile, like somebody dumped excrement on my head."

"You mustn't let it get to you, darling."

"No, you're right. I mustn't. I'll be all right. I'm more worried about you. She could take everything away from you—your money, your daughter..."

"But not you."

Vicky gave him a hard look. "She's going to try. She's going to drive wedges. Like..." Her mouth balked momentarily. "...'mistress.' If I thought that's all I meant to you..."

"Vicky, no, you mustn't." He pounded his fist into his palm. "God damn her."

Victoria walked to the window and stared out at nothing. Then she turned. "Jeffrey, if I'm going to face this ordeal with you, you'll have to tell me what it was she said to you the night you left her. What you meant by her 'curse.' If I know, at least I can prepare for it, *we* can prepare for it, deal with it. I don't want any more shocks like this one. I don't want to underestimate her."

He hesitated a moment, then waved his hand airily. "It wasn't that big a deal."

She didn't believe him. "Just tell me."

"She said—she predicted, I guess you'd say—I'd come back."

"Come back? To her, you mean?"

"Yes. Crazy, huh? I told her it would be a cold day

58

in hell before that happened. I mean, this woman has got some truly off-the-wall notions. The idea that I could..."

Vicky listened to him protesting, noting that the more he talked the less convinced he sounded. Amanda's parting shot had penetrated to the heart of Jeffrey's fear. And on further reflection, Vicky realized it penetrated to the heart of her own. The woman was very shrewd, very shrewd indeed. *Formidable*. Jeffrey's word had been most accurate.

"Jeffrey, I think that, deep down, you believe she has the power."

"To make me go back?"

"To make you do anything."

"That's silly. I'm here, aren't I?"

"Some of you is here. And some of you is still back there. We have our work cut out for us, Jeffrey Keating."

The discovery of Jeffrey's whereabouts began a period of harassment they thought would never end. Both phones rang day and night. If they turned off their phones, Amanda would send them telegrams and mailgrams. Then there were the deliveries. The doorman would buzz them from the lobby with urgent deliveries by messenger. The parcels contained favorite items from Jeffrey's wardrobe with pieces torn or cut off or holes punched through them; cruel messages in Amanda's elegant script, such as one telling Jeffrey how his daughter had come down with a fever and begged Mommy to bring Daddy back; a box containing Jeffrey's set of Joseph Conrad, with the last fifty pages torn from each book; an envelope with photos of Jeffrey and Amanda on their honeymoon.

Jeffrey and Victoria stood up to some of these measures better than others. They would laugh at Amanda's latest hijinks, but later the hurt or strain would show up on one or the other's face; they would tell each other it didn't matter what Amanda did to them or took from them as long as they had each other, but there were moments when they were overcome by Amanda's vicious dismemberment of all she and her husband had shared; in the night they held each other tightly, made

59

love with mad intensity, yet nothing quite totally purged the room of the woman's presence.

One day Victoria expressed a need to talk about it to someone. They had been together two weeks and seen no one but each other, and Victoria thought it would be a good idea to begin widening their acquaintances, start assembling a network of friends to ease them out of their awful isolation. Jeffrey thought it was a splendid suggestion and brought home his friend Renee, certain the two women would hit it off beautifully. How could she not adore Victoria?

Easily.

The evening, dinner at their apartment, was a disaster. Renee was hostile, negative, nervous, and disapproving from the moment she walked into the room, and it was all Victoria could do to remain polite. It wasn't until dessert that Victoria perceived what was going on: Renee was jealous. Armed with this insight, she listened to the woman talk shop with Jeffrey to the exclusion of her hostess. Victoria spent the rest of the evening in the kitchen cleaning up meticulously, counting the minutes until Renee said her good-byes. So that was it as far as Renee and Victoria were concerned.

Vicky did have some friends, but only one close enough to share her heavy burden with, and that was Willa.

Willa had been her best friend for five years, ever since Victoria had moved to the West Side after college. Willa had lived there then; she was divorced, older than Victoria, and full of practical advice about how to manage in New York City. Victoria, who was from a small town in Connecticut, looked to her as a kind of surrogate big sister. Eventually, the eight-year difference in their ages didn't seem to matter and they became best friends. Willa had moved from the building to a loft in TriBeCa before the area had become popular, so they did not see each other as often as they would have liked. Willa's live-in boyfriend, Matthew, had left his family three years earlier, and Willa had had to contend with Matthew's wife and three small children. So Victoria knew she'd have some practical, clearheaded advice. She phoned her that night.

"Darling," Willa said, "I'd begun to think you were dead. What happened?"

"You won't believe this, but I'm living with a man who just left his wife."

"I guess I don't set a very good example of moral turpitude, do I? Or moral turpentine, as Matthew would say." Willa's Matthew was a painter. Willa herself was an aspiring actress who landed occasional small roles in off-off-off-Broadway shows that never ran for more than three nights.

"I need your help," Victoria said.

"You've got it," Willa said.

"Lunch? Saturday?" Lunch was one of their traditions. As struggling working girls, they rarely got to go to restaurants they wanted to sample so they went to lunch together once a month at places that made Gael Greene's heart beat faster in *New York* magazine. The lunch arrangement had ended when Willa moved downtown, but occasionally they revived it for an odd Saturday or school holiday.

"Where?" said Willa. "Something soothing, I think. Japanese?"

They arranged to meet at the Japanese restaurant at the Waldorf Astoria, Inagiku.

"Willa will know what to do," Victoria told Jeffrey as he left for work one morning.

"I don't know why anyone should know," he said resignedly.

She watched his back as he went down the hall, wondering if he really knew his wife after ten years of marriage. He had underestimated her every reaction. What would happen next? She hated to contemplate the immediate future.

Willa was waiting in the front part of the restaurant, near the bar, seated in a low-slung chair sipping a tall, fruity-looking drink. She leaped up when she saw Victoria. "Vic, darling," she cried out. Willa was very dramatic. Vicky had gotten used to her conspicuous public displays, but it had taken some time. Willa loved being noticed. She wore clothes that guaranteed she would be noticed. Today she was dressed in a long hand-knit sweater that had designs of fire-red dragons intertwined with purple orchidlike blooms. The sweater covered skintight black leather pants and a silky black tunic worn with high-heeled gray snakeskin boots. Willa always looked terrific. She assembled much of her wardrobe by shoplifting. She was proud of her forays and would speak of them as other women might discuss a shopping trip. "I nicked this from Bloomingdale's," she'd say, or, "Today I hit Saks." Victoria was convinced she'd get caught one day but she never did. And despite security precautions, heavy antitheft tags, guards, alarms, floorwalkers, and store detectives, Willa was always dressed to the teeth in hot merchandise.

They took a table in a quiet corner. There was a tranquilizing serenity about the place, waitresses in kimonos and sandals and obis, tables polished and set simply, elegantly dressed diners murmuring.

"So. You've found a man. Tell me all about him. Aren't you divinely happy?"

"There's a lot to tell."

Willa shook her head, hearing the underlying depression in Victoria's voice.

The waitress came over and Victoria ordered a white wine spritzer, Willa a refill of her rum punch, then they ordered lunch—sashimi for Willa and shrimp tempura for Victoria.

She told Willa how she and Jeffrey had met, how he had pursued her, and how she had fallen in love with him. Willa got her to talk about how she felt about him sexually. She did not mention Amanda or Daria.

"So far it sounds perfect. Where does the married part come in? You know, considering how you describe his looks, his apartment, his business, and his cock, I think being married isn't something you could hold against him."

"I was getting to that," Victoria said as the waitress shuffled over and placed before Willa a lacquered tray of sashimi, raw fish cut into various exquisite patterns, and a platter of tempura before Victoria. Victoria wished her appetite were better.

"This wife is a real—"

"Ballbusters, we call them. Go on," said Willa, her mouth full of sashimi.

"She apparently made him spend everything on her,

on her wardrobe, on the apartment—it was *two* co-ops—on a summer home.

"This guy sounds like the catch of the century. Too bad you met him after."

"After what?"

"After she got to him first. What else?"

"He doesn't see her realistically. She's nasty, destructive, mean, and he believes her incapable of it."

"What does this broad look like? Candice Bergen? Jane Fonda?"

Victoria shook her head. "Wrong type. More like Sophia Loren. Absolutely gorgeous. Auburn hair, green eyes. A knockout."

"Hmmmm, this is getting interesting. But beauty doth not improve the bitch beneath."

"Is that a quote?"

"Yeah, it's something that all actresses learn on day one. It does not, however, get you jobs. It simply makes you feel better. You're a good person, Vicky, so I'm not surprised a decent guy would want you. But this wife sounds like trouble."

"She's been waging a campaign of inspired harassment," Victoria said. And she went on to describe the phone calls, packages, and letters, culminating in the destruction of the books.

"You know, you shouldn't let that bother you. Ex-wives are all alike. Matthew's once sent him all the pictures she had of the kids torn into shreds. Pictures of her children, for Christ's sake. Their little heads were torn off. It was really pathetic; talk about your castration fantasies. Then she sent him pictures of the two of them together intact. Weird. You have to take the upper hand with this lady. Let her know you're the boss fast. Tell her to go to hell the next time she calls."

"It's not that easy," Victoria said.

"I didn't say it was easy," said Willa. "At least not for someone of your temperament and upbringing. Me, I could tell her off in a minute. You got a problem, send her to me. I'll take care of her. Listen, if she can't hold her man, that's not something you should worry about. What about the kid?"

"I haven't met her yet. She's extremely pretty. She looks a lot like her mother, in fact."

"That could be creepy," Willa said. "I'm lucky that Matthew's three are all boys, although his ex could easily be one of the guys, if you know what I mean. When do you start being stepmommy?"

"I'm not sure. Isn't it a little premature for me to be meeting his daughter? I mean, we've only been living together for three weeks."

"Yeah, but you love him. The kid comes as part of the package."

"You know," Victoria said, "I think he misses her horribly. I'm afraid she'll be even tougher than the mother."

"Don't worry about everything so much. Just tell me how happy you are."

"Oh, I am, Willa, it's just..."

"Just what? Why aren't you eating your shrimp?"

Victoria put her chopsticks down and put her hands to her face.

"Oh, I get it," said Willa. "It hasn't been all that romantic, has it? He left her for you, but now all you can think about is what she's going to do next."

Vicky nodded.

"And," Willa continued, "you don't talk about love so much these days."

Vicky nodded again.

"Kid, you just have to get through this part and go on to the next. The ex will calm down, you'll settle into a nice life. Is this guy good for you? Is he being nice to you? You know, if he's a bastard I'll get Matthew to beat him up. Matthew is very strong from stretching all those canvases and schlepping them around. You could do worse than have Matthew on your team."

Vicky put her hands down and smiled. Her eyes were filled with tears but she was not crying. "I guess I thought I was the only one who ever went through this. I've never had anybody hate me in my life. I feel so guilty all the time, like I deserve to be punished."

"You dodo," Willa said. "*You* punished because he had a shitty marriage? Honey, you're the one that's saving his life. Now pull yourself together. If he's going through a bad time, you be the strong one. After all, you didn't leave your home. You *are* home. You have all your nice things intact, your own environment. Environments are very important, you know."

"It's certainly inferior to what he had before."

"Oh, tell me," said Willa excitedly. "You *know* what a frustrated acquisitor *I* am. I'd love to hear."

"Well, I said it was grand, but maybe that isn't enough. It's more like one of those decorating magazine places, sleek and very organized, everything in its place, a kitchen without a crumb in sight, let alone a pot or pan, bedroom very plush and female, no sign a man lives there."

"Where do you think the stuff comes from? Angelo Donghia? Any Breuer-style chairs? Roche-Bobois?"

"I wouldn't know that, Willa. Ask me if it's from the Columbus Avenue Bazaar, then I'll know. But they had this painting..."

"His or hers? Theirs?" Willa asked.

"She bought it for him. I never saw anything like it. The most beautiful landscape, a painting of a meadow, but it was so transcendent, as if it were heaven. I got lost in that painting."

"Doesn't sound like what Matthew does. His stuff could be a meadow, but then it could be a six-car wreck on the New York Thruway, for all you can tell from his brush strokes." Willa sighed deeply. "Believe me, if I understood his painting I'd have most of our problems solved, including what to make for dinner."

"What does dinner have to do with it?" Vicky asked.

Willa shrugged. "It's just this fantasy I have. One day I wake up and experience an epiphany—complete understanding floods in—and I go into the studio and stare at his latest painting and it says to me, 'Pot roast.' Then I go make a pot roast and after a day of laboring on this masterpiece, Matthew comes in and says, 'That's exactly what I was thinking of all day.'"

"Don't tell that to Matthew. He'd be insulted," Victoria said. She liked Matthew, finding him lively, if incomprehensible, and very sexy in a dark, hirsute, hulking way.

"What do I get now? He takes my meat loaf and mashed potatoes and makes sculptures out of them. One day when they write the catalog copy for his retrospective, they'll say, 'Instrumental to his vision was the food prepared by his lover, Willa, whose last name escapes us at this time, but whose chicken Marengo belongs to the ages, captured forever in Matthew Staunton's haunting *Chicken Marengo with Broccoli and Rubber Tire.*'"

Victoria laughed. "Willa, I love you. You always make me feel better."

"I guess what I'm saying is, we all feel like adjuncts sometimes. My career is nowhere, so everything seems to go into Matthew's. You've found someone you obviously want very much; why else would he have moved into your inner sanctum? You guarded your privacy more jealously than anyone I've ever known."

"I know," said Vicky. "That's why I'm a bit confused. I keep thinking, who is this person? Then I remember that I fell in love with him on an elevator, before I even knew his name."

"Better when you don't know their names. Their complications come with them."

They had some perfumed tea, then Willa pulled out a mirror and put on lipstick. "Well, I'm off. I'm going to Alexander's. Want to come?"

Victoria shook her head. She never went into department stores with Willa. Too dangerous. They could get her for being an accomplice.

"I'm not ripping off today, dope," said Willa. "I don't shoplift Alexander's," she sniffed. "Not up to my standards. I need some underwear and they have the cheap bikini stuff that turns Matthew on."

"Thank you," Victoria said impulsively.

"For what? For listening? Hey, that's what I'm here for. Now remember, don't get upset when she pulls this crap on you; you've got to expect a certain amount of flak in the beginning. But it doesn't last forever. She'll find someone, honey; if Matthew's ex could, anyone can. And you say that she's certifiably gorgeous. When that happens you'll be home free. But tell your friend Jeffrey to watch out for those divorce lawyers. They're a tricky lot. Matthew was lucky. He doesn't have anything, so they couldn't make him give too much away. But they tried. They'd have taken his balls for alimony if he'd let them. It's a rotten world out there." She threw down a twenty-dollar bill and waved at Victoria. "Must run."

Then she leaned over and kissed Vicky on the cheek. Vicky could smell her heavy, flowery perfume. "Love you," she said. "Bye." Then she was gone and something in Victoria sagged a bit. She waved to the waitress and asked for the check, then picked up her handbag and left the restaurant, heading for home.

When she walked in the door, she called out to Jeffrey. "In here," he replied, and she went into the kitchen. He was standing at the counter, sleeves rolled up and arms plunged into a bowl of dough. "Hi," he said with more cheer than she'd heard all week. "I missed you."

She was gladdened by the sight of his face, and her spirits lifted as she threw her arms around him and kissed him. "As soon as I punch this dough down, I'm taking you to bed. I feel terrific. Making bread is very therapeutic. Oh, and something nice happened. I spoke to Daria and she said her mother's going to let her see me tomorrow."

"Tomorrow? Sunday?" Victoria said.

"Yes, and I want you to meet her," he said firmly.

"Tomorrow?" she repeated. Suddenly she was nervous. But why? After all, she taught children every day, worked with them in camp. Children weren't threatening to her; one reason she'd become a teacher was to be in contact with children. She believed they kept you young, kept your perception of the world fresh and innocent. But Daria wasn't just any child, she was *her* child, the child of the woman who was tormenting them. "You don't think it's too soon?"

"No, of course not. How could it be too soon? I want her to meet you. I know she'll love you as much as I do. And Vicky," he said tenderly, putting his doughy hands around her, "I *do* love you. I'm sorry things have been so difficult this past couple of weeks. It's just that there's been so much pressure. But things will go back to normal, you'll see." Then he returned to his bread dough and began punching it again. "I'll be inside in a minute," he said.

Victoria walked into the bedroom and took off her wool jacket. Back to normal, he said. What did normal mean? They'd scarcely had a normal moment together!

She sat on the edge of the bed, waiting for him to join her. Perhaps they could talk about this some more.

But they did not talk. He came into the bedroom and sat down silently beside her. He pressed her gently to the bed and looked down at her face. His eyes took her in, lovingly, and she relaxed under his gaze. When she was with him she knew she had made the right decision. She had always liked to be in control, to know what to expect. With Jeffrey there was unpredictability, but it didn't bother her. She trusted him and was able to surrender to him. It was actually exhilarating. She wanted to lose herself in him, to feel her body opening up as it never had, to feel the unfolding of her soul. What frightened her with Jeffrey was that she felt she was giving away ground, ceding space that could never be regained. If he betrayed her trust, it would be very bad. She knew it was love, for perhaps the first time in her life. She gave in to it, putting her arms around his neck and thrusting her body up toward him. He enfolded her with his long arms and told her he had dreamed of her all his life. This, this was her reward for the days and nights of anxiety; this, in the end, would be the payoff. The only question was, would they survive until then?

They made love for an hour. Their first orgasms were quick and strong. Neither Jeffrey nor Victoria held back. Then they began again, Jeffrey still erect and amazed at his potency, Victoria strangely unsatisfied. This time it took longer; they built up to a high peak, a wild and uninhibited place; and when Jeffrey clutched her as he convulsed, she was afraid he would tear her apart in his arms.

When it was over, they lay together on the bed, Jeffrey stroking her hair and talking about Daria.

"She's a terrific kid, bright and interested in everything. I know you're going to adore her."

Victoria thought of the photo of Daria and her mother in their matching sundresses. Inevitably, Daria was going to resent her. "Are you sure you want to bring her here?"

"Why not?"

"Well, for one thing, there's nothing for her to play with. I might have a deck of cards somewhere, but aside from that I can't think of another thing. Maybe we should take her somewhere? Or maybe you should be alone with her. I'm sure she'll be confused and upset. My presence might make things worse."

"She's not confused," Jeffrey said. "She said to me, 'Mommy says you have a girlfriend and I want to meet her.' See? She's already excited about seeing you."

"Oh, I think that may be wishful thinking on your part, Jeffrey. Maybe I'll put on some clothes and walk over to Broadway and buy a few things she can play with."

"That would be terrific, Vicky. I'll see to the bread. We'll have some fresh with dinner, okay?" He looked a little forlorn when she put her clothes on again.

"I'm not sure how hungry I'm going to be," she said.

Outside, in the cool air, with the afternoon light growing dimmer, she summoned up the picture of a happy, trusting little girl holding her hand as they crossed the street. She knew so well the feel of that small hand in hers. Then she thought of the phrase, "Mommy says." Could she listen to what Mommy says every time the child opened her mouth? Who was Mommy, anyway? Someone who sent vile letters and destroyed precious things.

In the small stationery store two blocks from her apartment, she bought a box of Crayolas, the big box, sixty-four colors, a fat Walt Disney coloring book, a box of Pickup Sticks, a tray of watercolors, and a pad of blank white paper. At least the child wouldn't be bored, she decided. Then, as an afterthought, she threw in two candy bars. Schoolteachers know the value of bribery, and this kid was going to be the most difficult pupil of all, because she was going to have to be initiated into the vicissitudes of real life at the tender age of six. Victoria, almost trembling with anxiety, was not eager to begin.

Chapter Three

JEFFREY LEFT THE APARTMENT early to pick up
Daria, as eager as if he were visiting a lover. He put
on a fresh shirt, shined his shoes, and whistled. Then
Victoria realized, sleepily, that he was also going to be
seeing Amanda. She wanted to warn him not to go up
to the apartment, that perhaps there would be a scene,
but she refrained from doing so, afraid that he would
think her foolish if nothing did happen.

After he left, Victoria took a long, hot shower, then
went through her small wardrobe to pick out something
to wear. She wanted to look older to Daria, a bit ma-
tronly, in fact, so that Daria would think of her as an
adult with some authority. No jeans then, something
more staid, more official looking. She selected a tweed
skirt and a plain Oxford cloth shirt in pale blue. Then
she took her cup of tea, went into the living room, and
sat down on the rocking chair. She rocked quietly, sipping her tea, while she waited for Jeffrey and his daughter to return. They seemed to be taking an inordinately
long time just to go crosstown and back. As the minutes
stretched into an hour, then two, she began to panic.
Something awful must have happened. But why hadn't
Jeffrey called? She wished she could call there, but what
would she say? This is the mistress, I want to speak to
Jeff? She bit her lips and stood by the window, craning
her neck at the street, trying to will them into appear-
ing. Almost two and a half hours after Jeffrey had left
the house, she heard his key in the lock. "Hi," he called
brightly. "We're here. Sorry we're late. Daria wanted
to have breakfast out on the way over, and we had a
special little talk." He turned back toward the hall.
"Come on, Daria. Come in."

A small figure appeared in the doorway, the auburn-haired child she had glimpsed at school, dressed in a green jacket, blue jeans, and tiny saddle shoes. She was clutching a doll to her chest and her head hung down.

"Come and say hello to Daddy's friend Vicky right now." Jeffrey coaxed her into the room and shut the door behind them. Then he propelled her across the living room toward the windows where Victoria stood. "This is Daria," he announced. The child looked up at Vicky with a flash of bright blue eyes that seemed to laser straight through her. "Hello." Victoria started. It was a six-year-old's rendition of her mother's honeyed voice. It was disconcerting to have this miniature Amanda inhabiting her living room. You'd better get used to it, she told herself, and said, "Is that your dolly? What's her name?"

"This is my doll," Daria said, holding it out. It was a Russian doll, full-skirted, with a gaily smiling face and a babushka tied around its hair. Its painted eyes were blue, its hair red, its bee-stung lips arranged in a perky smile. The doll looked like Amanda also. Victoria felt assaulted from all directions and wondered if the mother had purposely sent this effigy crosstown? Daria laughed, then turned the doll upside down to show it had no legs and, for that matter, no insides. Beneath the spreading skirts of red and gold was a quilted liner not unlike the fabric of which potholders are made. Victoria stared at the doll, suddenly bottomless. "It's a tea cozy," Jeffrey explained. "You put it on a teapot."

Daria held the doll by its waist and flipped it up and down, up and down, its head pitching skyward, then its empty bottom showing. Why was it so unsettling? Victoria walked away, toward the kitchen. "I'm going to make myself something to eat. Does anybody want some lunch?"

"We had brunch out," Jeffrey said. "Daria had waffles and bacon and I had scrambled eggs and Daria's leftover waffles."

"Okay," Victoria said, feeling a bit dejected. "Why don't you give Daria some of the things we bought for her so she'll have something to do?" She turned around as she spoke and saw Jeffrey seated in the rocking chair

71

and Daria crawling onto his lap, still clutching her doll. It was going to be a long day.

She fixed herself a tuna sandwich and poured a glass of white wine from the half-gallon bottle they kept in the refrigerator. Then she took her sandwich into the living room and forced herself to get to know the child who might possibly become her stepdaughter one day. If she didn't love Jeffrey so much, she might never be able to tolerate her; other people's children, no matter how charming, are still other people's children.

Daria turned out to be an active, nosy little thing; more than once during the day Victoria caught her opening closet doors, dresser drawers, peering into the dark recesses of the low kitchen cabinets. Daria would give her a broad smile and flash her blue eyes. But she never said anything. "Just curious, huh?" said Vicky, closing the door or drawer while Daria beamed up at her. Vicky spent much of the time surreptitiously following the child around while Jeffrey, content to have his daughter in the house, read the Sunday *Times* business section, did the crossword puzzle, and looked over a contract with a new client.

Victoria, finally feeling guilty, took out the crayons and watercolors and paper and tried to get Daria to draw a picture. Daria sat down solemnly and looked at Victoria with her round eyes. Then she proceeded to draw an elaborate representation of a house with several stories, a large tree out front, and figures out on the lawn. When she was finished, she explained that this was her house and the other figures were her mommy and daddy and that the small orange blob on the grass was her goldfish, Sandy, who had died last year after she forgot to shake food in its bowl for the third time in a row. "Can I have a Coke?"

Victoria suggested that milk might be a better idea, but was overruled by Jeffrey. "Sure, she drinks soda all the time," he said, beaming at his child. She beamed right back. Victoria sighed and said, "I'll get the Coke."

Dinner consisted of Daria's favorite foods (by special request), Burger King Whoppers, french fries, more Coca-Cola and for dessert, jelly doughnuts, all purchased on Broadway by the doting father. Daria took only one bite of her hamburger, ate half a package of cold french fries, drank two Cokes, and ate three jelly doughnuts. "Does she always eat like this?" Victoria asked.

"Oh, no, this is good for her," Jeffrey said proudly. "She's really enjoying her food."

When Daria left, Vicky fell into a deep depression. She felt left out, spied upon, felt she had allowed something alien to enter her home. How could she attribute all of this to a small child? She felt guilty and confused. She had always loved children and found their innocence precious and endearing. But *this* child?

When Jeffrey returned he was glowing with pride. "Isn't she terrific?"

"Yes," said Victoria. "Just wonderful."

She went to bed with a heavy heart, knowing that she had to make the adjustment. But when she fell asleep, she dreamed the Russian doll had come to life, kicking up its embroidered skirts to reveal emptiness and flashing its blue eyes and pouty grin.

The next day a strange thing happened. Vicky had stayed late at school to finish marking some papers and heard a commotion on a lower floor. She left her classroom and went down the stairs, coming upon two eighth grade students quarreling over a jacket. One accused the other of stealing her school blazer. Victoria spent several long minutes settling the argument, aware that she would be kept even later at school finishing those papers which she did not want to bring home. She wondered at the laziness of mothers who sent their children to private school, where everyone wore the same uniforms, and didn't mark their child's name in the clothes. After the two girls tried on the jacket, one of them found her barrette in the pocket, so Victoria returned to her work upstairs. When she got back to the classroom she sensed that someone had been there. "Hello? Hello?" she called. No one answered. She stared at the desk. The papers were in order, yet she was sure they had been touched. A student making mischief? "Anybody there?" she called out, and she heard a reply, "Miss Lewis?" It was the voice of the school janitor, Mr. Everding. He was an older, patient man who had seen hundreds of children come to the school as tiny girls and leave as young women. He was kind to the children and helpful, always glad to aid in looking for lost note-books or orthodontic retainers or whatever they had misplaced. He came to the door of Vicky's classroom and said, "Someone came up here a few minutes ago looking for you. Told her you were in the building but I couldn't say where. One of the mothers. She didn't wait too long."

"Was she here? In the classroom?"

"Out in the hall. But she seemed to know which room was yours."

"What did she look like?" Suddenly Victoria was afraid.

"Handsome woman," Mr. Everding said, scratching his head, trying to remember. His manner said, Gee, I've seen so many mothers it's hard to tell them apart.

"What color was her hair?"

"Red, from what I could see of it. She had some kind of hat on. And a pretty kinda tan coat, with fur here, and here," his gestures indicating the sleeves and hem. "Very pretty lady."

"Thank you, Mr. Everding," Victoria said, concealing her uneasiness. "Mr. Everding," she called out, "are you going to be on this floor for a while?"

"I expect so," he said.

"Well, could you come and do my room next? I'm just about to go. I won't be in your way for long."

She finished her papers quickly while Mr. Everding swept the floor, wiped the blackboards clean, and adjusted the window shades. She thanked him for staying near, then she gathered up her bag of books and took her coat from the rack. "Would you just watch me as I leave the building?" she asked the custodian in a small voice. "I'm a little nervous today."

He looked puzzled but nodded, "Sure." Then he stationed himself by the window. Victoria hurried down the stairs, not pausing to check each landing, and out the door, which shut behind her loudly. She looked up and down the street but saw nothing unusual; then she looked up at the window, waved at Mr. Everding, staunch guardian of her well-being, and headed toward the crosstown bus and home.

On the bus she thought about the visitor to her classroom and knew it had been Amanda Keating.

Jeffrey soon began meeting with his lawyer, Amanda, and Amanda's lawyer to hammer out a separation agreement. The evening after the first of these meetings Jeffrey came home looking particularly grim.

"I need a drink," he said, and without even taking off his coat he went to the hall closet where Victoria kept the liquor and took down a bottle of scotch. Going into the kitchen, he poured it into a glass, straight, no water, soda, or ice. He gulped some down, then poured out more. He clutched the glass and stared at Vicky. He had a strange expression on his face.

"What happened?" Vicky asked.

"She wants everything. I get nothing. At least according to her version of the agreement."

"Well, what did you do?"

"I told her nothing doing, she can't have part of my business. And she can't have half the co-op *and* half the summer house. Can you imagine trying to share the summer house with her? She'd probably camp out there every weekend and claim that our half was Tuesdays, Wednesdays, and Thursdays."

Jeffrey told Victoria he wanted to be generous, to make sure Daria was well taken care of, but they had not bargained for total intransigence on Amanda's part.

"She won't listen to reason. She won't bargain. She gave her lawyer a list of her expenses and it's phenomenal."

"But can't she go to work?"

"She does work, part-time, at that gallery I told you about." This was Amanda's little thrice-a-week job at an art gallery on Fifty-seventh Street. Jeffrey joked that Amanda enjoyed it because the gallery was located across the street from Bendel's.

"But she could go to work full-time."

"And do what? She has no training at all. She hasn't held a real job since we married, and before she worked for me she was a receptionist somewhere, at a switchboard. She claims that since I supported her for ten years, I'm supposed to support her now."

"It doesn't sound as if you reached any compromises."

"Oh, sure. I'm getting my painting." He gulped more scotch.

"Are you going to ask for anything else?" Vicky asked quietly.

Jeffrey shook his head. "I can't see the point. Everything that's there seems to belong there. If we started dividing every piece of furniture it would turn into a silly fight. I have to protect my business. By law, she's supposed to get fifty percent of our assets, but I can bargain her away from claiming any part of the business, and that's the most important thing to me. Let her have the co-op, what does it matter? I'll try to get the summer house, which I always liked better anyway. You'd love it; it's really a charming place."

East Hampton, thought Victoria. We'd go to East Hampton every summer. The idea was both depressing and exhilarating. She had mixed feelings about that whole Long Island social scene. She'd never fit in.

"Jeff," Vicky said all at once. "Remember you told me you were going to call some of your old friends once you were seeing the lawyers? Maybe now you should begin getting in touch with those people." She was eager for Jeffrey to reestablish some of his old ties instead of living isolated in her apartment, hearing only from his ex-wife.

Jeffrey shrugged. "Yeah, I guess so." He drained his scotch and poured some more into the glass.

"You'd feel better if you did," Victoria said.

He looked at her as he took another swig. Then he wiped his mouth with his hand and said, "They don't want any part of me, didn't you know? I'm a wife-abuser, a criminal. They won't have anything to do with me."

"What?" said Vicky, incredulous.

"Oh, I called a few people. They practically hung up on me. They asked me how I could do this to Amanda, how I could do this to Daria. They were scared, kiddo, they were closing ranks. Divorce frightens them. Maybe it'll come knocking at their doors. Meanwhile, they don't want to hear from me."

"Everyone?" Vicky said. "They all said that? What kind of friends are they?"

"I guess no friends at all," he said tiredly. "They don't want to hear my side. Amanda got to them first. She told them I had run away with another woman; well,

76

that part's true, I guess. And that it had been going on for a long time, which is, as you well know, a lie. But they believed her. Why shouldn't they? They're her friends now. The woman scorned."

"I can't believe that all your friends would turn their backs," Victoria said.

"Believe it," Jeffrey said curtly. "We'll just have to make some new friends."

Victoria recalled how he had told her of his special circle of friends, couples who shared so many evenings together. Some of the people had been his friends from before the marriage. How could they be so callous and unfeeling? Jeffrey was clearly devasted by their hostility.

"Isn't there anyone you haven't called? Perhaps it's just those few people you saw most often, who are most involved," Vicky began.

Jeffrey laughed. "That's just the point. They were all my best friends." Then he smiled. "But you're right, there are some people, a few guys I knew in college, an old friend from high school. I hadn't been as close with them, but they never knew Amanda all that well and I don't think she'd call them. They weren't chic enough for her. I'll give them a call soon."

"Now," urged Vicky. "Tonight."

"No, honey, not tonight. Tonight I'm a little drunk, and I'm here with you and we'd better batten down the hatches because we're in for a long haul."

She did not tell him that earlier that week she had been desperately afraid in school, where someone had appeared mysteriously at her classroom and disappeared just as mysteriously. She did not want him to think she was becoming paranoid as well. Suddenly Amanda lurked behind the behavior of all his friends, determined his state of well-being, the condition of his ego and self-esteem. There had to be a way to break this power, to show Amanda she could not control their lives.

"I know," said Victoria. "We'll give a party."

"For whom?" Jeffrey said morosely, starting on his fourth scotch.

"For our friends. Between us I'm sure we know enough people to fill this apartment. We'll keep it very simple,

77

just wine and some fruit and cheese. You could bake bread. We can surround ourselves with *our* friends and you don't have to sit around thinking about the ones that got away."

"If you think so," Jeffrey mumbled.

"I think so," said Victoria, and she got a lined yellow pad and a pen from the file cabinet in the corner of the living room and sat down at the coffee table and began making her list.

She planned the party for a Saturday evening two weeks away, not on one of the weekends they were supposed to see Daria. Jeffrey's visiting rights had evolved into an informal every-other-Sunday arrangement; by choosing that Saturday, Victoria could be sure that the child would not discover the remnants of the party from the night before. In fact, she made Jeffrey promise they would hide all the party goods they bought so Daria could not tell her mother anything. During the next few days, Jeffrey provided her with the names and addresses of a dozen people he thought they should invite; Renee, his college friends and their wives, a few friends from his old job, and his secretary, whom he said was the soul of discretion. Victoria invited Willa and Matthew, three teachers from school, her friend Gail Harrison from Jeffrey's old building, and the codirectors of the summer camp she'd worked at the past three summers. The guest list totaled twenty-eight people. "See?" Victoria said proudly as she wrote out invitations. Twenty-two people accepted, to Victoria's surprise; she never expected that many. Jeffrey had been pleasantly surprised that his college friends were sympathetic and supportive. "They'll just have to fit in here," she said to Jeffrey, who was unperturbed about the party plans and strangely calm after his evening of drinking the previous week.

He seemed resigned to his fate, like a rat caught in a trap, and this made Victoria angry. She kept thinking, if only he knew the truth, that he didn't have to give everything away, he'd be so much better off. She hoped that seeing all the people together at the party would give him a sense of security and a foundation from which he could construct a new life. Vicky knew he spent much of his time living in the old one.

Willa phoned, excited, and offered to come early and help with the preparations. Victoria accepted, then talked to her about Jeffrey's settlement. "The way it sounds now, he'll be stripped completely bare by the time they're through. What can we do?"

"Do you want me to ask Matthew to talk to him? He could do it the night of the party without letting on we asked him to. Matthew's a very good actor. Take it from one who knows."

"All right," Vicky agreed reluctantly. "But only when the place is crowded and they can go off somewhere quietly. Otherwise it'll look like a setup."

"Don't worry so much," Willa said. "It's bad for your sex life."

"Hah," said Victoria, whose sex life had become a bit irregular of late, what with Jeffrey worried and distracted most of the time. "Maybe we should have held an orgy."

"Too late," said Willa. "You bought the wrong invitations."

She cleaned the house all Friday afternoon after school and spent Saturday shopping. She walked over to Zabar's, where she bought several kinds of cheese—an herbed Brie, a Port Salut, and a Bleu. Then she bought three breads, a variety of crackers, Greek olives, roasted peppers, pate de campagne, and cornichons. Satisfied with her purchases, though they cost much more than she'd expected, she went on to the liquor store where she ordered several half gallons of Boucheron, to be delivered later that afternoon. She bought a chrysanthemum plant for the coffee table and small fragrant soaps to put in the bathroom. When she got home there was a note that said, "Back in a few minutes, love, J." She wondered where he could have gone. She put down her heavy shopping bags, then realized she had forgotten the plastic glasses. She raced out again, banging the apartment door behind her, ran to the elevator, and bumped into Jeffrey as he was coming out. He was carrying a long, white florist's box. "Damn," he said. "It was supposed to be a surprise."

"I forgot the glasses," she said.

"I'll get them. Here," he said clumsily, thrusting the box at her and disappearing back into the elevator.

She stared at the box as she walked back to her apartment, then when she came in she ripped off the bows. Inside was a great deal of fluffy tissue paper with a note on top. "To V.," it said on the envelope. She opened it up. A card inside said, "I owe everything to you. All my love, Jeff." She felt her eyes filling with tears. She pulled aside the tissue and saw a dozen long-stemmed roses. They must have cost a fortune. "Oh, Jeff," she said, and then the world was all right.

That night everything was in place. Her gateleg table was pulled out, the cheeses, crackers, and breads arranged on top, a vase filled with Jeffrey's roses set back, their fragrance filling the room. The chrysanthemum plant sat on the coffee table next to bowls of little olives, a tray of mixed nuts, and some paper cocktail napkins. Victoria had decided late that afternoon to make one hot hors d'oeuvre, and she had spent the last hour before the party filling mushrooms with a ham and cheese mixture. Then she had dressed in her black pants and red tunic and waited for everyone to come. Willa, as promised, was first, fragrant with Bal à Versailles and wearing long black palazzo-style pants and a low-cut black top that revealed her cleavage. Vicky knew she had gotten dressed up especially to impress Jeffrey; this was to be their first meeting. Willa had told Vicky she wanted to meet Jeffrey when everything was just right, not in some coffee shop somewhere, so they had agreed that the party would be just the place.

"So, this is the man," Willa said, studying Jeffrey with embarrassing candor. He looked irresistibly handsome in dark slacks and a white silk shirt. "I like him. Yeah, I like this one a lot." She threw her arms around him, pressing her breasts against his chest. "Welcome to the family," she said. "You'd better take good care of my friend."

"I'm trying," Jeffrey laughed.

"You'd better, or I'll get Matthew after you. This is Matthew, my live-in hit man. He's a painter but in his spare time he beats up people who take advantage of my friends." She introduced a dark man, at least six feet three inches tall and weighing two hundred pounds, wiry hair on his arms and on his chest, exposed by the V of his unbuttoned shirt.

His muscles rippled as he extended his hand. "Don't listen to Willa. I'm really a pussycat."

"He chews wineglasses," said Willa. "Show them how you chew wineglasses."

Matthew shook his head. "All I do with wineglasses is drink wine from them. I think I'll do that right now."

Matthew and Jeffrey brought the women some wine, then returned to the food table to sample cheeses. "I see you've done everything," Willa said. "Isn't there anything for me to do?"

"You can hold my hand," Vicky said.

"You nervous?"

"Kind of. This is our social debut as a couple."

"It's going to be gala."

"If anyone shows up. Oops, the doorbell."

All at once the guests began to arrive—Jeffrey's friend Renee, accompanied by a shy, accountant-looking fellow; Gail Harrison from Jeffrey's building, overweight but lively and warm; the old college friends of Jeffrey's who proved to be kind and supportive and who told rollicking stories about their friend's pranks in the good old days. The room began to fill with people laughing pleasantly, talking, sipping wine, and nibbling on cheeses, crackers, nuts.

Vicky smiled benignly and went into the kitchen to heat up the stuffed mushrooms. She took them out of the refrigerator and put the tray into the oven, then set the timer so she wouldn't have to stand in the kitchen while they heated up. Her ears buzzed and fingertips tingled from the two glasses of wine she had drunk a little too fast. The mingled dialogue from the living room reached a crescendo, and her heart swelled with each decibel. Everything *will* be all right, she told herself.

Then all at once the sound level dropped to a hush. At first Vicky thought it was one of those odd moments at parties when, for no reason at all, everyone stops talking at the same time. But the noise didn't pick up again. It was the oddest sensation. Then the silence was broken by Jeffrey's voice at the front door. "What are you doing here?" he was saying to someone. His tone was angry, peremptory. "What do you want?"

81

"Why, darling, you know I adore parties," a female voice said.

Victoria's knees went rubbery and she had to lean on the counter to keep from collapsing. The voice, all honey and poison, was unmistakable. *Oh God, tell me it isn't true,* she prayed. She caught her breath and her balance and ran a hand through her hair, then moved cautiously into the living room. Amanda stood at the front door, regal, slender, frighteningly erect and composed, titian hair cascading around her face and shoulders like a *Vogue* cover come to life. She wore a matching designer coat and dress in an expensive plaid fabric, something Victoria had seen advertised in the Sunday *Times* fall fashion section. She was absolutely breathtaking. But her eyes were hard, cold, crystalline, hate-filled. Behind her stood a young man in his mid-twenties, athletic-looking like a dancer. *Gigolo,* Vicky thought, but he looked like he could take care of himself. Out of the corner of her eye Vicky noticed Willa's boyfriend Matthew sidling protectively toward her, hammy fists balled for action. The other guests stood transfixed in a tableau vivant of apprehension and shock.

Victoria stared at the figure in the doorway, filling her eyes with Amanda, and suddenly their gazes locked. Victoria felt scorched and withered by a gust of hatred. Then a mocking smile widened the corners of Amanda's mouth, as she made a gesture that encompassed the entire room. She looked at Jeffrey. "So this is what you left me for. This crummy apartment, this crappy little party, that mousy girl in the tacky top and last year's pants. What a joke." She turned to her companion. "Come on, honey. They told me this was a grown-ups' party."

She snorted, pivoted, and departed with a rustle of expensive fabric. Victoria felt the energy of the party leave the room in Amanda's wake.

The party had resumed after Amanda's departure, but it was a hollow imitation of the vibrant affair that had been in progress. Amanda's presence lingered, dominating conversation, tainting the food and tincturing the drink. It even poisoned a friendship. When

Jeffrey, Victoria, and their guests began speculating on how Amanda had found out about the party, Victoria had tactlessly said, "The only person here who knows her is Gail. They live in the same building."

Gail's hand flew to her chest. "Vicky, surely you don't think that I—"

Victoria realized her error. "Oh, no. I didn't mean *you* told her!"

"I've never said two words to the woman," Gail said defensively, panning the room for supportive faces.

"I'm sure you haven't," said Jeffrey. "Vicky wasn't accusing anybody."

"I hope not," she said, but for the rest of the evening she was hurt and broody, and she was the first of the guests to leave.

When the last guest had department, Jeffrey found Victoria standing forlornly in front of the bathroom mirror. "She's right," Vicky said to his image in the mirror. "It *is* a tacky top, and they *are* last year's pants. And..." Her chin began to quiver. "...I *am* a mousy girl!"

"Vicky, no, no, you mustn't let her get to you that way," he said, spinning her around and pressing her tightly to him. He held her until her wracking sobs had subsided, then pulled her by the hand into the bedroom to make love to her. But he couldn't hold his erection, and their lovemaking ended in debacle.

"That's never happened to me before," he said through the hands pressed to his face as he sat on the edge of the bed.

Vicky caressed his back comfortingly. "She got to you, too."

"Yes, she got to me, too. Darling, we must keep her out of our lives—out of our hearts, out of our minds."

"Out of our bed," Victoria said flatly.

"Yes. Particularly out of our bed."

Jeffrey got his erection back, but the evening had been lost to Amanda Keating.

Amanda broke off divorce negotiations the following Monday, leaving Jeffrey and Victoria in a perpetual state of tension despite the improvement in their social life. They began to see their friends for quiet dinners, an occasional movie, and once, a Broadway show. They went to see *42nd Street,* charging the tickets off as a business expense. After the show they had a drink at O'Neal's near Fifty-seventh Street on the Avenue of the Americas.

"How are you going to get her back to the negotiating table?" Vicky asked.

"I'll starve her out," Jeffrey explained. "I'm cutting my checks back to the bare minimum. Just enough for her to pay the maintenance on the co-op and feed herself and Daria—and that gigolo."

Vicky's eyebrow arched. "Does that upset you, that she has a lover?"

"You mean am I jealous? No. I'm just worried about Daria's reaction to seeing a strange man in Mommy's bed."

Vicky gazed steadily at him. "Maybe just a little jealous?" she said teasingly.

He shrugged. "Only in that it bugs me that she's giving him freely what I had to beg for. I was a terrific husband. I gave her everything she wanted, everything she needed. I didn't ask for much, but whatever it was, she denied it to me. This guy probably freeloads off her, uses her, is inconsiderate, never gives her a thing, and she fucks his brains out. You explain it. It's a mystery."

"It's supposed to be. It's a very alluring mystery."

"What does that mean?"

"I don't know. I think you're still attached to her, in a way. I think you're more hurt and jealous than you admit. It's all right," she added, covering his hands with hers. "I understand. It doesn't mean you're going back to her or anything."

He looked at her. "Is that what you think?"

"No, of course not," she protested, but too loudly. "Well, sometimes I fantasize about it."

He leaned over the table and pressed her cheeks tenderly with his fingertips. "Vicky, you're a goose."

"It wouldn't be the first time a man went back to his wife after having an affair," she said. Her mouth pouted and her eyes began to mist.

"Vicky, Vicky, don't you know how much I love you? When you say 'affair,' it's like someone stabbing my guts. This isn't an affair. I want to marry you!"

84

The mist in her eyes turned to pools that spilled off over her cheeks. "Do you? Still? We could live together, like we are now. That would be okay."

"Are you denying my proposal?"

"Is this a proposal?"

"It's my fifth. You accepted the first four, so I didn't think I had to make another."

"I need reassurance."

He reached into his pocket. "Will this help?" He produced a powder-blue box, the unmistakable signature color of Tiffany's. Vicky rubbed her eyes and opened the box. Inside was a small hinged case, and inside that was a ring, a rosette of diamonds and rubies on a platinum band. Vicky gasped as several diners nearby looked at them interestedly. "It's not an engagement ring, and it's not a wedding band; obviously those are out of the question until the divorce comes through. So call it . . . a commitment ring."

She slipped it on her finger and held it up to the light. "Oh, Jeffrey, I didn't need any sign of your commitment. It's the most beautiful thing I've ever seen."

"When things get dark, look at it."

"Yes. Yes, I will. Oh, Jeffrey, get that divorce as soon as you can. I want to be your wife more than anything in the world. I want to have your children."

"I promise," Jeffrey said. "I pledge it."

Though Victoria could not precisely gauge the extent of Jeffrey's attachment to his estranged wife, his attachment to Daria was so powerful it worried her. He indulged the child terribly, disciplined her halfheartedly, and seemed incapable of objectivity about her. Victoria attributed it to his guilt about leaving, even though it wasn't his daughter he'd left but his wife. Victoria held her tongue though, recognizing the explosiveness of the issue; she did what she could to correct the child's worst tendencies. It was not easy; she wasn't Daria's mother, or even her stepmother. When Victoria denied Daria something, the girl simply appealed to her father and received it.

One Saturday morning Vicky went downstairs to get the mail. There were some department store flyers and a bill from the phone company. Vicky opened it in the elevator. When she read the amount, her eyes widened. "Huh?"

A man in the elevator smiled. "Rates went up again."

"By two hundred dollars?" She felt absolutely wobbly-legged when she stepped off the elevator and stood in the corridor examining the bill. The charges for her line were $238.72. They were usually around forty dollars. The extra two hundred dollars was for long-distance charges.

She called out for Jeffrey when she got into the apartment.

"I'm in the kitchen. You want cheese in your omelet or caviar and sour cream?"

"You'd better hold the caviar. We're going to have to hock the jar to pay my phone bill." She showed it to him. "I thought you were going to use your own phone to make long-distance calls," she said.

"I do. But I didn't make those calls. I don't know anyone in Hawaii. Eugene, Oregon? Don't know anybody there either." He went down the list, shaking his head. "Looks like the phone company crossed your line with somebody else's."

"Either that or..."

"Or what?"

"Daria. Look they were all made the weekend she was here. In fact, I remember coming into the bedroom and finding her on the phone having a make-believe conversation. At least that's what I thought it was. Does she know how to dial long distance? I mean, pressing 'one' first?"

"I can't believe she did it. She's just a kid."

"A kid can press eleven buttons on a telephone, Jeffrey. It doesn't call for prodigious manual dexterity. How am I going to pay this bill?"

"Call the phone company. Maybe if you tell them the truth they'll cancel it or forgive some of it."

"I was hoping you'd say you'd pay for it. After all, it's your child. I was also hoping you'd say you'd have a talk with her. A few more visits from her and my savings will be wiped out."

"You're right," he said. "I'll take care of it—if she really did it. I'm from the innocent-until-proven-guilty school. Now, how about those omelets?"

86

Victoria decided to ignore his barb about her assumption of Daria's guilt. She knew she was right—but she also knew there was no point in pursuing the matter.

The following day, a rainy Sunday, Jeffrey picked up Daria and brought her back to the apartment. The child clutched her Russian doll as usual. He played Tiddly Winks and Chutes and Ladders with her for a while, then settled down to read the *Times*. Vicky played cards with Daria, ignoring the fact that the girl cheated openly and changed the rules constantly. Then Daria got bored, and so did Vicky. "I'm going to read the paper with your daddy in the living room. You can stay in here and play quietly with Sasha, okay?"

"Okay," Daria said, waving her doll around like a ventriloquist's dummy. "We have to call Sasha's parents in Russia."

"Do you?" asked Vicky. "Do you know how to call Russia?"

"Sure. My mommy showed me. You just press 'one' and then ten numbers."

"Yes, said Vicky. "That's exactly how you get Russia."

Vicky stalked into the other room and removed the sports section from Jeffrey's hands. "What's going on?" he said.

She took his hand, pulled him to his feet, and led him to the bedroom door. There was Daria, talking to Russia, or somewhere. Jeffrey marched in and removed the phone from her hand. Her face tightened with guilt and she began to cry. Jeffrey put the phone to his ear. "Who's this?" He listened. "Ma'am, that was my daughter fooling with the phone. I'm sorry. Where are you, anyway?...Really? How's the weather out there?" He suppressed a laugh. "Well, I'm really sorry again, ma'am." He hung up.

"Where was she?" asked Vicky.

"Encino, California. She couldn't tell me how the weather was because the sun hasn't come up yet." He turned to Daria, who was sobbing uncontrollably. "Honey, honey, it's all right. No more phone calls though, okay? Okay, sweetie?"

87

"Mommy said I could," she sniffed.

"In your other house, you can."

"No, I can't make them in my other house. She said I could make them here. She told me how."

Jeffrey and Victoria exchanged significant glances. "Well, sweetie," Jeffrey said, "I'll talk to your mother about it. But no more phone calls, all right?"

"*She* doesn't like it, right?"

"She? Who's she?"

Daria pointed at Vicky.

"She has a name, honey. It's Vicky."

Daria looked sullenly at Vicky.

"How about saying her name? Say, 'Vicky,'" her father pronounced.

Daria shook her head. Vicky looked at Jeffrey, silently praying he would be firm. But Daria remained intransigent, and Jeffrey shrugged.

"Give her time," he said.

Vicky's shoulders slumped. How much time will it take, she wondered dejectedly. But she pushed the thought away, unwilling to torment herself any more. It *would* take time.

Later in the week Vicky met Willa for an early dinner. Willa, who had a crush on Zubin Mehta, had a pair of tickets to the Philharmonic at Lincoln Center. She'd promised to take Matthew because they were doing something by Elliott Carter (whom Willa couldn't stand); otherwise, she sighed, she'd have much preferred to take Vicky. They had dinner at The Saloon, a huge barn of a restaurant on Broadway across from Lincoln Center, where waiters on roller skates brought the orders.

Vicky told Willa about Daria's long-distance spree, but Willa waved her hand disdainfully. "You can't get crazy from the shit children pull. When I was her age, I glued my mother's false eyelashes together. The fettucini here is fabulous."

"If I thought it were just mischief, it wouldn't bother me," Vicky replied. "But I keep thinking that maybe the tensions of the divorce are beginning to affect her. I've seen some divorced children in my class—"

Willa waved futilely at a waitress. "I think a lot of

that is crap. Children are always looking for a reason to misbehave. I mean, they're fucking savages! So they use divorce as an excuse. Divorced parents let them get away with it because they feel so guilty. I say, slam them down."

"I suppose you're right. Jeffrey just won't slam Daria down, though. If he slams anyone down it's me. He resents it when I insist he discipline his daughter."

"Hey, nobody said it's easy. You bought yourself some ball of wax when you took up with that man."

"I love him, Willa."

"You'd better, honey, with that queen bitch on your backs."

"She put Daria up to making those calls."

"'Beware the wrath of a woman scorned.' Waitress?" They finally got someone to take their order. "You've got to break Jeffrey in. He's got to be on your side when the kid acts up; otherwise, the kid'll divide and conquer. Or, rather the bitch will, because she's using the kid to exploit every weakness in your relationship with Jeffrey. I'd say she's done a fine job so far."

"Jesus," said Vicky. "You are one smart lady."

"I know a thing or two."

"What do you think of this?" Vicky said, producing an oversized piece of drawing paper from her handbag and unfolding it. It was a picture drawn by Daria, of a haunted-looking house in total disrepair, with broken windows, torn curtains, collapsing roof, mysterious dark figures flitting about, and standing over it, a giant woman with red hair and an angry expression. "Daria says it's her house. Creepy, isn't it?"

Willa studied it, making muffled grunts through a piece of bread. "That's her mother, right?" she said, pointing to the red-haired giantess. "What's this red thing here? Looks like a lampshade covering a stick-figure baby?"

"That's her doll. That babushka doll I told you about, the one with no bottom, like one of those cozies they put over toilet paper rolls in people's bathrooms. Sasha. I don't know who the baby is."

Willa stared at the picture for another minute. "Broken home," she said, handing it back to Vicky as the food arrived. "Reigned over by her mother. The doll? I don't know. Maybe it's her, the kid. The kid needs to reign over someone too; otherwise her mother would totally dominate her. I don't know, I'm no psychologist. I'm just a hungry actress loading up on carbohydrates so I can rape Zubin Mehta after the performance. He's playing Wagner and Brahms and"—she curled her lip—"Elliott Carter. I think I'd rather listen to Jimmy Carter. Have I helped?"

"Oh, yes. Thank you. Boy, am I glad I have you as a friend. I need your objectivity."

"Hell, I can do more than that. If that bitch gives you a hard time, you tell ol' Willa. I'll show her what true bitchery is."

"What could you do?" Vicky laughed.

"I'll fix her ass. I'm not afraid of her." Victoria stopped laughing as she realized Willa was serious.

The doorman smiled at Vicky when she got home, then snapped his fingers and said, "Wait, there's a package for you. I think it's for...uh...your friend." He could not bring himself to say "the man you live with." Poor Joe, Vicky thought. He got out a clipboard and showed her where to sign for it. It had been hand delivered by some teenaged kid, he explained. Vicky wondered if it was something Jeffrey had ordered without telling her, perhaps something for the apartment. But then, why would it be sent by hand instead of mail or United Parcel?

The doorman went to the small closet near the mailboxes where deliveries were held and removed a large, square, flat package that seemed not to weigh too much. He handled it with great delicacy. She looked at Jeffrey's name and their address and apartment number written in heavy black marker. Beside it, in red marker: "This End Up." "The kid said you're not supposed to tilt it," Joe said, handing it to her precisely as instructed.

She carried it onto the elevator, holding it like a pizza or birthday-cake box. It was too heavy to be pizza or birthday cake. She smiled at her own thought, knowing she wouldn't eat anything delivered in such a mysterious manner. When she got to her door, she set the package down on the floor, found her keys, opened the door and held it open with her behind as she picked up the package.

She set it down on the gateleg table and turned on the lights. She wondered when Jeffrey was getting home. He'd said he'd be working late, until around eight-thirty or nine. It was eight-fifteen. She sighed and went to inspect the package again. There was no return address. She hefted it again, weighed it in her hands; it was the shape of a poster, but heavier. She wondered whether she should open it without Jeffrey, and finally, overcome with curiosity, compromised by slitting a corner of the wrapping with a steak knife. Peering, she saw a layer of plastic bubble-wrap. Underneath was something crimson. Cautiously, she poked the sharp point of the saw-toothed blade into the plastic liner, puncturing one of the air bubbles with a pop. Suddenly a viscous red liquid spurted out of the hole, covering the knife and her hand and splashing her clothes, the table, and the rug. It began oozing out of the hole and spreading in a puddle on the table.

Vicky's first thought was, *Blood.* She heard herself scream as lurid fantasies raced through her mind, thoughts of hacked-off limbs, ghouls bleeding their victims white. But the liquid had a familiar odor. It was paint. She shuddered, wondering what object had been immersed in paint and who had sent it. The answer to the latter question was already dawning on her as she went into action, running into the kitchen and yanking ten or fifteen pieces of paper towel off the roll over the sink, then rummaging through the cabinet beneath the sink until she found an old, half-filled can of turpentine. The odor and oily texture of the paint indicated it was enamel. Tough paint to clean, she said to herself, rushing back to blot up the puddle and stanch the flow from the punctured parcel. Then she got down on her hands and knees and started scrubbing the carpet with turpentine-soaked paper toweling. She managed only to make things worse, pushing the paint deeper into the fiber and shredding the towel into frayed pieces that stuck to the tacky paint. "Shit, shit, shit," Vicky muttered between clenched teeth. Suddenly she felt a hand on her shoulder. She screamed, falling backward

91

from her squatting position and sprawling across the carpet.

"Jesus, it's only me," said Jeffrey. He looked down at the red stain on the carpet. "What happened?"

Victoria sat panting on the carpet, hand over her heart. "You scared me to death! I didn't hear you come in."

"Look at you," he said, offering his hand. "You're as white as ivory." He helped her to her feet and moved to embrace her, but she pushed him away.

"I have wet paint on my clothes. You'll get it all over yourself. Oh, God, am I glad you're home."

"What did you spill?"

She told him about the package. Gingerly he examined it, frowning. "Looks like we'll have to operate. Nurse, bring me some newspapers and the rubber gloves. Keep some rags handy, and an intravenous of turpentine. I'm going to change into some old clothes and scrub."

Two minutes later Jeffrey reappeared from the bedroom in a pair of Jordache jeans and a Lacoste polo shirt. Vicky laughed. "Is that what you call old clothes?"

He grinned. "I left my old-old clothes behind in the holocaust. Amanda didn't consider them worthy of returning to me shredded."

"You may not be so lucky this time," Vicky said, nodding at the package.

"You think this is from her?"

"Do you have any other ill-wishers? God, I hope not. One is more than enough."

Jeffrey prodded the package with the knife. "It's like someone dipped something in a bucket of paint, then wrapped it in plastic before it could dry. See, it's starting to dry where you opened it." He delicately lifted the package, held it while Vicky laid newspapers under it, then set it down and began slicing through the paper and plastic wrapper. The blood-colored paint seeped out, running onto the newspapers and soaking into the levee of balled-up paper toweling she'd placed on the perimeter of the table. As he peeled off the last layer of plastic, they discerned the shape of the item within. It was a picture frame. The picture was face down, so that the sides of the frame and the canvas floor formed a cavity into which paint had been poured to the brim. Vicky fetched a large plastic trash bag and they tipped the painting into it, spilling the excess paint until the cavity was drained. Then Jeffrey looked at Vicky.

"I think I know what this is."

"I do, too."

"I don't want to look. I might close my eyes when I turn it over. Tell me if I'm wrong."

He turned the picture face up. Though it was totally disfigured, Jeffrey recognized the canvas Amanda had given him for a gift, the lovely nineteenth-century landscape. "Oh, Jeffrey darling, I'm so very sorry," Vicky said, hanging her head.

"I didn't know her hatred went this deep," he said, containing tears with blinks.

I did, thought Vicky. But when she spoke, she said, "I didn't know anyone's did."

Chapter Four

JEFFREY'S LAWYER DIDN'T seem very troubled by
the destruction of the painting. "When you've handled
divorces as long as I have," he said, "you've seen everything." Victoria, for one, wanted to know what "everything" meant. Sometimes she believed that Amanda
was the only vengeful ex-wife in the entire city of New
York, that everyone else was completely civilized and
treated the whole matter like an English garden party.

Vicky kept waiting for Jeffrey to lose his temper, to
reach the point where he said, "This is enough, no more."
But after the painting incident, Amanda's behavior took
a peculiar turn: she became completely cooperative.
Meetings were quickly arranged between lawyers to
take advantage of Amanda's new frame of mind. Jeffrey
was skeptical but grateful. Vicky was wary and afraid
to hope.

One afternoon while teaching class, Vicky was called
from the room to the telephone. The headmistress dis-
approved of personal phone calls at school; Vicky was
apprehensive until she heard a jubilant Jeffrey. "The
papers are signed," he said. "We'll celebrate tonight.
By the way, I got through to you by saying I was your
brother and I'd had another child. Bye."

Vicky hung up, then turned to the scowling Mrs.
Dolittle. "My third nephew," she explained, straight-
faced. "Alexander Jeffrey." Mrs. Dolittle glared at her.
"Your class is waiting, Miss Lewis."

She danced up the stairs and to celebrate allowed
the children to discuss their favorite TV programs for
the rest of the hour. "Dallas" won, hands down.

But Jeffrey's jubilation seemed ill-founded to her
when Victoria read the agreement that night. The pic-

ture grew worse and worse. Amanda was to receive the co-op, including all its contents, Jeffrey only the summer house, worth nowhere near the same amount. There was heavy child support, heavy alimony, life insurance, health insurance, home insurance, a large bank loan and department store debts to be paid, stock to be exchanged, savings to be divided. Jeffrey would be left with very little.

"But I've got the business," he said. "And she'll get married, wait and see. She's not the type to live alone for long."

Vicky lowered the papers and stared at Jeffrey. The agreement was a giant ball and chain that would hobble them. Where would they get money for themselves to live? Her salary was low. Jeffrey's only stretched so far. How could they afford a life of their own?

"We won't be able to move," Vicky said quietly. It was all she could bring herself to say. Amanda had exerted herself once more and gotten exactly what she wanted.

"But we have the summer place. It'll make a big difference summers, especially when we have Daria in August."

A month with Daria. She'd forgotten about child custody. She was afraid to look.

"Vicky, it's over. There's nothing she can do anymore. In one year the divorce comes through. I don't have to negotiate with her again."

"And your painting? Was that mentioned? Are you to be compensated for that? And the clothing she destroyed?"

His helpless shrug said it all. "I have to get over to the old apartment and clear out the rest of my things. By next month, the papers say."

"Weren't you supposed to make her pay for the painting to be fixed?" Vicky persisted, feeling a too-familiar anger rise.

"She denied everything," Jeffrey said.

They opened some wine and halfheartedly toasted their "triumph," but in bed that night, once again, Jeffrey lost his erection. "It's no good. I'm too uptight. It's been an exhausting day."

"It's all right," Vicky soothed. "I understand."

95

His problem persisted another week, then abated, but Victoria became anxious about their lovemaking, always afraid it would turn into disaster. Jeffrey refused to talk about it, never used the word "impotence," as though he feared putting a name on it. But Vicky knew something deeper was inhibiting Jeffrey, someone's presence in their bed.

Determined to exorcise Amanda's spell, Vicky began a campaign to find out more about the woman. She questioned Jeffrey about his relationship, about his ex-wife's past, and he told her a few things. He mentioned that his parents, who lived in California, had never liked Amanda.

"Why not?" Vicky asked.

"They didn't think she was good enough for me."

"In what respect?"

"Not from the right background."

Amanda, Vicky discovered, came from a small town in upstate New York, a town situated near Elmira and surrounded by colleges. Amanda grew up aware of haves and have-nots; haves went to college, drove convertibles, went to pep rallies and football games in pretty clothes. Have-nots, "the townies," lived in little wooden frame houses; their fathers were unemployable (Amanda's had lost a leg in an accident at an auto assembly plant), their mothers watched TV all day long and sipped vodka from orange-juice bottles. Amanda's parents had both died by the time she was seventeen and her only living relative, an aunt in Schenectady, offered to take her in. She had a little money saved and Amanda was able to convince the aunt that it would be well spent sending her to secretarial school in New York City. She came to New York, enrolled in a typing and steno course, and lived at the Y. Six months later she got a job working as a receptionist for a law firm. Two years later, she was working in a similar position for a public relations firm. Jeffrey's public relations firm.

"So she came to New York to conquer the world," Vicky said.

"I guess so," Jeffrey said. "It's hard to remember what she was like then. But that beautiful head of hair and long legs! Skirts were shorter then, and she'd sit with those legs crossed."

"But what were you like?"

"Me? Like I am now. Nice guy, affable, a prince among men."

"No, really. Why did you marry her?"

"Why does anybody get married? To be married."

Vicky quietly absorbed this small bit of information. A few of her questions had been answered. A girl who'd had virtually no family, who'd been deprived as a child and had to struggle for everything she had—certainly explanation enough for some of Amanda's excesses. She would be more hostile than most when her world was threatened. Still, these explanations didn't add up to a justification of Amanda's unremitting vindictiveness. There was an element in her character that could not be attributed to upbringing, environment, or other influences cited by psychologists as the causes of deep anger. Certainly, being left by her husband must have been dreadfully provoking—Vicky sometimes fantasized herself in Amanda's place, and it made her immeasurably anxious—but she wasn't the first woman ever left by a husband. No, there was an aspect of Amanda's reactions that went beyond conventional behavior, something that touched on the spiritual. "Spiritual," Vicky uttered aloud, knowing that it sounded false when spoken aloud. Yet spiritual sickness was the diagnosis with which she was most comfortable whenever she thought of Amanda. Now that the separation agreement had been signed, though, maybe Amanda would calm down, get on with her life and let everyone get on with theirs. For the first time in a month, Vicky relaxed.

That turned out to be a mistake.

A discouraging new phase began in Vicky's and Jeffrey's lives, a run of bad luck. Vicky had never thought about luck or fate before. She believed people made their own fates, that their actions determined events. She had always felt in control. But when the bad things began to happen, she found that nothing she did altered them. It was, in a way, more disturbing than Amanda's harassment because it couldn't be blamed on anyone, at least not directly. In all the things that happened in the subsequent months, Amanda was never far from Vicky's consciousness. She found herself wondering whether Amanda was not, in some almost supernatural way, affecting events. But whenever the word "supernatural" crept into Vicky's thoughts, she resolutely dismissed it.

It began with small, odd incidents, the ones Vicky later thought of as omens. On the way to school one morning she was almost run over by a car going through a red light. She'd been so immersed in thought she hadn't even heard it approach until its horn blared as it brushed past her skirt. She arrived at school trembling. There she was summoned by Mrs. Dolittle and told that one of the parents had complained about Vicky's treatment of her daughter. The girl was the daughter of the heir to a furniture-chain fortune, and she was spoiled and lazy beyond redemption. Vicky had marked her work severely in the hope of bringing about more parental involvement. The parents had gotten involved, all right, threatening to withdraw their generous contribution for the construction of a science and computer annex.

But it was something else Mrs. Dolittle said at the end of the distasteful interview that distressed Vicky even more. "I must say," the headmistress remarked as she rose to her feet, "that this incident, combined with complaints by some other parents about your morality, doesn't present a very encouraging picture for renewal of your contact with us."

"My morality? Who's been complaining about it and what have they said?" Vicky could feel the hot flush of her blood rising up her neck and into her cheeks.

"I think you know perfectly well what I'm talking about. Now, if you'll excuse me..."

Vicky had walked out of Mrs. Dolittle's office on rubbery legs, and how she got through the rest of the day she couldn't explain because she didn't remember getting through it at all.

As if that weren't enough, a few days later Vicky found a number of tenants clustered around a notice that had been posted in the lobby of her building. She edged through the perimeter of the crowd, craning her neck to see, but she could only make out the word "conversion" on the sign. "What's going on?"

"Looks like we're going co-op," said a young man in jogging outfit.

"What does that mean?"

"It means you have two choices: bankruptcy, or moving to Queens."

Joe, at the desk, handed her a large envelope from the landlord containing the co-op offering plan. She studied it perfunctorily and slumped. Of all times to throw a co-op at her. What would they do if they had to buy? They couldn't afford it. It was hopeless.

She sat in her living room as the daylight faded, feeling depressed. Only a few months ago she'd thought how lucky she was not to get depressed often. Now look at all the things she had to worry about: money, her job, Jeffrey, Daria, Amanda, where she and Jeffrey were going to live, her writing. She hadn't written any stories since Jeffrey moved in. The thing she loved best to do had gone by the wayside. She felt like a failure. For once she wished she were back in her old home in Connecticut with her parents taking care of her, with stability and serenity in a world of simplicity and order. She'd thought a lot lately of calling her parents, but decided not to do it when everything was going wrong. It would take too much explaining, too much justifying. They were old-fashioned people with a simple morality. Talking to them might only make her feel worse.

Her phone rang. She didn't move, afraid to answer. It persisted, and finally she got up and went into the bedroom. Her voice was tentative and fearful when she said hello, so certain was she that the phone bore bad tidings.

"Victoria? It's your mother."

"Mom! My God, I was just thinking about you! This is incredible! Is everything okay? Is Daddy all right?"

"We're fine." Her mother's voice sounded far away and strained. "But we're real worried about you."

"Why?" What did they know? How did they know?

"We received a most upsetting phone call last evening from this woman, Mrs. Keating. Victoria, she said some awful things. I didn't recognize my daughter in what she told me. Is any of it true?"

Victoria felt sick to her stomach, as though someone

had just thrown something vile in her face. How had Amanda found her parents? "What did she tell you?"

"She said you stole her husband. Said he left his home and his daughter for you. Victoria, your father's so upset, he doesn't want to come to the phone."

"Oh, that disgusting woman!" Victoria wailed, sobbing. This was precisely why she hadn't wanted to talk to her parents. *And Amanda knew it.* Victoria heard herself forming oaths in her mind that she had never uttered in her life. "Mother," she said in a firmer voice, "the woman is a pathological liar. She was hateful to him. He left her, yes, but I didn't steal him. He fell in love with me, I couldn't help it. He wants to divorce her, I can't help that either. I love him. I want to marry him."

"He's married to somebody else."

"He's getting a divorce, I told you."

"And you're living with him, meantime?"

"Yes. Mother, it's not the way it looks."

"What about his daughter? What about that poor child?"

"She's well taken care of. And she's certainly not poor." Victoria almost smiled. Of all the players in this game, Daria was the one on whom pity was wasted most. She was a shrewd, manipulative little girl who knew exactly how to exploit her father's tenderness to get her way. "What did Amanda Keating tell you about *her*?"

"She said her daughter cried her eyes out every night for her daddy," said Victoria's mother. "She said she may have to send the child to a psychiatrist."

"She said that? You listened to her?"

"Of course I listened to her. What am I supposed to do?"

"She's a liar, Mom. She's a sick, horrid woman."

"That may be so, but I haven't heard you deny one thing she said."

"It's far more complicated than that."

"It doesn't sound complicated from where I sit."

"Mother, whose side are you on, anyway?"

"I don't know why she called us. We have nothing to do with it."

"She wanted to upset you. She wanted to turn you against me. She wanted you to worry."

"Well, I must say, she's succeeded in that. Do you want to come up here? If you're in some kind of trouble, we're here to help you."

"Thank you, but no, not right now. I have some things to work out. But I want you to have faith in me, Mom. It's nothing at all like that woman described. Jeffrey is a wonderful man, you'd love him. I'm not a home wrecker. As soon as some things get straightened out, I'll come up and see you. Until then, please believe everything is all right. And tell Daddy not to worry."

"Hah. What am I supposed to do if she calls again?"

"Hang up on her. Don't listen to her...her...shit."

"Victoria!"

"I'm sorry, Mom. I'm absolutely enraged. I have to go now. This call is costing you a lot of money."

"Please take care of yourself, won't you?" her mother pleaded, sounding on the verge of tears. "Call us soon?"

"I will. Please believe in me."

"I do. I know you wouldn't take up with the wrong kind of man."

"That's what I've been trying to tell you."

There was a pause. Her mother was struggling with a thought. "I could come into the city, meet this fellow if you think it would help. Square things with your father, you know?"

"Thank you, Mother. Just the offer means a lot to me. But no, give me a little while longer to work things out on my own."

"If that's what you want."

"Tell Daddy not to be disappointed in me."

"Sure, darling. You know how much we love you. If we get upset, it's because of that. We're always on your side."

She set the phone back on its cradle and fought to suppress tears of despair that seemed to well up out of someplace deep in her chest. But the phone never gave her a chance to gain control. It rang almost immediately and Vicky snatched it up, hoping it was Jeffrey.

"I hear you're going co-op," said the unmistakable voice. "Lucky you! Now you can own that fleabag apartment. I'm sure your lover will be thrilled."Amanda chuckled and hung up.

Victoria was so stunned she held the phone in her hand for several minutes, gazing at it as if it were a foreign object. How had Amanda known about the building going co-op only hours after it had been announced? How did she always seem to know everything, right down to the most intimate detail, about their lives? Was her phone bugged? Their apartment wired? Was Joe the doorman an informer? Daria? Jeffrey himself? If this weren't the last quarter of the twentieth century, Vicky would have sworn there was something supernatural in Amanda's prescience.

Drained of emotion, she curled up on the bed in fetal position, phone still clutched in her hand. Moments later, she heard Jeffrey's key in the lock. She rushed into his arms. His embrace was limp, his kiss perfunctory. "I really needed this co-op," he said with a profound sigh. "Where's the offering statement?"

Vicky handed him the envelope with the landlord's plan. Experienced as he was in co-op plans from the conversion of the building he'd lived in with Amanda, his fingers quickly found the schedule of prices, and he searched for the price of their apartment. Then he sat down heavily. "This calls for a very large glass of undiluted scotch."

Vicky poured him a drink and made a diluted scotch for herself. "How much are they asking?"

"A hundred thirty thousand for this—"

"Fleabag," Victoria said.

"I never called it a fleabag."

"No, your wife did."

"Amanda? How the hell did she get into the act?"

"I don't know." She told him about Amanda's call.

"That calls for a second large glass of undiluted scotch." He drained his glass and handed it to her.

"Please don't get drunk. I need you sober tonight. I've had such a terrible day. Everything seems to be going wrong. Amanda also called my parents. She upset them terribly."

"Your parents? Jesus Christ! How did she track *them* down?"

"Jeffrey, what kind of a woman are we dealing with

here? This is no longer just another case of a woman scorned. It's not even a case of mental imbalance. I think this is a case of someone who's out to destroy us."

He put his arm around her. "I think that's excessive. Have some more to drink and you'll go back to your 'woman scorned' theory." He grinned and let out a deep breath. The alcohol was relaxing him. He tapped the co-op plan. "I wouldn't worry about this. These things take a long time to go through, and the prices you end up with are usually far below what the offering plan states. It may even turn out that the tenants will defeat the plan entirely. I can be of help in organizing them."

"That would be wonderful." Vicky began to relax, seeing his confidence.

"As for Amanda, I don't know where she's getting her information, but we're just going to have to let these things roll off our backs or we're going to end up basket cases. I don't think she's out to destroy us. She's just striking out at whatever threatens her. Our best strategy right now is just to harden our armor and ignore her." He reached into his pocket and handed her a small envelope. "Maybe this'll cheer you up."

Vicky opened the envelope and brightened. "Oh, Jeffrey. The Philharmonic!"

"Beethoven, Stravinsky, and the Tchaikovsky Violin Concerto with Itzhak Perlman. Willa's pal Zubin Mehta conducting."

"Willa will be purple with envy. Oh, Jeffrey, this is so exciting. What's the occasion?"

"It's the commencement of National Screw Amanda Week. We'll observe it with feasting, raucous celebration, lovemaking in exotic positions, and sacrifices to the gods."

"Oh, Jeffrey, I love you so," murmured Victoria, snuggling into his arms. This time his embrace was not tentative. He carried her into the bedroom and ravished her, peeling away the layers of her fear until only her exquisite vulnerability remained. She heard herself uttering dirty things, felt herself bestowing her body, saw herself using her hands and mouth to give pleasure in ways she had never thought possible. The vigor of their sex was that of a revival, where all evil influences are purged, the soul redeemed, the promise of a new day

103

reaffirmed. They fell asleep in a tangle of limbs and bedclothes and slept from nine until seven the next morning. When they awoke they felt a closeness they had not known since the beginning. Despite all the terrible things that had happened the last few days, Vicky knew a truth now that she had never realized with as much clarity: that as long as she and Jeffrey had each other, they were proof against just about anything the world could throw at them.

Victoria fastened the tickets to the refrigerator door with a magnet shaped like a bagel. Every morning while sipping coffee before she left for work, she stared at them. They had become a sort of symbol of the promise of their new beginning, the falling away of bad luck and the restoration of normalcy and routine.

And indeed things did begin to improve. They had a lovely Christmas, exchanging modest but meaningful gifts: a morocco-bound volume of Conrad's *Lord Jim* for Jeffrey, unearthed at a dusty bookshop downtown; a tiny, exquisite gold locket for Vicky. Willa lucked into an understudy's job for *Annie* and treated Vicky to lunch at Le Cirque for her Christmas gift. Vicky felt extravagant and ill-dressed, seated in the restaurant eating the thinnest, tenderest slices of veal. Willa was expansive, loving and drunk on two Gibsons and a bottle of expensive Burgundy. Vicky began to feel less afraid.

By the time the evening of the concert arrived, Vicky had actually dared to allow herself to think she could relax her vigilance. For the last few months she had lived with a knotted stomach and a clenched jaw, anticipating trouble from any quarter. Perhaps, as some of her friends and indeed Jeffrey himself had predicted, the danger had peaked and the dice would start rolling in her favor.

She'd bought a new dress with the rest of her parents' Christmas money, a long-sleeved silk chemise with tiny flowers printed on a maroon background. Jeffrey promised to take her to an elegant restaurant after the concert, the Cafe des Artistes, a few blocks away from Lincoln Center.

His face brightened when she stepped out of the bedroom in her dress. He looked quite elegant himself, in a dark suit with a navy blue Dior tie and a flamboyantly contrasting silk handkerchief in his breast pocket.

They arrived at Avery Fisher Hall well before the start of the concert; Vicky wanted to walk around the plaza. When it got too cold they went into the lobby and had a drink at the bar. Concertgoers milled about them, their conversation cultured and witty and urbane. The air was festive, crackling with excitement and anticipation. It was her deepest look yet into the kind of life-style she might have with Jeffrey, and the prospect made her giddy.

They held hands as the usher showed them to their seats. Jeffrey had gotten the orchestra, center, toward the rear. Vicky looked up excitedly as they sat down, watching the crowd flow in, staring at the well-dressed men and women who were, most likely, the fashionable subscription crowd. She clutched her program with excitement. Then she leaned over and murmured, "Thank you," with her lips buried in Jeffrey's neck.

"Don't be silly. You deserve it. In fact, we'll do it more, if we can afford it."

"That would be wonderful," Vicky enthused.

The program was to be the Stravinsky first, the suite from *Firebird,* followed by an intermission; then the violin concerto with Itzhak Perlman, then another intermission and the Beethoven Sixth. She wished the violin concerto came first; she was most excited about seeing Perlman play.

The houselights dimmed and applause rolled across the house when Zubin Mehta appeared. Then it spread as the maestro bowed and turned to the orchestra. The Stravinsky began and Vicky settled back in her seat. It was thrilling to be present in person hearing the orchestra and watching the famous conductor at work.

When the music ended, Vicky applauded vigorously. Then, as the audience rose to its feet for the first intermission, Jeffrey asked her if she wanted to stay in her seat or go for a drink.

"I think I'll go to the ladies' room," she said.

He nodded and stood to let her pass him, secretively cupping her buttock as she did.

Vicky joined the throng making slow progress up the aisle. She hoped she would not have to wait too long in the bathroom. She had the uneasy feeling that every woman in the audience had the same destination. She reached the lobby and was directed by one of the ushers toward the ladies' room. Once inside, she joined the line waiting patiently for stalls. The women in front of and behind her were friends and they chattered about clothes, husbands, dinner, and Zubin Mehta. Vicky noticed that only two people were behind her in line; apparently bathroom-goers slipped out of their seats quickly. She became afraid she would miss the bell that signaled the end of intermission, but no one seemed concerned so she assumed she would be finished in time. When her turn finally came, she slipped into the cubicle gratefully, and placed her handbag on the fold-down shelf. It was then that she glanced down and saw a pair of feet directly outside her door. The feet, wearing elegant high-heeled, sling-back pumps in gray lizard, tapped impatiently as they waited. Why wasn't this woman waiting back in the corner where the line formed? Why was she standing in front of Vicky? Then Vicky saw the bottom of the woman's coat hanging at the middle of her calf. It was camel-colored suede with a fur trim.

She remembered this coat from the description given by her school porter, and by Jeffrey; it was unmistakably Amanda's.

She froze inside her cubicle, not moving. What could she do? The feet did not move from their position, right in front of her door. There were other stalls free; why had this woman picked hers? Why, unless it was someone who was waiting for her to come out, waiting to do what? Would she be attacked there in the ladies' room at Avery Fisher Hall?

She could hear the warning bells dinging outside the rest room. The intermission was over. The voices in the bathroom increased in tension, water ran in the sink; she heard the sound of paper towels yanked from the dispenser, then the door slamming. Almost everyone had left the bathroom now.

Except for Vicky. And the woman with the fur-trimmed coat.

If I scream, no one will hear me; then she'll know she has me trapped, Vicky realized.

But suppose it wasn't Amanda? Suppose this was just a woman waiting to use the bathroom? She would feel ridiculous if she opened the door and discovered some lady with gray hair standing there, angry because she was taking so long. But the stalls next to her were empty, weren't they? She wasn't aware of any sounds. Why was the woman waiting here? What was happening?

She heard the far-off sound of applause. Oh, God, she was missing the concert. She was going to miss Itzhak Perlman, in person, playing her favorite concerto. How could she get out of here?

She wished she had come in with a girlfriend. She wished she had some protection. She felt the silk dress growing damp with nervous perspiration beneath her arms. She was going to ruin it, her brand-new dress. She decided that she would raise her handbag up, like a club, burst out of the stall, hit Amanda in the face (if it *was* Amanda) and race out the door. She writhed with frustration. She hated herself for being afraid. But what else could she do? There was absolutely no one to help her.

She looked down and she saw that the feet had disappeared. Where had the woman gone? She bent down, low, and tried to peer beneath the stall door and walls. She could see nobody. Was she safe? She was afraid to look. She had to get out. She glanced around and ran out of the rest room and toward the aisle where the usher tried to stop her; the performance had begun. But Vicky shrewdly concocted a story that her husband was a doctor awaiting an important message. She moved past Jeffrey, whose face was tense with concern. "What the hell happened?" he whispered sharply.

"I'll tell you later," she whispered back, eliciting shushes from several members of the audience. She opened her bag, removed a wadded tissue, and dabbed her palms and forehead. She tried to concentrate on Itzhak Perlman, but her fear continued to clutch her throughout his performance. She remembered what Willa had said: "I think you're getting a little paranoid." Had Amanda become such an obsession that Victoria saw her everywhere? She began to wonder how many women wore such a coat. It was not one of a kind.

Still, why did the woman park herself outside Vicky's stall when others were free? She felt foolish, but her fear would not recede.

She returned her attention to the music but could not concentrate. Perlman concluded his performance to a wild ovation, and Jeffrey rose to his feet shouting, but Vicky was lost in a funk. "Can we get some air?"

"Sure," he said, wrapping her coat around her. "We can walk around the plaza. You don't look so hot."

They descended to the plaza level and strolled for a few minutes in the bracing air.

"Now, you want to tell me what happened?"

"You're going to yell at me."

"Why would I do that?"

She took a deep breath and let it out in a puff of white vapor. "I thought I saw Amanda in the bathroom. Waiting for me."

He frowned. "Why didn't you leave?"

"I was in the stall."

"*In* the stall? Then how could you see her?"

"I saw her coat. The fur-trimmed one you said you bought her two Christmases ago?"

"But how did you know it was her?"

"I didn't *know*, exactly. She stood outside the stall, directly in front of me. You see, in the ladies' room you stand on line in one corner near the door waiting for stalls to become free. Nobody plants herself in front of someone's stall."

He stared at her.

"I knew you'd yell at me."

"Who's yelling? I haven't said a word."

"You're yelling internally," she said.

"Internally I'm saying there are probably ten thousand women who own that coat."

"Not *that* coat," she said stubbornly.

Jeffrey continued to stare at her.

"I know it sounds crazy," Victoria said.

"Even if it was Amanda, what did you think she'd do? Push you down the toilet? Attack you with a sanitary napkin at point-blank range?"

"Please don't make fun of me, Jeffrey."

"Well, I do think you're being slightly—"

"Paranoid," Vicky said miserably.

"You spoiled the concert for yourself."

"And for you?"

Jeffrey shrugged. "I enjoyed the performance, but it takes the edge off things knowing you were so upset."

"Oh, Jeffrey, I'm so—"

She pulled up sharply and gasped. "Look!"

She pointed to a couple standing near the doors of the hall. Vicky's heart tripped. The woman wore a fur-trimmed, camel-colored suede coat with high-heeled sling-back shoes. Her auburn hair glinted in the radiance of the lobby lights behind her. Jeffrey did a long take and his eyebrows knit. They edged a little closer to get a better look at her face. Then the woman turned toward them. Vicky's nails dug into her companion's arm.

"Is that your Amanda?" Jeffrey asked with a laugh that was nearly contemptuous.

Victoria looked hard. Then she slumped. "Not even close."

"Not even close," he said, shaking his head. "Come on, let's go back inside."

Vicky trailed behind him like a dishonored Oriental wife. The evening was ruined.

Chapter Five

IN MARCH Jeffrey suffered a bitter blow.

They were relaxing in the living room with a glass of wine when the phone rang. Jeffrey's phone. They were both certain it was Amanda. "Don't answer it," Vicky pleaded.

"I'll get rid of her," Jeffrey said, scooping up the receiver. "Yeah?" There was a long pause. "Oh, Mother, I'm sorry, I thought it was..." His face darkened and his knuckles whitened around the telephone. Vicky knew something was seriously wrong. "All right, Mom, all right, stay calm. I'll be out there on the first flight." He asked her some questions about doctors and diagnosis and prognosis and Vicky concluded his father had had a heart attack.

He hung up and confirmed her conclusion. "Not major, but serious enough to lay him up. My mother's just to the left of hysterical. I've got to go out there for a few days." He called information, got the numbers of American and Trans World Airlines, and booked a night flight to Los Angeles.

"Do you want me to go with you? I will," Vicky offered.

"Can you get away from school?"

She reflected and made a face. "We're about to go into exams before the Easter vacation. It might be tough."

"Don't do it if it's going to hurt your standing."

"Well, things are still kind of delicate. But I so wanted to meet your parents."

"This is not the time to meet them, darling. And I wouldn't want you to jeopardize your job." He hugged

110

her. "I'll be gone maybe three days; I'll call you every chance I get."

"Sure."

He looked at her. "What is it? You're worried about something."

She shrugged. "We haven't been apart since you moved in."

"Maybe my absence will make your heart grow fonder."

"It couldn't possibly be," she said, pressing her cheek to his chest.

She followed him around as he packed, wondering whether she should say what was on her mind. Finally she said it, but obliquely. "You don't think anything could happen while you're away, do you?"

He tilted his head, at first not comprehending. "Happen? You mean with Amanda? She has no reason to call."

"That's never prevented her from calling anyway."

"You'll handle it, I'm sure."

Victoria blinked at his easy dismissal of her fear. She was by no means sure she could handle it. She was by no means sure she wouldn't fall apart if Amanda started something while Jeffrey was away. She longed to tell him how afraid she was, but how could she add to his burden of worry? She decided to unplug Jeffrey's phone, unplug her own except at predetermined times when Jeffrey was to call, and to get out of the house as often as possible until he returned, see some friends, hit some movies, do some shopping she'd been putting off. These tactics would minimize her exposure to Amanda, but with Amanda you never knew what she was going to do, or when, or where.

"Take care of yourself," Jeffrey said, embracing her hard. "I'm going to miss the hell out of you."

"Same."

"I'll call you every evening at eleven, New York time. I love you." And he swept out of the house, lugging a compactly packed suitcase. She closed the door and locked both locks.

In the next three days while Jeffrey was gone, she realized several things. The first was how much, how truly much, she loved him. His absence from her life,

111

from her bed, was wrenching, and despite what her
friends said, there were none of the benefits of being
alone, of doing the things she couldn't do when he was
around. There was nothing she wanted to do without
him. His phone calls demonstrated that he felt the same
way. They talked for scandalously long times, but neither could break off the conversation, which dwelt on
the minutest details of their daily lives. Vicky's heart
and body ached for him.

Another thing she realized was that she had indeed
become certifiably paranoid about Amanda. She looked
for her everywhere, expected her to call or visit or turn
up or manifest herself somehow, to take advantage of
Jeffrey's absence. Yet nothing happened that week, not
so much as a whisper from Amanda. It was entirely
possible that Amanda didn't know about Jeffrey's father.
And why would she?

This was perhaps the only benefit of Jeffrey's absence. Vicky was able to see how jumpy she'd gotten,
and to laugh at herself for having become so crazy on
the subject of Amanda. Amanda's uncanny prescience,
Victoria could now see, was simply a matter of good
spying; her "presence" at Vicky's school or at Lincoln
Center had never been proven; and, during this blessed
three-day respite, Vicky began to put Amanda's wrath
into perspective. Of course, Amanda's wrath, as Vicky
told Willa over drinks at Teacher's on Broadway one
of those evenings, was "wrathier" than that of most
other women, but when Vicky put herself in Amanda's
place, trying to imagine what it would be like after ten
years of marriage to have her husband leave her and
her child, it became a little easier to appreciate what
made Amanda so vindictive.

There was one upsetting incident that week, upsetting and puzzling. The first night Jeffrey was away,
Vicky got nervous and stayed up as late as she could,
reading. Close to two in the morning she shut off the
light and fell into a deep sleep immediately. But after
what seemed only a few moments, she heard laughter,
laughter she knew only too well. She struggled to wake
herself, like a swimmer thrashing to the surface and
gasping for air because he had dived too deeply. As she
came out of it she heard someone moving in the living

112

room. She held her breath, listening. Cautiously she slid out from under the covers and glided to the bedroom door. She looked into the living room, ears cocked, fist clenched, breath held. In the moonlight the living room looked eerie, but she saw no movement. She flicked on a lamp. The living room was empty. She searched the kitchen and even opened all the closet doors. Nothing.

She concluded she'd been dreaming. But Amanda's laughter had been all too real, and Vicky could have sworn she'd heard a burglar or someone in the next room.

The following evening, Jeffrey called and said, "Are you all right?"

"Yes, why?"

"I dreamed someone broke into our apartment."

Vicky drew her breath in with a hiss. "I dreamed the same thing!"

"Weird. But you're all right. You lock both locks when you're home, plus the chain?"

"Yes, don't worry. No burglars." Just Amanda's spirit in the next room, laughing, Vicky said to herself.

She dismissed the coincidence of her and Jeffrey's dreams. But a time would come when she remembered them.

By the time Jeffrey returned, Vicky had achieved some understanding, objectivity, and calm about Amanda, and felt better able to face any trouble that might now arise. Which was a good thing, because almost from the moment Jeffrey put his suitcase down, Amanda rose like some magnificent hooded cobra that had been lurking in ambush. And Vicky realized that she had been lulled almost fatally into a false sense of security, and that the biggest mistake she'd made was to stop being paranoid.

Jeffrey looked awful as he stepped into their apartment. He'd lost weight, almost ten pounds; his clothes hung loosely on his frame, and his shirt collar gapped around his throat. His complexion was slightly yellow; in spite of being in one of the garden spots of California, Palm Springs, he had obviously not set foot outdoors once during his entire visit. His embrace was halfhearted, not because he wasn't glad to see her but because he seemed to have lost some of his strength.

113

His face was haggard, with circles of fatigue under his eyes. "You look—so tired," she said, carrying his suitcase into the bedroom and opening it to unpack for him.

"It's been exhausting. I had to do everything for my mother; she was near hysteria the whole time. He had a crisis one morning and I thought we'd lost him, but he's okay now, and—"

Jeffrey's phone rang. About an hour before he arrived, Vicky had plugged it in again. "That must be my mother, checking up on me. She's always nervous when I travel." He picked it up. From the way his jaw tightened Vicky knew it was not his mother, knew it had to be only one person. "How did you know that?" he said tersely. After another pause he said, "Well, if you knew, why are you bugging me about late checks? I'll put them in the mail tomorrow." Another pause. "That's not in our separation papers.... You think so? Well, take me to court then." He abruptly hung up. They stared at the phone, waiting for the familiar pattern. A moment later it rang. Jeffrey picked it up and listened, in case it really was his mother this time. Then he slammed it down and unplugged it. Automatically, like an actress who has played in a long-running show, Vicky proceeded to shut off the phone in the other room. She reached it just as it began ringing and removed the clip that attached the wire to the receiver.

Jeffrey sat with face in hands on the edge of the bed. "I can't take this the minute I walk in the door," he moaned.

Vicky got on the bed behind him and began kneading his shoulders. His neck and back muscles were tense and knotted. "The funny thing is, this is her first appearance since you went to California. The minute you walked in the door. Of course, I did have your phone unplugged while you were away, so I don't know if she was trying to reach you."

"She wasn't," he said, flexing his shoulders pleasurably under Vicky's massage. "She knew where I was and why."

"How? How did she know?"

"Renee might have told her when she called the office. It doesn't make sense because I'd told Renee specifically that Amanda was not to be told anything, and

Renee hates Amanda anyway. She wouldn't give her the time of day. I just don't know."

"What was she complaining about?"

"The checks are five days late. I forgot about them in the emergency."

"And that business about something not being in the separation papers?"

"She wants me to pay for repainting the apartment."

"Unbelievable. What does she think the alimony is for? I was glad you told her to take you to court. She mustn't be allowed to think she can cadge more money out of you every time she—" Vicky stopped mid-sentence and removed her hands from Jeffrey's neck. He fell back with his head on her lap, fast asleep.

Over the next few weeks Amanda bore in on Jeffrey relentlessly, as if she knew his resistance was weakening. She phoned him constantly to complain. She started a lawsuit. She propagandized Daria about her father's cheapness, about his cruelty, about his indifference. She pushed and prodded Jeffrey, already worried sick about his father, until his health began to fail. Vicky tried to get him to relax, but he was always tense as a guy-wire with anxiety over his father, over flagging business, over Daria's well-being, over Vicky's well-being. He didn't eat properly and had lost even more weight. Victoria began to worry that he might collapse.

For some time she'd been wondering who among Jeffrey's and Amanda's old friends might serve as a go-between to appeal to Amanda, to ask her to moderate her demands on Jeffrey and take some pressure off him. Uncertain whether Jeffrey would approve of such a plan, she sounded him out circumspectly. Unfortunately, there wasn't anyone who sounded very suitable. Jeffrey had come to the depressing conclusion that most of his friends either had been Amanda's, or had been simply business acquaintances who would not stand by him when the going got rough. Of the remaining people in Jeffrey's former life, Amanda had painted such an awful picture of him that none of them would associate with this heartless beast who had philandered on his long-suffering wife, taken up with some money-grubbing tramp, and abandoned his family without any means

115

of support whatsoever. As Jeffrey had once said, Goebbels himself could not have done a better propaganda job. Finally, Vicky abandoned the idea of using an old friend.

There was someone else who might be enlisted, however. For some weeks Daria had spoken of a new boyfriend of her mother's, a man named Mitch, who Daria said was kind. She'd even shown Vicky how Mitch had written his phone number in her Snoopy address book, "in case I ever have a problem," Daria reported solemnly. Sensing a possible ally, or at least a nonhostile presence in the other household, Vicky had copied the phone number from Daria's address book one night while the child slept. Perhaps this was the time to call him and try to prevail upon him to get Amanda to ease up. Daria had described him as a nice person, gentle, softspoken. Naturally, as Amanda's lover his loyalty would be to her, but as she depended on him he might have some influence over her behavior. Early one evening, while Jeffrey was still at work, Vicky decided to try it.

She searched through her drawers and found the paper with the number on it hidden under a pile of nightgowns. She picked up her phone, then put it down as doubts began to gnaw at her. Why would Mitch give her the time of day, let alone agree to act as her gobetween? What would happen if Mitch told Amanda that Victoria had called—she might redouble her campaign against Jeffrey. These and other worries assailed Vicky and she realized what a dangerous stunt this could turn out to be. But, as Jeffrey was fond of saying, high risk, high rewards. If Mitch was sympathetic and did manage to influence Amanda, the benefits could be incalculable.

Fortified by this conclusion, pleased to be taking some action, she dialed the number. Her mouth had dried up and she licked her lips and cleared her throat several times. The phone rang five times and she was just about to hang up when someone picked it up.

"Is this Mitch?"

"Yes." He pronounced the word quietly, with just a touch of curiosity in his voice.

"You don't know me," she began, feeling foolish at once as she realized she must sound like some girl calling for a date, someone he'd met at a party. "I mean, you do know me in a way. We just haven't met." She felt she was compounding the awkwardness with every word she uttered. She could feel her face flushing. Mitch listened silently at the other end of the line, waiting for her to clear up the mystery. "Oh, hell," said Vicky, taking a deep breath. "I'm Victoria Lewis. Vicky? Jeffrey Keating's...um..." She silently cursed the English language for failing to furnish an acceptable word for what she was. Mistress? Girlfriend? Lover? Roommate? Fiancée?

"Ah," said Mitch in a tone that put her at ease at once. "You're Jeffrey Keating's Um."

"Yes, and I understand you're Amanda Keating's Um," she laughed.

"Well...how may I be of help? And how did you get my number?"

"I have to protect my source," she said. "And as far as helping me, I hope you won't think I'm being presumptuous, but I'm at my wit's end with Amanda, and Daria described you as a nice person, so I thought maybe you could intercede for me, I mean for Jeffrey. He doesn't know I'm making this call, but I had to do something because things are getting desperate."

"Desperate?"

"She's driving Jeffrey to the wall. He's getting sick. She's harassing him so, I don't know if his health can take it much longer. And you know, if that goes, he won't be able to make a living, and if he can't make a living he can't pay her alimony. So it's in her best interests to stop driving him crazy."

"I agree with you," he said.

"You do? Do you really?"

"God yes. I tried, believe me. I told her, 'You have his money, what the hell more do you want, his blood?'"

"What did she say to that?"

"She didn't say anything. That's when I realized."

"Realized what?"

"That she does want his blood."

Vicky's spirits rose. In spite of Mitch's last remark, the fact that he was in sympathy with her, that he might be able to mediate somehow, gave her a glimpse of hope that she'd despaired of finding these last few weeks since Jeffrey returned from California.

"I realized something else, too," he said after a moment.

"What's that?"

"That Amanda Keating is a bad lady. A *very* bad lady."

Vicky felt her stomach plunge sickeningly. She sensed what he was going to say next, and felt the energy drain out of her body as though a plug had been yanked.

"I'm not her...I'm not with her anymore."

"Ah, I see. I'm sorry."

"Don't be. I'm well rid of her."

"I wish I could say the same."

"Amanda is beautiful, enchanting, seductive. She's also deadly. I really feel for you, Vicky. If I were still seeing her, I'd be glad to help. But, well, she dumped me for somebody else. And I wouldn't bother appealing to him if I were you. He's a real shit, and I wouldn't be surprised if he's been reinforcing her the last few weeks. The two of them, whew," he whistled. "Bad medicine."

"God, this is awful."

"Yes, it is. Ray was my best friend."

"I'm sick."

"No sicker than I am. If it's any consolation to you, I think Jeffrey did a good thing, walking out on her. I just hope the price isn't too high. Good luck."

Victoria put the phone down and stared into space. She remained in that hypnotic attitude for fifteen minutes, eyes focused but unseeing on the detail of a Vermeer reproduction on the wall directly in front of her. A decision was being distilled drop by drop into her mind, and when at last she blinked, she knew she had to confront Amanda face to face.

She held back a few days to see if Jeffrey's condition and spirits improved. But he became increasingly apathetic. He had a bad cold he couldn't shake and a steady cough that kept them both awake into the small hours for several nights running. His weight had dropped almost fifteen pounds from what it had been when he'd moved in with her, and his elegant clothes hung limply on his body. Just to look at him made Vicky want to cry. His muscles had lost their tone, and when she wrapped her body around his as he slept, she felt little of the resilient firmness of the man she'd taken up with. They did not, of course, make love.

Sometimes at night when they couldn't sleep they talked about Amanda, Vicky probing for some insights that would help her get a sharper fix on her rival's motivations. One night he said, "Amanda's biggest problem is confidence."

"You mean overconfidence?"

"Over? Hell, no, under. Not even under. None whatsoever."

"Amanda?" Vicky said, dismayed.

They were lying in the dark, flat on their backs, staring at the light patterns on the ceiling as traffic passed beneath their bedroom window. "It's hard to imagine, I'm sure. But her lack of confidence affects everything she does." He paused to cough, a long series of wracking, hacking coughs. Vicky rubbed his back until his chest cleared, then he dropped back on the mattress. "It's what makes her such a bully. And this infatuation she has with beautiful things—furnishings, clothes, art—it has to do with her not really knowing who she is. She gets her identity from expensive things, hides behind them."

Victoria took it in, wondering if Jeffrey's theory might be valid. If Amanda lacked confidence, it would explain the paradox of why, if she didn't love her husband, she was so angered by his leaving. It wasn't the loss of a loved one that grieved her. It was the blow to her ego! Jeffrey represented all those material objects that gave her an identity and the security that went with it. Amanda's rage was aimed as much at herself as at Jeffrey or at Victoria.

So Amanda might be vulnerable after all. But how to penetrate her armor and exploit that vulnerability? The answer was, you had to be very strong with her, very firm, more self-confident than she. Can I do it? Vicky asked herself. The answer was, she didn't have much choice. With Jeffrey's health and spirits deteriorating, she'd have to find the strength in herself.

She lay back on the pillow and went over her plan, thinking up different contingencies, dealing in her mind

119

with each one, rehearsing the dialogue over and over, projecting herself into Amanda's role so that she knew the enemy intimately, thought like her, anticipated her.

Restless, she got up and went into the living room. She took some notepaper from her desk drawer and wrote out the script she had composed in her head. She looked at it, imagining herself to be Amanda opening the note, studying it, reacting to it. Vicky concluded the the text was fine, but the handwriting evidenced uncertainty, tentativeness. She took some scratch paper and rewrote the note a dozen times until the script looked bolder, more confident, yet casual, a duchess summoning a subject. When she was satisfied, she took a fresh piece of notepaper and wrote a final draft. She reread it with satisfaction. It said: "Amanda: Please meet me at twelve-thirty on Tuesday, March eighteenth at Il Parmegiano on West Fifty-sixth Street. I think you'll want to hear what I have to say. Victoria Lewis."

She had thought out every word, from the salutation (not "Dear Amanda", just "Amanda"; Amanda was not dear to her, nor did Vicky wish to dignify her by calling her "Mrs. Keating") to her own signature (her full name, not "Victoria" or "Vicky"; by using her own full name but addressing Amanda only by her first name, she established a subtle psychological advantage).

She addressed the envelope and put a stamp on it.

She'd selected a restaurant because Amanda would be inhibited from making a scene in a public place. She chose a school holiday, at the beginning of spring recess, in mid-March. That way they could meet on a weekday. A weekend was no good because Jeffrey would be around and she'd have to lie about where she was going, and she was a terrible liar. She'd give it all away and Jeffrey would forbid her to go.

Il Parmegiano was a businessmen's restaurant in the crowded district of the West Fifties between Fifth and Sixth Avenues. She figured that at twelve-thirty the place would be jammed with lunchtime diners, mostly men. She felt safer setting up a rendezvous with Amanda in a place heavily populated by men, among whom Amanda might be expected to behave herself.

Victoria arrived early at twelve-fifteen and asked to

be shown to her table immediately rather than wait at the bar. The maître d' showed her up a flight of narrow stairs to the upstairs dining room where he seated her in the back. The table was, she noted nervously, in a row of tables pushed against the wall. She seated herself on the banquette with her back to the wall. Smiling, she recalled that gangsters always sat with their backs against a wall in public places so no one could shoot them in the back. She ordered a glass of wine from the waiter and glanced around at the other diners. The tables were filled with men in gray or black pin-striped suits, heads bent low, drinks at their right hands, breadsticks in their left, gesturing, conferring, looking powerful and busy. A few women occupied several scattered seats throughout the place but there were no tables of women only.

She waited nervously for Amanda's arrival. She had told the maître d' that she was expecting a tall, red-haired woman as her luncheon guest; he was to bring her upstairs immediately. But at twelve-thirty Amanda did not show up. Vicky waited, five minutes, ten minutes more; then she began to wonder how long she could wait. The waiters poured water in her glass and brought the bread basket and butter, as if urging her to eat. By then it was twelve-fifty. Unnerved and feeling foolish, she ordered another glass of wine. Then Amanda appeared.

Vicky knew she had arrived even before she saw her, as the noise level dropped palpably and several heads turned toward the arched vestibule near the stairs. Vicky's stomach churned as a charge of adrenaline rushed through her system, but she fought back the panic and struggled to maintain the cool confidence that she knew was the only thing standing between herself and defeat.

Amanda wore a simple but expensive mauve sweater-dress beneath an elegant dyed beaver coat, plum color trimmed with fox. A Hermès scarf was draped with studied casualness from her throat. Her red hair was superb, the finishing touch on someone who could have stepped from the cover of the Italian edition of *Vogue*. Vicky had determined not to try to compete with Amanda in couture, and had dressed in what she felt most secure in, a forest-green long-sleeved dress, a string of pearls, an antique gold bracelet inherited from her grandmother.

The maître d' seated Amanda, and Vicky could feel the nimbus of frigid air that still clung to her from outside. "Vodka martini straight up," she commanded the maître d', who bowed and disappeared. Then Amanda focused her eyes on Vicky, staring at her silently to make her uncomfortable. At length she said, "Well, the long-awaited confrontation scene between the wife and the mistress. I suppose you want to play it civilized, like a Bette Davis movie."

Vicky had determined to show strength from the very outset, and had anticipated a nasty remark from Amanda for openers. "If you'll be good enough not to call me Jeffrey's mistress, I'll refrain from calling you his dumped wife," she said. She followed this with a sip of wine, then placed her hands in her lap so Amanda couldn't see them shaking.

If Amanda was wounded by Vicky's rejoinder she didn't show it. Instead, she looked at the man sitting on the banquette to Vicky's left and smiled. It was a very theatrical gesture, Vicky thought, for even if Amanda had lost the first skirmish she could always recoup her losses by capturing a man's admiration.

"What made you think I would show up today?" Amanda asked, nodding haughtily as the waiter set her drink down. She raised it to her lips, narrowing her eyes as she studied Vicky over the rim of her glass.

"Because I have something you want," Vicky replied.

Amanda didn't pause a beat. "It certainly isn't my husband," she said with a laugh. "You're welcome to what's left of him."

"You're a very cruel woman, Amanda."

"Perhaps, but I stop short of stealing other women's husbands."

"That wasn't stealing," Vicky said. "It was more like recovering abandoned property."

"That's a very good analogy, dear. If I abandoned Jeffrey, it's because he was worthless to me."

"If that's so, then why are you punishing him? You don't want him back. You're having too good a time with your Mitches and your Rays."

Amanda's eyelids twitched ever so faintly at the mention of her boyfriends, and Vicky exulted in the realization that for once her own spy system was the equal of Amanda's. "You don't think the crime of abandonment should go unredressed, do you?" she said.

"It's been quite handsomely redressed by your lawyers," Vicky replied. "You're receiving extremely generous alimony and child support, and that's what I invited you here to remind you of."

The captain appeared with menus tucked under his arm, but Victoria waved him away, taking charge of the situation with a command that later, as she reflected on the confrontation, was to leave her dumbstruck.

"Remind me of what? How generous it is?" Amanda said. "I don't think he's paying me enough. I don't think he can ever pay me enough."

"That's because your vanity is bottomless," Vicky answered. "But I'm here to tell you that, adequate or not, it's all about to be cut off."

"That would be very foolish of him. I'll take him to court."

"The courts can't get blood from a stone, Amanda. Jeffrey is a sick man. If something happens to him, his business will suffer. And if his business suffers, there'll be no more money to pay you with."

"Oh, but there will," Amanda came back, and for the first time her eyes were kindled. Oh, how they were kindled! They had blazed into angry flame that glowed through her narrowed eyelids. "There will because Jeffrey's life insurance policy is locked into the separation agreement. That's half a million dollars if he dies. He's worth even more to me dead than alive, except that if he dies I lose the pleasure of watching him suffer."

Vicky stared, genuinely shocked. She gazed once more into Amanda's eyes to confirm the conclusion that was forming rapidly in her mind, a conclusion she gave utterance to with a quavering voice that had lost all semblance of control. "My God, you're not just cruel. You're crazy!"

"How right you are, my dear." Vicky's heart began to trip as she felt control slipping from her grasp with every second that passed. She saw a waiter and signaled frantically for the check, but he didn't see her as he passed by. Meanwhile, Amanda had opened her clutch bag. For a moment Vicky thought that Amanda was going to take out a wallet to pay for the drinks, but instead she produced a little vial of clear liquid. The bottle was too plain to be perfume. It was more like a chemist's bottle with a cork stopper, which Amanda twisted and removed. "Let me show you just how crazy I am," she said.

Vicky realized that whatever was in that bottle, Amanda was going to toss it at her face. Her first thought was that it must be acid. Her heart hammered wildly in her chest, and she blinked and raised her hands to protect her eyes. What an idiot she'd been, to think she could reason with the woman, and now she was to pay for it forever with a mutilated face. Her life flashed before her just as they say it's supposed to, and for the first time she rued that she had ever let Jeffrey in the door. Her conscience had warned her about married men; her parents had told her what a sin she was committing.

Then her reason took command. Was Amanda so mad she would risk prison to get even? If she were going to throw acid in Vicky's face, wouldn't she do it where she couldn't be observed? Was she so vengeful she would sacrifice everything she had to salve her injured vanity? It made no sense.

She dropped her guard, opened her eyes, and gazed unflinchingly at Amanda, who tossed the contents of the bottle squarely in Vicky's face. For an instant her eyes stung and she thought she had grossly misjudged her enemy. Then she detected a familiar aroma, the unmistakably cloying odor of gin.

Through smarting eyes she saw Amanda's head thrown back in laughter, a gay tinkling laugh that contrasted with the heartless prank she'd just perpetrated. "Next time it will be real acid," Amanda said breathlessly.

Vicky dabbed her face with her napkin and slid out of the banquette. "I take it back, Amanda. You're not crazy. You're incredibly stupid. One day you'll realize how stupid. I hope to be there when that happens." Slinging her coat over her arm, she started for the exit.

"What's the rush, dear?" Amanda said throatily. "We haven't even ordered lunch. Or can't you afford it? I'll treat."

Vicky ignored her and walked in a calm, measured pace across the floor. The maître d' stepped forward from his post near the vestibule. *"Signorina?* Is something the matter?"

"Please, I have to go." She brushed past him, conscious that this scene must be played with dignity despite the unexpected turn it had taken. It would be a major mistake to let Amanda feel Vicky was fleeing. So when she lost her balance at the top of the stairs, her first thought was, Damn, I blew my big exit. Her second thought was that someone, something, had pushed her.

It happened so fast that Vicky, reconstructing it again and again in her mind later on, saw it was not as a sequence of events but as one intricate motion, like a complex ballet move blended of a dozen steps. She grasped for the banister but her coat got in the way and she pitched downward, not comforted by the realization that the stairway was carpeted. She heard her own cry as her shoulder and back struck the stairs first, saw her legs tumbling over her head, felt her knees and ankles strike the banister and then the stairs, watched her coat sail over her head, then felt the buffeting of half a dozen more stairs as she bumped the rest of the way, feet first, on her stomach. The last thing she saw as she did one last somersault was a corona of auburn hair at the top of the stairway. Then Vicky felt the darkness steal over her eyes.

How long she was unconscious she didn't know, but she awoke to a hubbub of waiters, captains, maître d's, and patrons. "Don't move her." "Call an ambulance." "Ask if there's a doctor in the house." "See if she's wearing a medical tag." Someone had his fingers on her pulse, another was waving a towel at her face. "She's coming to," someone else said.

The man with his fingers on her pulse was gray haired, kind-faced. "Are you all right?"

She took a deep breath and surveyed her body limb by limb. "My back hurts, but..." She flexed her spine. "I don't think...ow."

"Your back?"

"No, my ankle. Ooow."

He made her move every muscle. She seemed to have bruised her spine and ribs and twisted her ankle. The man asked her if she wanted an ambulance. She said no, she wanted Jeffrey, and she gave him Jeffrey's office number. The man gestured at one of the captains to make the call, then barked an order at the rest of the staff to return to work. "I'm the owner," he explained. He had a gentle voice. His accent was continental.

"I think I can get up," Vicky said, but he gestured to her to remain still.

The captain returned and said Jeffrey was on his way. His office was not far from the restaurant. Then they helped her to her feet and sat her down near the coat room. "Can you tell me what happened?" the owner asked. He said something to the captain and within moments he'd brought her a cup of tea.

"The woman I was with, we had an argument. She followed me out and pushed me down the stairs."

He glowered and said something in Italian that sounded like "barbaric." Then he turned to the captain. "You saw this?"

The captain looked puzzled, then turned to Vicky. "Your guest, she was the attractive woman with red hair?"

"Yes."

The captain conferred with the owner in Italian. Then the owner said, "The captain says your guest never left the table. Only when you fell did she get up and leave. She was most concerned. She offered to help."

Through her pain Vicky almost laughed. "That's not true! She followed me and pushed me."

The owner and captain looked at each other. Then the owner nodded and said, "*Si, signorina.*"

She knew they were patronizing her. "Why don't you ask someone else?"

"*Si, signorina,* but the maître d' too agreed. She was seated at the table, with her drink. You see? She paid and left, ten minutes ago."

Vicky was filled with horror of a magnitude she'd never known. What had happened? How had Amanda

126

gotten up and pushed her and yet not left the table? Was she seeing things?

"I think you're in shock, *signorina*," the owner said. Which was certainly true. Her ankle had begun to throb, and she knew it would hurt even more when the shock wore off.

The owner kept her company until Jeffrey arrived, teeth clenched and face pale. He examined Vicky, touching her ankles and knees, wrists and elbows, neck and spine, asking her where it hurt, asking her what had happened. "I'll tell you later," she said.

"The young woman apparently tripped," said the owner.

"Is that true?" Jeffrey asked her. "Were there any witnesses?"

"The restaurant is not to blame," Vicky said. She still could not grasp what had happened.

"Did she pay her bill?" Jeffrey asked, reaching for his wallet.

"It's taken care of," said the owner. He handed Jeffrey his card. "Please be my guests for dinner as soon as the *signorina* is recovered." He sent a waiter into the street to hail a cab and they carried Vicky out to a Checker. Jeffrey ordered the driver to take them to Mount Sinai Hospital's emergency room. Vicky protested. She didn't feel anything broken, but he insisted. He held her tightly as she began shaking uncontrollably in delayed reaction to her frightening experience. "Can you tell me what happened?"

She'd been debating with herself about how to tell him, what to tell him, but she decided to tell him everything and try to make him understand. "I invited Amanda to lunch."

"You what?" His incredulous stare was almost comical, a double take out of a Marx Brothers movie.

"It was the only way I could think of to get her off your back. Look at you, Jeffrey, you've dropped fifteen pounds, your eyes are bloodshot, and your complexion looks like death warmed over. She's literally worrying you to death. I had to try to stop her."

"I can fight my own battles."

"Please don't take it wrongly," Vicky said, squeezing his hand, "but this is one battle we've both lost."

127

He looked at her ironically. "You're no one to talk about lost battles."

"I learned something very important today. Against Amanda, you *can't* win."

"So what else is new?"

"No, Jeffrey, you don't understand. You can't win because she's...omnipotent."

He pursed his lips. "I wouldn't go that far."

"You would if you'd been there today."

The taxi pulled up to the Madison Avenue emergency entrance at Mount Sinai, and the driver helped Jeffrey carry Vicky up to the admitting desk. As the injuries weren't life-threatening, she and Jeffrey were seated in a gaudy orange waiting area where eight or ten other patients, surrounded by large families, slumped as they waited for their names to be called. There, Vicky told Jeffrey the entire story. As she spoke she watched his face. It was curiously impassive. She finished and waited for him to say something. When he did at last, she felt as if she'd been pricked by the blade of a knife.

"How many drinks did you have?"

"Two glasses of wine. Why do you ask?"

He shrugged. "You didn't have anything stronger, like martinis?"

"Martinis? *She* had a martini. I've never had a martini in my—Oh God, the gin."

"It'd be hard not to notice it," he said almost apologetically. "In fact, I can still smell it."

"She threw it at me." She looked for understanding in his eyes but found none. "You don't believe me, do you?"

He shrugged again. "Amanda's done some shitty things, but she's not into physical violence."

"Not into physical violence!" Vicky burst out as heads turned. "Jeffrey, she pushed me down a flight of stairs! She could have paralyzed me for life, killed me, and you tell me she's not into physical violence?"

"Darling, lower your voice."

"Talk about adding insult to injury. I literally took my pride, to say nothing of my life, into my hands on your behalf, and you don't even give me the benefit of believing me?" It all came pouring out now, the tensions, the frustrations of these last few months, the humiliation and now physical pain compounded by a horrifying sense of isolation. She sobbed uncontrollably, shaking off Jeffrey's attempts to comfort her. A nearby resident, a pretty girl in a blood-stained white coat, came over to ask what was the matter.

"She's just a little overwrought," Jeffrey said, holding his palm up, and the woman disappeared back into the warren of treatment rooms.

Vicky caught her breath and her sobs abated into hiccuping whimpers. Her eyelids began to droop and she felt drowsy. Her head nodded to her chest and she napped. It might have been for less than a minute until Jeffrey squeezed her arm and told her they'd called her name for X rays, but in the brief moment she saw something, understood something with astonishing clarity. It was what Willa had told her: that Jeffrey was still attached to his wife. Not in love with her, no; indeed, maybe he didn't ever love her. But attached nevertheless, the way slaves remain attached to the owner who abuses them, children to the parent who mistreats them, dogs to the master who beats them, the way the enchanted are attached to those who cast a spell over them.

The odd thing was that though this realization wounded and saddened her, she did not feel the threat was fatal to her love for, her life with, Jeffrey—at least, not unless she allowed it to be. Jeffrey's inability to break Amanda's grip on him didn't mean he cared any less for Vicky. It didn't mean he wanted to go back to Amanda, though he sometimes became wistful about what he'd given up. What it did mean was that Jeffrey had a serious character flaw that would have to be taken into account henceforth in their relationship. In due time, Vicky was confident, his strange fixation with Amanda would fade with the kind of nourishing love Vicky knew she could give him, love that was healthier, more sustaining, more fulfilling than the sadomasochistic bond that had held Jeffrey's marriage together.

Nevertheless, it would be insane to deny Jeffrey's extant feelings for Amanda. If she did deny them, Vicky would feel betrayed again and again, and these betrayals would poison their relationship. She would have to be patient and compassionate with him, knowing that eventually he would find the insight into himself and the strength of character to break the emotional shackles as cleanly as he had broken the legal ones. It was a new experience, accepting a man with so deep a fault. But she was up to the challenge, she was certain, as certain as she was of the throbbing pain that had led her to this moment of truth.

"No breaks that we can see," the resident said, studying the X rays intently. "But lots of bruises and contusions. That was a particularly aggressive flight of stairs you tangled with, Miss Lewis. I prescribe rest, aspirin, an ice pack on that ankle, and elevators."

Jeffrey was summoned and consulted, then he signed the papers and carried Vicky out to Madison Avenue, where he caught a cab and solicitously maneuvered her into it. "I spoke to Amanda while you were in X ray," he said.

"Yes?"

"I really gave her hell."

"Did you?"

"Of course, her version of the story is nothing like yours."

"I'm not surprised. Tell me about it."

"She says—and mind you, I don't believe this, I'm just telling you what she said—she says you got drunk and abusive and she threw a drink in your face."

"A drink?"

"Yes. Then she says you rushed out and tripped over your coat at the top of the stairs."

"And what did you say to that?"

"I called her a liar, of course."

"Good for you. Then what?"

"She said, 'I think you know me well enough to know I don't go around pushing people down stairs.'"

"And what did you say?"

He lowered his eyes.

"You do believe me, don't you?" Vicky said. "Whatever she may say."

"Well...I spoke to the owner of the restaurant, too. He, um..."

"Yes, I know what he says."

Jeffrey looked at her pleadingly. "Vicky, I...I wasn't

there. It's your word against hers. Even the witnesses say.... It's not that I don't believe you, but..."

His voice trailed off feebly.

Vicky felt more alone at that moment than she'd ever felt in her life.

If she could no longer discuss the incident with Jeffrey, there was always Willa. Willa was not sick of hearing about it. She did not say, "Well, I wasn't there," or "There were witnesses, Vicky," or "Maybe you shouldn't have had more than one glass of wine." Willa balled her fist and pounded it on her knee. "Why, that fucking bitch!" She sat on the edge of Vicky's bed. She'd come running when Vicky told her about the incident, plying her with half a dozen cheerfully wrapped inexpensive gifts she'd picked up at a stationery store—a little address book, a memo pad, some buttons with dumb sayings on them, a pen that wrote with grape-scented ink. Vicky's bed was littered with wrapping paper, and she felt better than she had since the run-in with Amanda.

"I'll bet Jeffrey wanted to kill her," Willa said.

Vicky lowered her eyes. "He was upset, of course."

"That woman's a menace," said Willa. "What *is* Jeffrey doing about her?"

"He's speaking to his lawyer."

"Lawyer? You don't stop that woman with lawyers. You certainly don't stop her with civilized lunches."

"How *do* you stop her?"

"You punish her. I don't mean docking her alimony check or serving her with papers." The actress hunched her shoulders and became Brando in *The Godfather*. "You gotta hoit da broad," Willa rasped. "You gotta hoit da broad *bad*."

"What do you suggest?"

Willa looked at her, evaluating her critically. Then she shook her head. "Nah. You won't do it, you're too well brought up. Jeffrey won't do it, he's still too conflicted. So maybe I'll do it. I'm just crazy enough, and it would give me intense pleasure."

"Do what?"

"Mess her up a little."

"Willa!" Vicky's eyes rounded.

131

"Nothing too flagrant, just a few marks on her face so whenever she looks in a mirror she remembers who she fucked with."

"Willa, I've never heard you talk this way!"

"Honey, I'd like to remind you of my humble up-bringing on Avenue B. I was the president of the Delancy Knights Sisterhood. We took care of our own."

"This isn't the Lower East Side. Willa, I refuse to let you do whatever it is you're thinking. I'll settle this my own way."

Willa looked at her friend and read the alarm on her face. "Sure, kid." She stretched, then gathered up the wrapping paper strewn over Vicky's bedclothes. "Well, gotta go to the theater. Understudying is hard work; you spend every waking moment hoping one of the leads will catch the flu."

Vicky laughed. "Good luck. Now, remember what I said. I'll deal with Amanda my own way."

Willa kissed her on the cheek. "Okay, okay."

"Promise me you won't do anything," Vicky said, grasping her friend's hand.

Willa pulled her hand loose. "Bye!" And she exited, leaving Vicky with a profound uneasiness fluttering around her stomach.

There are a lot of nuts in New York City, some of them homicidal. They get their kicks in particularly revolting ways, like setting fire to tenements and watching residents jump from blazing apartments, or torturing derelicts, or pushing people in front of subway trains. This particular nut had been making headlines for about two years in a unique way. He heaved masonry, heavy stones and bricks dislodged from the cornices of decaying buildings in the Theater District off the roofs during the height of pedestrian traffic. One of the strangest aspects of his pathology was that he never stuck around to see the devastation he wrought, never actually saw the stones strike his victims' skulls, crushing them like eggshells. By the time his victims hit the pavement dead, he was making his way down the escape stairs of the buildings he knew so intimately, and blending into heavy crowds flowing west across Broadway and Seventh Avenue toward the Shubert, the

Broadhurst, the Music Box, and the O'Neill. His gratification came simply in tossing the slabs over the top, his satisfaction from hearing about it on the news and reading about it in the papers.

He'd killed or injured eight people since first acting out his mad fantasy, and despite intensive detective work, he'd never been caught because of the randomness of the times and places that he struck. Tonight he selected a cheap hotel between Broadway and the Avenue of the Americas on West Forty-fourth Street, and the time was seven thirty-eight P.M. He'd scouted this location the previous week and found a suitable concrete slab resting on a brick retaining wall that rose chest-high from the floor of the rooftop. The mortar had long ago weathered away and lost its cohesiveness, and the slab adhered to the wall only by gravity. Earlier in the evening he had fought with himself, one part of his soul wrestling with the other for control of his compulsion, but the outcome was never in doubt, and after chain smoking half a pack of Marlboros he stepped onto the tar roof, walked up to the slab, and pushed it with just the right amount of energy necessary to make it arc to the center of the sidewalk below. The screams and shrieks that greeted his ears as he padded off the roof told him he'd scored a direct hit.

That evening he watched the eleven o'clock news on CBS and heard Rolland Smith announce the ninth victim of the madman they were coming to call the "Rooftop Killer." She was a pretty actress understudying a role in a Broadway musical. Willa Somebody-or-other. He felt a pang when they flashed a photograph of her, and he started to cry. Then he switched to NBC to see if they were carrying the story there.

Vicky was watching the eleven o'clock "Eyewitness News" on ABC. When Willa's picture was flashed Vicky was so dumbfounded she almost didn't hear the story. She heard the word "murder" and her first thought was that Willa had murdered Amanda; her second was that Willa had murdered the actress whose part she coveted. Then she concentrated on the news story.

Jeffrey was in the living room when Vicky started to scream and scream. He thought a burglar had gotten

133

into the bedroom and he scooped up the first hard object that came to hand, a heavy glass ashtray that sat on the coffee table. He found Vicky in front of the television set, hysterically screaming and crying and pulling her hair with grief. It took him fifteen minutes to calm her down to the point where she could speak coherently, by which time her throat had been rasped to a mere croak.

Chapter Six

DESPITE HER INJURIES, Vicky insisted on going to the funeral, which was conducted at the Park West Chapel on West Seventy-ninth Street. It had been arranged by Willa's parents, Willa's live-in lover Matthew being of no practical help at all. Supported by Jeffrey, Vicky arrived early and hobbled up to the closed coffin before the service began. She looked at it dumbly, pondering the riddle that compounded the mysteries of life and death that are usually celebrated at funerals.

As she studied the unadorned coffin, stained a deep reddish brown and bathed in the light of a single spot recessed in the ceiling of the chapel, Vicky could almost hear Willa irreverently saying, "Dead, she was a star!" From somewhere deep inside her Vicky continued the dialogue with her dead friend. "Willa how did this happen?"

"You read the papers. Some nut," she imagined Willa replying, caustic in death as she had been in life.

"But Willa, consider the sequence. You leave me vowing to mess Amanda up and that night you're struck dead by a piece of masonry thrown off a building."

"For Christ's sake, Vicky, are you going to tell me that Amanda bugged your bedroom and overheard our discussion, then rushed into Times Square and schlepped over the tops of buildings in her ankle-length mink and I. Miller heels, searching for the precise place that I was going to walk under? Then she hauled this slab of masonry into position, spotted me a hundred feet below among six billion people pouring into the Theater District, and chucked the thing in a perfect arc directed at my head? Is that what you're saying?"

"Well..."

"Well, shmell. It was a loony-tune, like I said, and I happened to be in the wrong place at the wrong time. If I ever get my hands on that little shit...but I'm sure he's not going to the same place I'm going to. He doesn't have an Equity card."

"Couldn't Amanda have, well, directed this guy somehow?"

"You mean with thought waves? Vicky, I've had enough lunatics in my life the last couple of days. Do me a favor, just cool it? Be a good friend and say the usual prayers and let me rest in peace? I gotta go—I'm auditioning for *You Can't Take It with You*. Over and out."

Vicky felt a draft of cold air as if Willa's spirit had departed. "Oh, Willa," she sobbed, falling heavily into Jeffrey's arms.

In the weeks that followed, Vicky was tormented by dreams and finally phoned her doctor to ask for something to help her sleep. He prescribed Librium, and at last Vicky knew a week of blessedly blank nights of undisturbed sleep, free from menacing fantasies that haunted her nights.

During this time Jeffrey displayed enormous solicitude, shopping, cooking, cleaning, calling her constantly from his office, making her confinement as comfortable as possible. She could not have got through this period without him. And yet, though they drew closer to each other in that sense, in another sense Vicky felt a gulf between them widen. For, notwithstanding everything Jeffrey had said, everything Willa had advised in their last "discussion" at the funeral chapel, despite the dictates of reason and common sense, Vicky was now certain that Amanda was motivated by forces not entirely natural. Vicky choked on the word "supernatural," but if she did not utter it she thought it nonetheless. It was impossible for her to dismiss the link between Willa's announced intention to avenge Vicky's injuries and her death that same night. But how could she speak of these things to Jeffrey?

From that point onward Vicky became two people, the one she had always displayed to her friends and family, and another, a kind of underground Vicky that nobody knew. This alter ego believed in magic, in the power of certain people to read minds, to intuit events, to control behavior remotely by means of the will, to transport objects telekinetically, to cause events by wishing them. Of course, she knew only one such person possessed of such powers, and that person now became a perpetual fixture in Vicky's fantasy life, sometimes minimally, sometimes totally, but never out of mind completely for one waking moment or, for that matter, most sleeping moments as well. She found herself becoming alert and wary like some forest creature that is prey to a particularly malevolent bird. She always stepped tentatively out of her apartment, into her elevator, out of the elevator into the lobby, out of the lobby into the street. Her eyes darted here and there as she walked, she shrank a moment before entering buildings and shops. She watched for sudden movement in traffic, she looked behind her constantly, used store windows for mirrors, even checked the sky for falling masonry.

This was not, she insisted to herself, paranoia. It was simply a kind of pervasive caution based on her belief that the threat to her was genuine and not fanciful. It was also her secret, perfectly guarded from everyone including Jeffrey, whose sensitivity to her was not delicate enough to register the nuances of her defensive tactics. Oh, she did change her telephone number to a new, unlisted one (even asking the installer not to insert the little card with the phone number on it into the window on the phone, a precaution against Daria's prying eyes). But this, she explained to Jeffrey, was due to some obscene calls she'd received from teenaged boys.

But Daria was to spend more time with them, not less, they had been informed. Amanda was going on a vacation to the Caribbean in mid-June and Jeffrey was expected to take care of his daughter. Hoping to mitigate anxiety in this first test of their ability to cope as a threesome, Jeffrey proposed that they spend that week in East Hampton at the summer house, getting it into shape for July and August visits. Vicky readily agreed, not relishing the prospect of caring for Daria alone. She was also exhausted from her trying year and felt that a week away, even helping to paint a house, would be welcome. As the school year neared its conclusion, her workload increased even more. There were term papers to grade, final exams to prepare, class evaluations to draw up, and the graduation ceremony to face. Each upper class had to contribute something to the graduation ceremony; her class had voted to prepare a scene from George Bernard Shaw's *Saint Joan,* but Victoria discovered, too late, that no one in her class knew how to act. They came from the "Charlie's Angels" school of emoting, delivering lines with sensuous squirms and great tosses of their ponytails.

Vicky was so preoccupied that she did not notice that she had missed her period. When it finally occurred to her that she was a week late, she attributed it to increased work and tension. When it was two weeks late and her breasts began to feel sore, she knew she had to go to the doctor. After a blood test and a wait of several hours, she learned she was pregnant.

"Me?" she said to the doctor, who had called her at home, later that afternoon. "I'm pregnant?"

"Why not?" said the doctor. He knew she was not married. She felt his hesitation and said, "This is wonderful news. I'm going to tell my fiancé right away. He'll be so glad." When she hung up she knew that Jeffrey would not be entirely glad, for they had no room and no money. But she also knew she wanted to go through with it. She was going to have his baby. She decided to wait for Jeffrey to come home. When he arrived she sat him down and brought out a bottle of wine and two glasses, then set out some canapés that she had prepared in the kitchen before he came home. He looked askance at her. "What's the occasion?"

"Oh, it's an occasion, all right." She downed a half glass of wine in two gulps and poured another. Immediately the warm tingle of alcohol suffused her body, and she felt herself relaxing. Jeffrey chewed a slice of brown bread with cream cheese and scallion, but looked at her with consuming curiosity.

"So? What's up?"

She giggled. "Remember that movie we saw last week on the late show, when the woman told the man, 'Sit down, I have something to tell you,' and you laughed and said, 'That never happens anymore'? Remember? You said nowadays men are much more in touch with their women and always know when it's their period and it never comes as a surprise to men to learn the woman is pregnant. Right?"

Jeffrey was now leaning forward intently. He'd set the hors d'ouevre down on the plate and stopped chewing mid-bite.

"Well," said Vicky, raising her glass to her lips again, then setting it down as she remembered her doctor's injunction against too much alcohol. "Uh, I have something to tell you."

"You're pregnant, aren't you?" he said. His face and body reflected more than a small degree of ambivalence. He was grinning, but the grin seemed forced and strained, like that of a beauty contest runner-up when the winner's name is announced. His arm and leg muscles tensed to spring out of the sofa and embrace her, but they seemed counterbalanced by another set of muscles that restrained him, causing him to hesitate, then rise clumsily and hug her without genuine enthusiasm. And then his words gave him away as well. "Honey, I'm really happy for you." He kissed her on the cheek.

She stood frozen in his embrace, searching his eyes. They smiled but without sparkle. "Happy for *me?* What about yourself? For us?"

"Oh, sure, that goes without saying."

"It did go without saying!" She separated from him and pushed him back onto the sofa. "You're not happy about it, are you?"

He shook his head exaggeratedly. "It's not that. It's simply that, well, the reality of it hasn't really sunk in. I mean, right now, it's just an eeny-teeny...what the hell's the word we used in zoology?...blastula, not a huggy little baby that wets and laughs and says mama-dada."

"Jeffrey Keating, you are not being honest with me." She poked her index finger in his chest. "Now, you'd better level with me or we are in extremely big trouble." She conquered the impulse to cry but she wasn't sure she could do it twice. "Is it the money?"

He nodded defeatedly, hiding his eyes from her. "I just don't know how we're going to afford it. I was thinking that when the divorce came through we'd get married, have a good time for a year or two, rebuild the

139

finances. Maybe by that time Amanda would have re-married and I'd have the alimony monkey off my back. That's when I contemplated a baby." He tilted his head. "What happened? I thought you used—"

"Diaphragms are ninety-eight percent effective," she quoted her doctor.

"Terrific. That's the way my luck's been going lately. Amanda probably snuck up here one day and punctured your gadget with a pin to even up the odds."

Victoria gasped, as if her direst fantasy had been read by Jeffrey and made into a joke. "I can't con-ceive—"

"You did conceive," he replied instantly.

"If it's only the money, I've figured out how we can do it. Between my Blue Cross and some benefits I get from a policy the school carries, plus your major med-ical, plus something from my parents—"

"Your Blue Cross and school policies will cover only a fraction, believe me. I can't put you on my major medical because we're not married. And I'm by no means certain your parents will want to contribute to bringing a . . . bringing *this* child into the world. But that's not the point, darling. Even if we cover the doctor bills, there's the little matter of maintenance. You know, like food? Clothing?"

"I have some ideas about that as well. Where there's a will, there's a way. I'm just worried that you don't even have the will."

"I'm sorry, honey. It comes as a shock. I haven't ad-justed yet. Husbands in a lot better circumstances than mine often have difficulty adjusting too, you know."

"It's not just the money though, is it? Let's get it all on the table, okay? So I know whether I should keep the child or . . ."

She couldn't finish the thought, but she waited for Jeffrey to make some sort of protest. He didn't, and his silence revealed the depth of his conflict. Into that si-lence she said, "It's Daria." She seized him by the wrist and dug her nails into him. "I'm right, aren't I? You're worried about Daria."

He grimaced, but she would not release his wrist. "Daria will adjust, I'm sure."

"You don't really believe that," Vicky asserted.

"How do you know what I believe?" He shook his arm loose from her grip, massaging it. Four red welts glowed angrily on the white skin of his wrist. "Aiiiieeee, white woman fight like tiger," he said with a grin. It faded fast as he gauged her solemnity. "If you've seen one case of sibling jealousy, you've seen them all."

"No, not this one. Not Daria. Daria is a special case, and you know it."

"Special? How?"

"Because she's her mother's emissary. She bears Amanda's messages of hatred into this house. And she bears information back to her. You're afraid Amanda is going to inflame Daria's sibling jealousy. You're a-fraid Daria won't love you anymore for bringing a kid brother or sister into the world, and Amanda's going to be standing on the sidelines cheering her, coaching her, polarizing her feelings, turning her against you."

Jeffrey fell back into the sofa, breathing hard. He did his Viennese psychiatrist bit: "A most interestink theory, Frau Doktor." But his wounded eyes belied the joke. She watched them fill with tears, and sympathetic tears of her own seeped into her eyes. She put her arms around his neck and pressed his head to her bosom. He did not sob or even whimper, but the heaviness of his breathing and the hot dampness she felt spreading across her shirt where his head rested testified to the depth of his pain and fear. At last he spoke. "God damn her. God damn that woman."

"We'll fight her, my darling. We'll fight her every inch of the way. You're not going to lose Daria, I'll see to that."

"And I'll have another child," he said brightening as if the idea had just been introduced to him.

But Vicky understood what he meant. "It will help when the pain of separation from Daria gets to be too much. It'll be good for you. It'll help you see things more clearly, deal with them more firmly."

"If he's a boy can we name him Rover?"

Vicky laughed. "If he's a boy you can name him any-thing you want. Oh, Jeffrey, take me to bed and make good love to me."

Her desire was urgent, and she knew that it stemmed from something beyond the physical. Her underwear

141

was damp with the special excitement, and, sensing it, Jeffrey stripped her and slid into her with no foreplay of any kind. She heard herself moan from the depths of her soul, and it seemed no more than twenty seconds before she cried that she was going to come. Jeffrey lifted himself off her until the tip of his swollen organ merely hovered on the rim of her vagina. He held himself back until she begged him to complete the act. Then he plunged into her to the very hilt, and she came with a ferocity that startled and almost unnerved them both. Jeffrey went almost berserk with arousal, slamming into her for another minute before releasing his lust in a series of convulsive gushes. He collapsed, full weight, on top of her. She bore him easily, joyously.

"Jesus," he breathed. "I think the whole building heard that one."

"The whole building? The whole neighborhood!"

"The whole eastern seaboard!" he laughed, and they laughed together in tearful gales.

They talked on and on into the night, Jeffrey's enthusiasm waxing as they resolved each anticipated problem. At length they grew drowsy. They kissed one last time, and moments later Vicky heard his rhythmic, sibilant breathing. She couldn't fall asleep yet, however. Something was still bothering her. She finally remembered what it was. She opened the drawer of her bed table and removed the plastic case containing her diaphragm. She opened it, removed the rubber ring, and held it up to the light filtering into the bedroom from the street.

At first she saw nothing through the membrane stretched across the ring. Then she noticed it: a pinprick of light shimmering through, just a little off center. It was not a puncture so much as a tear at a point where the rubber might have had a defect or abrasion. But there was no question about it; the diaphragm had been punctured.

She spent the rest of the night with her eyes open, staring into the darkness, wondering.

Spring ambled toward summer and Vicky observed her personality altering along with her body. Though forever alert to the menace of Amanda, she was able to relax more, and she spent the crystal days of May dreamily. She experienced some nausea and discomfort, but it was not nearly as bad as she'd been led to believe by some of her friends who'd been through pregnancy. She noticed herself reacting more equably to things that used to drive her up the wall. Jeffrey's monthly checks to Amanda ceased to bother Vicky. She reasoned that the money brought them the freedom to be together. She handled the tumult of exams and graduation plans with complete composure. Her values seemed to be changing. The most important thing now was maintaining the body that protected the baby; everything else was of little consequence.

In honor of graduation exercises, she decided to buy herself a new dress, something without a waistline, with a belt she could remove later when she needed the extra room. She checked the ads in the *New York Times* and at last saw exactly what she wanted, a loose spring style in a blend that looked like silk. The price was reasonable; the dress was at Saks Fifth Avenue, on the fifth floor. She decided she would go after school on Monday to buy it.

Monday was a perfect early June day, warm but with a breeze so that the sun was still comfortable. Vicky strolled leisurely toward Fifth Avenue; she wanted to enjoy every moment. She walked on Madison Avenue looking in all the windows of the boutiques, admiring the bright colors showing for spring and summer, cheerful pinks, yellows and turquoises. Everything made her happy this day, and when she passed women pushing babies in carriages and strollers she wanted to stop and tell them her secret. She hadn't told anyone yet; she felt superstitious about revealing pregnancy this early. She'd wait until she was closer to her third month. Until then, she was content sharing the secret with Jeffrey.

At Fifty-seventh Street she walked over to Fifth Avenue. She went into Doubleday to look at books on pregnancy, but when she picked them up and flipped through them they seemed to have nothing to do with her. The pictures and illustrations dealt with women who actually looked pregnant, who threw up in the morning and who worried about varicose veins. Except for diagrams of cells dividing, there wasn't much about the

143

first few weeks. She drank lots of milk; she didn't think there was too much else she should do.

She walked down to Saks and stared in the windows. Beautiful sports clothes were displayed there, terry-cloth lounging outfits, tennis clothes, bathing suits, white pants, and colorful T-shirt tops. She wondered if she should buy something new for their visit to the Hamptons. Jeffrey had told her it was much too early to swim. Jeans and an old shirt would do; they were going to spend most of their time tidying up the place and touching up paint, oiling hinges, patching screens, and the like. She sighed; you didn't need white pants for that, certainly.

She took the elevator to the fifth floor and searched for the dress that had been advertised. A salesgirl directed her to the right department and she selected two styles to try on. In the dressing room, she saw that the dresses weren't quite right; neither style was as flattering as she'd envisioned. She dressed again and went out to look for something else. Wandering around, she saw nothing that interested her on that floor, so she went to the escalator and rode down to the fourth. She still had plenty of time to wander through the store; she loved Saks and enjoyed just walking around and looking. She decided to stroll through a few floors before leaving.

As she rode the escalator down to the second floor, she idly watched people moving up the escalator to the third floor. Suddenly her eye caught sight of a halo of red hair. Heart pounding, she tore her eyes away and stared straight ahead. Amanda. She looked down at her feet and prayed that Amanda had not seen her. She wasn't going to get caught anywhere, even in a crowded department store, with that woman around. She ran to the down escalator and stepped hurriedly on the topmost tread. Pushing past some of the shoppers, she descended to the first floor and walked quickly toward the nearest exit. As she neared an elevator bank, she saw a down elevator opening. In the crowd stepping out she spotted the red hair again. *She's following me,* Vicky thought in a panic; *she saw me and got on an elevator to beat me to the main floor.* Vicky backed away and turned, running toward the escalators again. She

144

glanced behind her and could see, quickly, the flash of red hair approaching. Red hair and a lavender sweater, she noted in panic, closing in behind her on the escalator. She ran onto the up escalator and pushed past several shoppers to the second floor. Then she made her way to the third, jostling, pushing by, trying to be nonchalant but actually in a panic. On the third floor landing she stopped by a display of mannequins wearing the latest fashions; she heard the distinctive "bing" of the elevator bell and knew she had to move quickly. Amanda seemed to know exactly where she was. She rode the escalators up to the seventh floor. Stopping there, she paused to catch her breath. She felt a faint stirring in her abdomen; it felt as if she were going to get her period. That was impossible; she was pregnant. She ignored it and pressed on to the eighth floor. The elevators on eight opened and again she saw that sweater and hair. "No," she heard herself cry, and she ran toward the down escalator, running in panic, moving as quickly as she could, down the moving stairs as if they were stationary, trying to go as fast as possible. When she reached the fifth floor, she rounded the corner to get the escalator to the fourth floor when she saw Amanda coming toward her again. She hurriedly turned around and stepped onto the down escalator and began to walk up against the flow. The passengers cursed as she wove through them. Vicky was sweating and winded as she got off and made her way to the bottom of the next down escalator. Just as she stepped on, a mother and daughter were getting off. The child lost her balance as Vicky bolted past her. The mother shrieked. Vicky looked behind her and saw the child's pinafore caught in the folding step of the escalator as it ground toward the end. She turned around and grabbed at the child, pulling her dress with all her might. The dress tore. The mother was screaming, "Oh, my baby, oh no." Bypassers and the other people on the escalator shouted for someone to stop the machinery. Vicky yanked the pinafore off the girl's shoulders. Just as she did, the dress jammed the stairs and stopped the escalator.

The little girl was crying; her mother held her, rhythmically murmuring, "It's all right. It's all right." Shoppers crowded into a tight perimeter, exchanging explanations of what they saw or thought they saw. No one had actually seen Vicky board the down escalator the wrong way, and it had all happened so fast even the child's mother couldn't explain the sequence to the security guard and floor manager who'd pushed through the ring of onlookers. Several women praised Vicky for her heroism and quick thinking in rescuing the child from possible mutilation. Vicky listened to the hubbub impasively, sitting with one leg tucked under her and massaging her abdomen to ease the cramps. They became stronger, and the fear that something had happened to the baby surged through her body, borne on streams of adrenaline that made her heart thunder and her eyeballs pulsate. She looked around for Amanda but couldn't see much from her position on the carpeted floor.

The guard helped her to her feet and took her name and address and phone number and some notes about her role in the incident. Vicky did not tell the truth. She felt guilty about lying, but thank God the child wasn't hurt, and when she overheard the store manager sending the girl and her mother to the children's clothing department for a complimentary replacement of the ruined dress, Vicky felt relieved. The cramps, however, were getting worse.

The guard helped her out of the store and summoned a taxi. She took it directly to her doctor's office. He examined her and frowned. There was a slight stain. It could mean nothing, or it could mean a problem was developing. He ordered her home and to bed. She was to call if the cramps worsened or if there was any bleeding. Numbly, she left his office, hailed a cab, and rode home. She took off her perspiration-damp clothes, got into bed, and stared at the wall. She had done this to herself, she thought; she had brought this upon herself with her obsessiveness and paranoia. Oh, that had been Amanda, all right, but for Vicky to bolt blindly, jeopardizing people's safety, jeopardizing her own, jeopardizing her baby's...

The phone rang—her new unlisted number. She picked it up. No one spoke. No one had to. Vicky put the receiver down and bit her lip. "Amanda," she said aloud, "has my number." It was a good pun, but it wasn't funny.

She was losing the baby.

The bleeding increased. It was dark brown and viscous, and it was accompanied by severe cramps. Impassively she followed the doctor's instructions, avoiding baths and sex, staying in bed, eating sensibly. She did not cry. She tried hard not to attribute her miscarriage to Amanda. Miscarriages happen because there is a defect in the embryo or in the mother's childbearing system. If the embryo is healthy and strong, even intense stress or physical abuse cannot dislodge it. If it is not, no amount of care and pampering will make it survive. The fact that she'd become aware of the cramps immediately after the incident in Saks didn't mean it was caused by the incident in Saks. It was a coincidence.

That was what the rational part of Vicky's brain told her.

The other part told her something quite different.

Jeffrey was terribly upset. He stayed home from work for two days, running errands for her, catering to her every wish, reassuring her that when she went back to the doctor everything would be all right. He delivered graded term papers to her school and collected the final exams for her to mark. Vicky was not sorry to be missing school; she didn't particularly want to be around children right now. Jeffrey told Mrs. Dolittle Vicky had a bad case of the flu. As she had seldom missed a day in three years of teaching, her excuse was accepted without question. Her class sent a floral arrangement, an enormous get-well card that opened into a dozen large sections, and the school yearbook. Vicky leafed through it, gazing at former students now going on to be seniors and eighth grade students, next year's crop of pupils. Browsing through the photos of the youngest children, she stumbled on a photograph of the first grade and caught sight of Daria Keating.

The first graders were standing in the little garden behind the school, arranged in a semicircle, holding hands. Daria was on the far right. The other girls stared at the camera, squinting into what must have been a strong sun judging by the shadows cast on the grass, some with their eyes nearly shut. They were cute children, awkward in their extreme youth, a different awkwardness from the adolescent kind Vicky was accustomed to in her thirteen- and fourteen-year-olds. But then there was Daria, standing alone; Daria, who had dropped the hand of the girl next to her and stood apart from the rest of her class. She looked past the camera, and on her face was the smile that Vicky had seen once before, on the face of Daria's mother in the Italian restaurant. The picture literally chilled her, and she asked Jeffrey to throw an extra blanket on top of the quilt.

The bleeding diminished, and by the time she returned to the doctor it had stopped. Jeffrey sat nervously in the anteroom and stalked into the consultation room as soon as the doctor had completed his examination.

"I'm afraid Vicky's lost this one," he said. He was in his fifties, well-tanned and manicured, but his eyes were compassionate and his mouth tense with disappointment.

"Shit," said Jeffrey. "I was really starting to get into it."

"It's not uncommon," the doctor said. "There's been no harm to Vicky's system. The spontaneous abortion was complete and there's no need for a D and C. You can resume your normal activities and try again. You'll have as many children as you want."

"Poor Rover," Jeffrey said as they stepped into the warm spring air outside the doctor's office. "He never had a chance."

Oh, my darling, if you knew even the half of it, Vicky said to herself.

They turned their attention to the week in the Hamptons at Jeffrey's summer house. Jeffrey was to pick Daria up from Amanda's apartment next Thursday evening; Amanda would take off for the Caribbean the next morning. Jeffrey would put in half a day at the office Friday morning, then come home and help Vicky pack and shop. He'd pick up the rented car early in the evening, and Saturday morning bright and early they

148

would take off. The weekend weather prediction was good.

Vicky waited apprehensively for Jeffrey to return with Daria. Finally they arrived, giggling over some private joke. Daria looked unkempt, her clothes wrinkled, her hair unbrushed and snaggy. One of her sneaker laces had been broken and hastily knotted together. Her hands were dirty.

"Is that how Amanda delivered her to you?" Vicky asked Jeffrey.

He looked at Daria as if noticing her appearance for the first time, then shrugged. "I had a cab waiting. I didn't really look."

"It's disgraceful," Vicky said, lifting the suitcase and setting it on the couch. "Did you check to make sure she has everything? The last time, she forgot half her clothing and all her underwear."

"I told Amanda..."

"You can't count on Amanda," Vicky said.

"I packed myself," Daria interjected. "Mommy says it's my responsibility."

"Did she at least check what you packed?"

Daria shrugged and exchanged a look with her father, which Vicky caught. "This is not a joke, Jeffrey." She pressed the catches on the suitcase locks and opened the lid. "Damn," she groaned, examining the contents. Everything was jumbled together, and as she sorted the items she repeated the oath. "Look at this. Two winter sweaters, a pair of heavy corduroy pants and mittens. Just what we need for early summer weather. *No* shorts, *no* tops..." She poked around the suitcase, producing a slipper. "Where's the other slipper?"

"I couldn't find it," Daria said. She looked at her father for support but this time got none. Jeffrey looked embarrassed and dismayed.

"Well, I suppose you can hop all over the Hamptons," Vicky snorted. "Look at this underwear—soiled, frayed, and it looks too small. Is this how your mother dresses you?"

Daria's chin began to quiver and her eyes moistened. "It's not her fault," Jeffrey said.

"I never said it was. Her mother should never leave it to Daria to pack. But at least you could have checked

149

the suitcase. I know, I know, the taxi was waiting," she cut him off, slamming the suitcase lid down and collapsing on the sofa, breathing heavily. "Now what do we do?"

"I'll go to Gimbel's East right now and buy her some things."

"Take me with you," Daria whimpered.

"No, you stay here with Vicky."

"No, I want to go with you," she insisted, her eyes round with fear.

"Vicky's not going to hurt you. She's just upset." He moved toward the front door but Daria clung to his leg.

"Don't leave me," she cried. Her face was turning red and her fists clenched and unclenched rapidly.

Jeffrey kneeled and held her. "Tweety bird, what's the matter?" He looked helplessly at Vicky. "She's never acted like this."

"I just want to go with you," Daria bawled, almost hysterically.

As convincing as Daria's performance was, Vicky didn't buy it. The child certainly wasn't afraid of her. Sure, Vicky was displeased with Daria, but that was no cause for hysterics. It was a play for her father's attention, to distract him from examining Daria's behavior too carefully; if he did, he might become as irritated with her as Vicky was.

She wondered if Jeffrey saw through the ploy. From the way he was fussing over Daria, Vicky doubted it. "It's all right, Jeffrey. Take her with you," she said at last.

Daria beamed as if she'd been spared the gallows, and Jeffrey hustled her out of the apartment before Vicky could change her mind.

That was the start of their week together.

The next day Jeffrey picked up their rental car, which turned out to have battery problems. It stalled, dead, in front of Vicky's door, and he had to get it jumped, return it to the car place, and wait an hour for another vehicle.

They loaded it up and Jeffrey, already weary, told them to climb in. Daria, in the new Sasson shorts and Gloria Vanderbilt shirt Jeffrey had bought her at Gim-

150

bel's East, climbed into the backseat. Vicky was relieved; she'd been afraid she'd have to battle Daria for the right to sit next to Jeffrey. Daria was apparently content to sit in the back with her bag of bribes, a ball, a jar of bubbles, a book of stickers, a new Smurf figure, six packs of Bubble Yum, and, of course, her doll.

There wasn't too much traffic once they got on the Long Island Expressway. And the traffic thinned the farther away from New York they got. The drive was pleasant; Jeffrey kept remarking on the difference off-season driving made in one's outlook. "The whole thing of going out to a house on weekends is insane. You spend more time in your car than you do on the beach. And once you get there, you talk for hours about getting back, when to leave, what route to take, when and where to buy gas. Everything's getting so crowded. The only way to enjoy it is to go when almost nobody else does."

Daria was quiet and kept to herself, chirping to her babushka doll, Sasha. Vicky, lulled by the uninteresting scenery along the expressway, closed her eyes and was about to drift into a catnap when she overheard Daria's dialogue with the doll.

"I'm going to kill that bitch."

"Sasha, that's a very, very bad word," replied Daria. "You should say, 'female dog.' And it's not nice to want to kill anybody. I'm going to tell Daddy what you said."

"Go ahead and tell him. *He* won't do anything."

"He will too."

"No, he won't. He's afraid to."

Vicky's eyes flew open and she looked at Jeffrey. He sat obliviously behind the wheel, the sound of Daria's voice muffled by the rush of air past his open window. She nudged him and he looked at her quizzically. "Listen," she murmured to him, reaching across his body to roll up his window. But by that time Daria had lapsed into silence. Jeffrey looked at Vicky again, but she said, "Never mind, I'll tell you later." He shrugged and rolled his window down again. Vicky strained to hear another discussion between Daria and her Sasha, but the child remained silent until Jeffrey veered off the expressway onto a smaller highway running south toward the ocean.

"Uh-oh," Daria singsonged to Sasha, "we're almost there."

"Don't worry," Sasha said in a squeaky falsetto, "he won't punish you."

"He will too," Daria replied. "I helped."

"You only helped a little bit."

Vicky nudged Jeffrey. "Did you hear that?"

"Yes. What does it mean?"

"I doubt if it means anything at all. She's always making up conversations."

"Not like that one." She turned in her seat and looked at Daria. "Punish you for what, honey? What did you help do that you're afraid you'll be punished for?"

Daria blinked as if coming out of a trance. She looked at Vicky with round, innocent eyes, clutching Sasha. "I have to pee," she said.

"We're almost there," Jeffrey said.

"I can't wait."

Jeffrey sighed and thumped the steering wheel with the heel of his hand. After the delay in getting on the road this morning, he was anxious to get to the house. But he spotted a gas station and pulled in. "Would you do the honors?" he asked Vicky. Needing to stretch her legs anyway, Vicky helped Daria out of the car and asked the attendant for the key to the ladies' room. He handed her a paddle-shaped piece of wood with a tiny key dangling from it. Vicky took Daria into the ladies' room, where the child entered a stall, clutching her doll.

Vicky waited. And waited. "Are you all right?"

"Yes."

Vicky waited some more. "What's going on?"

"Sasha had diarrhea," Daria said lugubriously.

Vicky opened the stall door and found Daria fully dressed, holding the doll over the toilet rim. "Daria, for God's sake!" she snapped, clutching the child by the wrist and yanking her out of the bathroom.

Daria started crying. "Sasha isn't finished. We can't leave until she's finished!"

Jeffrey was standing arms akimbo beside the car, looking very grouchy. "*Now* what?"

"I don't want to go to the house," Daria wailed.

"Huh?" He looked at Vicky. "What's with this child?"

"She's been behaving very strangely. First last night, and now this." Vicky gave a big shrug.

"I'm afraid," Daria snuffled, gasping for air. Jeffrey

152

held her, caressing the back of her head until she took one last stuttering breath and relaxed.

"Afraid of what? What are you afraid of, little girl?" he asked.

"Nothing," Daria said, climbing docilely into the backseat.

Jeffrey looked at Vicky over the roof of the car. "Is this a phase of child development I'm supposed to understand?"

"Something's going on, but I don't know what," Vicky said.

It was midafternoon when they reached the Hamptons. As they approached the ocean, Vicky rolled her window down to the bottom so she could smell the tang of the sea mingled with a faint touch of rotted vegetation. The town of East Hampton was a jewel, with a gorgeously manicured green, a duck pond, expensive homes, and chic shops. Beyond it, between towns, gas stations and fast-food places mingled with A-frame cottages in natural wood, clustered in colonies on scrubby plots of grass and ivy. The trees were low and unattractive, the branches and leaves bent inland in the teeth of a perpetual prevailing wind from the sea.

In due time Jeffrey turned right off the highway, pulling over a hill that revealed the full expanse of the sea beneath gentle rolling cumulus clouds. Then they descended and turned into a rutted lane containing seven or eight houses. A few were painted white or pastel, the rest were of natural or stained wood. Unlike the cottages occupied by summer renters, these showed signs of year-round tending, with recently cut lawns, docked hedges, pruned rose bushes, and bright window boxes planted with geraniums, petunias, ivy, and impatiens. Only one house seemed unoccupied, a low saltbox with split cedar shingles at the very end of the lane. Grass had grown tall and seedy in the front yard and some rambling roses twined around a rustic fence. "There she be," Jeffrey beamed as the car jounced over a couple of ruts and braked to a halt in the driveway.

"Oh, Jeff, it's charming," Vicky said, clapping her hands.

"You may not think so when you see all the work

we have to do. But it's fun, actually, and good exercise. Right, Daria?"

No answer came from the back of the car. Jeffrey twisted in his seat and looked at his daughter. "She's asleep," he said.

"Maybe we should let her sleep awhile longer until we've unpacked some things. She's been so cranky."

"Fine," Jeffrey said, hopping enthusiastically out of the car and opening the trunk. He handed her a pair of keys on a ring. "Here, why don't you open up and I'll start carrying this stuff inside." Jeffrey surveyed several cartons of summer clothes, provisions, tools, paint, spackle, electrical tape, waxes and polishes, and gardening implements.

Vicky raced up a flagstone path half covered with weeds and fit the keys into the locks on the front door. The door budged sluggishly on its hinges and she peered into the gloom. The windows were all shuttered and pencils of light filtered through the slats. She could make out nothing. She stepped inside, groping for a light switch, but when she flipped it up nothing happened. She stepped farther inside, closing her eyes for a few moments to help them adjust faster to the darkness. When she opened them again she frowned.

There was nothing to see.

The walls and floors were bare. She looked up and saw an electrical conduit running along a rafter, but there was no fixture attached to it, just a couple of capped wires. She moved slowly through what she assumed was a living room. She made out a fireplace with an empty mantel and no screen, no grate, no andirons, no tongs. There was no furniture of any sort, no pictures on the walls, no carpets. She kept wondering if perhaps Jeffrey hadn't explained things to her correctly, or if she'd misunderstood. Was the furniture all stored in another room? She padded through an open door into a bedroom. It, too, was empty. She backed out of it and entered the kitchen. An old stove and refrigerator were there but nothing else. The cabinet doors were flung open and the shelves were completely empty. "This is a joke," she muttered, but her heart had begun to pound as she recognized that something was very wrong. She glanced in the second bedroom, then the bathroom, then

154

ran out the door, shielding her eyes against the strong late afternoon sunlight. "Jeff, you have to come in here. Now. Instantly. Put that stuff down and come here at once," she commanded.

"What's the matter?" he asked. "Mice?"

"Thieves," said Vicky. "There's nothing inside."

He dropped the box he had lifted and rushed past her, taking the flagstones three at a time. She heard him shuffling from room to room, groaning at first, then cursing, then bellowing like a wounded animal. He reappeared at the door, his face ashen. "Fucking bastards! Fucking cocksuckers!"

He stumbled down the path, looking stricken. She caught him in her arms. He was breathing so hard she thought he was hyperventilating. "I think I'm going to cry," he whimpered. He leaned against a fence post, trying to compose himself. "Were there any signs of forced entry? Was the door pried? The windows broken?"

"No."

He shook his head in disbelief. "We've been cleaned out. I mean cleaned out. An army of ants couldn't do a number like this. We have to call the police." He looked down the lane. A few houses down, an old woman in a cotton dress was watching them. Jeffrey hailed her and took two steps towards her. Then he snapped his fingers. "Daria."

"She's still asleep," Vicky said.

"Just as well. If she saw that house now she'd get hysterical."

He approached the woman, who had shears in her hand and a little burlap bag over her shoulder. She was clipping dead flowers and pulling weeds out of a border beside her house. She was square-jawed and gimlet-eyed, a type Vicky had often seen in New England. Tugboat Annies, she called them.

"May I use your phone? We've been burglarized," Jeffrey said breathlessly.

"You can use my phone, but you haven't been burglarized, sonny."

"You don't think so, huh? If you can find so much as a teaspoon over there, I'll pay you a handsome reward."

The woman examined a drooping zinnia as if it had

personally insulted her and clipped it smartly, dropping the flower in her bag. "Oh, I'm not saying there's anything left. I'm just saying 'twasn't burglars what done it. In fact, I'm surprised to see you. Didn't think you'd be back."

"What are you talking about?"

"Oh God," Vicky groaned as the realization dawned on her.

Jeffrey turned and looked at Vicky. "Do you know what she's talking about?"

"I think I do, and I think I'm going to be sick."

"'Twas your wife. At least, I thought it was your wife—seen you two every summer for years, leastways. Come here with a truck, bunch of young moving men."

"Amanda!" Jeffrey cried, clenching his fists. "Red hair?"

"Red hair. Fur coat."

"Amanda," he repeated, venom in his voice. "When did this happen?"

"March. On a Sunday. Those boys were real professionals. Did the job in under an hour. Picked it clean."

"Why didn't you stop her? Call the police?"

She glowered at him. "'*Twas* her house, wunt it? She *was* your wife, wunt she?"

"We're getting divorced. The house belongs to me alone. It's in the papers."

"Well, now, maybe your lawyer should of sent me a copy of the papers so's I could perform a citizen's arrest." The woman said it with a poker face, but Jeffrey flinched at her sarcasm. Her contempt for city people was clearly enormous. But then she softened. "Look, young man, I'm sorry, I didn't know you was in the midst of a divorce. When she and the little girl showed up here that day, I naturally thought—"

"The little girl? What little girl?"

"Your daughter. That *is* your daughter, right? Pretty thing with red hair, spit 'n' image of her mother?"

"My daughter was *with* her when she ransacked the house?"

"Yes. She even helped carry a few things out. I remember 'em telling her she'd have to join a union."

Jeffrey's face reddened. "This is too much. My circuits are overloaded." He looked around for something to lean against. Vicky seized his arm and led him to a picnic table beside the house.

"Let me get you a beer, young man. Miss?" asked the woman.

"That would be fine, thank you," Vicky said.

Jeffrey buried his face in his hands. Vicky caressed his neck. The tendons were stretched tight with tension. "Daria!" he gasped. "Daria!"

"That explains it," Vicky said.

"Explains what?"

"Her behavior last night and today. She's been entirely irrational, and now I know why."

"She was feeling guilty. She was afraid of what would happen when we got here. When did this woman say it happened? March. March. Of course."

"That's when your father was sick. When you went to see him. That's why Amanda was so quiet. She was doing *this*," Vicky said, jerking her thumb in the direction of Jeffrey's house.

It was then that Vicky remembered the dreams that she and Jeffrey had had on the same night back in March when he was in California. Dreams about burglary. And Vicky had heard that awful laughter...

The neighbor brought out three glasses of beer on a painted metal tray. "That's why I never got married," she said. "That, and the fact I'm fat and ugly."

"You're very nice," Vicky said.

"There's some furniture stores in East Hampton and Amagansett; you could pick some basic things up fairly cheap. Five & Dime's got some utensils—cheap lamps, bed linens. I'll be glad to lend you anything you might need to pass the night."

"That's very kind of you," Jeffrey said, emptying the glass down his throat. He seemed to have recovered from the first shock. "We may take you up on that offer." He looked morosely at Vicky. "I'll never replace some of those antique pieces. Not at the prices I paid for them originally." He shook his head, then faced his neighbor. "Do you object to profanity?"

"No, I've heard it all, used it all too."

"Good." He filled his chest with air and bellowed, *"SHIT!"*

157

As the curse echoed through the trees, the woman smiled. "You look better already."

"I have to get back to my daughter. She's sleeping in the back of the car."

"She's in the back of the car, but she ain't sleepin'," said the woman, nodding with her chin at the car parked under the branches of an oak tree.

They followed her gaze and saw Daria's head, eyes round with a combination of curiosity and fear. As soon as she realized they were looking at her, she popped down. "Thanks for the hospitality," Jeffrey said.

"Anytime. I'm Miss Potter."

"And I'm Jeffrey Keating. This is my fiancée, Victoria Lewis."

Miss Potter raised her glass in salute, and Jeffrey and Vicky returned to the car.

"What are you going to do?" Vicky asked.

"I'm going to call my lawyer, for starters."

"Hmph."

"What's that supposed to mean?"

Vicky stopped and faced him. "Your lawyers never do a damn thing. They can't. Her lawyer says she didn't do it, or you can't prove it, or it was a mistake, or she's sorry. Or he says sure, Amanda did it, sue us. I don't want to hear about lawyers. I want to know what you're going to do about that woman. *And* that child."

"What about the child?"

"What about her? She's an accomplice to the crime! She helped her mother plunder your summer home! *Our* summer home!"

"You're not going to blame Daria," Jeffrey said, stiffening. "What was she supposed to do, block her mother's path? Call the police? She's innocent."

Vicky gaped. "I can't believe I'm hearing this. She's about as innocent—"

Jeffrey menaced her with a sharply pointed finger. "You'd better be very careful what you say, Vicky. I'm ready to deck the next person who crosses me, and you happen to be very close."

Vicky held her ground, thrusting her chin out pugnaciously. "That's just dandy. Your wife and daughter strip you bare and I'm the one who gets punished. How long are you going to go on excusing their behavior?

Forgiving that awful woman for the horrible things she's said and done to me. Not just to me, to *you*. She's robbed you of your money, your possessions, your privacy, your dignity. She tried to rob you of your manhood when you lived with her. She's trying to rob you of me. She's setting your daughter against you. And what do you do? Stand there with your pants around your ankles begging for more."

Jeffrey brought himself up, fists clenched, and Vicky stepped back flinching, waiting for a blow, knowing she'd gone too far. But he did not hit her. Instead he pivoted sharply and stalked silently to the car. Vicky trudged after him. "Where are you going?"

"I'm going into town to forage for some things for tonight. You can stay here and think about this: Daria is only six years old and this divorce has been tough as hell on her, something you've never had to experience in your sheltered life. She lives with her mother whether we like it or not, and she has to adapt to her mother's ways or it'll become intolerable for her there. If she betrays us she does it with no malice aforethought. Now, if you don't buy that, if you can't live with me, father of that child, then maybe we'd better pack it in."

"Jeffrey, no!"

He climbed into the driver's seat and slammed the door. Vicky looked into the car and saw Daria curled on the backseat, eyes shut tight in sleep—shut too tight. She was about as fast asleep as Jeffrey was. And about as innocent, Vicky said to herself, completing the sentence she had dropped a few moments ago, as Amanda. A faint smile played at the corners of Daria's mouth.

"When will you be back?" Vicky asked.

"I don't know," Jeffrey snapped, starting the car.

"What am I supposed to do?"

"Guard the house against burglars," he replied, backing the car out of the driveway with a screech, then lurching down the lane with a roostertail of dust and gravel.

Fists clenching and unclenching, hot tears streaming down her cheeks, she watched the car jounce over the rutted road, then turned in the driveway to look at the forlorn house. Without Jeffrey it was as alien to her as a hut in the wilderness. She felt as if she'd been parachuted into some unfamiliar environment chosen at random, with instructions to survive off the land as best she could, and no explanation of the purpose of her mission. No, it was worse than that in some ways, because the environment wasn't merely alien, it was hostile. Amanda's raid had not merely deprived the house of its heart and soul, but had touched it with a defiling presence that lingered like the smell of lust at the scene of a rape.

She entered the house again, moving through it cautiously as she opened the shutters in each room and threw up the window sashes to air the place out. The strong sunlight and pungent, kelpy sea breeze dispelled some of the mustiness but failed to obliterate the less palpable odor of memories of Jeffrey's life with another woman, a happy marriage turned rotten, as if infected by damp rot. Here was the stove where Jeffrey sang over his Sunday breakfasts, here the window where he and Amanda had watched the weather roll in over the sea, here the place where the bed had been, where they had made love, where they had made joy, where they had perhaps made Daria.

And what was Vicky to make of Daria, she wondered as she stepped out of the rear door into a scrubby, ill-tended garden, about twenty feet square bordered by flagstones piled upon each other without mortar. Tall dune grass wisped out of the cracks, mingled with tiny purple wild flowers she couldn't identify. The floor of the yard itself was a coarse ivy. Some lonely green stakes in one corner bespoke the cultivation of tomatoes at some earlier date in this sad history. In another corner stood a swing and slide, rusting. Amanda had forgotten to take it, or perhaps had left it intentionally to convey some ironic message which at the moment went over Vicky's head.

She sat delicately on the swing, tested it with half her weight, then kicked gently, wondering what indeed was she to make of Daria. The child was indubitably under her mother's influence, but did that make her a co-conspirator? Children were no angels, that was something Vicky had learned quickly after becoming a schoolteacher. But few were truly devils. Most of them were monkeys, imitating their parents and peers, following the pack, adapting to the dominance of the strongest. Isn't that what Jeffrey had said? That Daria had to adapt to her mother's ways or it would be intolerable for her? What had the child done, really, but stand by, passively for the most part, while her mother dismembered the cottage? Undoubtedly Amanda had justified it all to the little girl, pacifying her, putting a good light on it, till at last Daria offered to help and her mommy said, What a good little girl!

Maybe Jeffrey was right? Where was he? She wanted to talk to him, work this out with him now. She stopped swinging, listening for his car. She was answered only by the breeze, and a gust with just a hint of rain. She stood and looked out to sea. Steel clouds were sliding under the fleecy ones and a wind was getting up. She shuddered and went into the house. It was chilly, damp, and musty inside, the moaning of mounting wind echoing in the empty house as if it were some outpost on the edge of the civilized world. The floorboards creaked as she followed her earlier path from room to room, shutting the windows she'd opened in anticipation of that first wall of wind and water that leads a squall off the sea. The sky had become almost black with an odd yellow cast, the clouds seemingly mixed with dust from some volcano or sandstorm swept up on the other side of the world.

The storm hit with tropical suddenness, battering the weather side of the cottage and drenching Vicky as she struggled with a jammed sash in the master bedroom. She cursed but finally hauled the window down and turned into the room, seeking a bed or chair to collapse into, but finding only the hard surface of the floor. She remembered that Jeffrey had unloaded a few cartons from the car before storming off, and she went to the front door where he'd placed them, just inside. They contained boxes of kitchen staples, no blankets. She cursed again, started to cry, then braced herself and tried to relax. She peered out the kitchen window in the hope of seeing his car. She saw only sheets of rain slashing the houses and trees on the lane.

Now she felt weary, inexpressibly weary, and slid down to the floor of the kitchen and closed her eyes.

The rain drummed on the roof and clattered against the windows. Under ordinary circumstances, in a warm, well-lit, furnished cottage in the country with your loved one nearby, there are few things as enjoyable as braving a summer storm. But here, in this desolate place, stripped of everything but ghostly memories by Amanda's despicable looting, the storm was as menacing as some wild creature attempting to claw its way into the house.

She lay, eyes wide open, hands wrapped around her shins, listening for the hopeful sound of Jeffrey's automobile above the wail of the wind and hiss of the rain, but rewarded only by a peal of thunder. She struggled to get comfortable and warm, and at last found some comfort from the warmth of her own body in fetal position. Despite the raucous noise of the storm, she was able to close her eyes and drift into sleep.

Somewhere in the depths of her slumber she felt something drawing close to her. Darkness had set in, and the storm had abated, but a cold wind whistled through chinks in the windows, and an occasional gust rattled the panes. Above these sounds she heard the creak of floorboards, and she clawed up through sleep to consciousness, hoping the sound would disperse with her dreams when she opened her eyes. From behind her eyelids she could make out the flicker of firelight, and it now became imperative for her to open her eyes. She reached deep inside herself for the energy but she was all but overcome by torpor, and by the fear of what she would see when she wakened. But something, someone, was definitely near; she could almost feel its breath on her face. Dimly she saw a spectral presence, bone-white and ghostly, drifting toward her, bony clawed fingers extended. Its eyes were hollow, its mouth twisted in a lurid smile. It came closer. Her limbs felt dead and helplessly immobile. It knelt to bestow a kiss on her. She felt its rancid breath on her face, but mingled with it was a hint of perfume, a scent she recognized all too keenly. The presence touched Vicky's mouth. She opened her eyes wide and saw it. She screamed. The thing shrieked.

It took only a moment to realize it was Daria's doll, Sasha. Daria was holding it only inches from Vicky's face when Vicky awoke. Her scream had frightened the child and sent her shrieking in terror out of the kitchen. In the entryway to the cottage Jeffrey stood holding a candle. Daria clung to his leg screaming hysterically, and Jeffrey, not knowing what had scared her, clutched a length of firewood like a club. "Vicky? Is that you? Who's there?" He stalked into the kitchen, holding the candle in front of him, raising the cudgel against a potential intruder.

"Jeffrey, it's me." She crouched in a corner of the kitchen, trembling.

"Daria, it's all right, it's Vicky. It's only Vicky."

He stooped to help Vicky to her feet. He set the candle and stick down and took her in his arms. "I'm so sorry," he whispered. "That was very bad of me to do."

"No, it's all my fault. I should never have spoken against Daria. I thought about what you said and you're absolutely right; it's not her fault."

"Hush, it's all right. God, your clothes are damp. You slept on the floor? I'll never forgive myself if you come down with something. Vicky, I'm sorry. I need you. I love you." He held her hard, his lips buried in her neck, and she could feel his tears trickling down her skin. She closed her eyes, reveling in his embrace, feeling as if they'd found their way back to each other's love.

Over his shoulder he saw Daria, watching them with big eyes shrouded eerily by the light of the candle.

"It's the best thing that could have happened," Jeffrey declared, holding the candle up to the barren rooms of his cottage. "Now there are no memories of the marriage to weigh us down here."

Vicky disagreed, but said nothing. The emptiness of the place virtually cried Amanda's name from every corner. "I wouldn't have felt weighed down by memories if she'd left us some forks and spoons," Vicky said.

Jeffrey laughed, then snapped his fingers. "Which reminds me—you must be starved. Here's something to tide you over till we go out to dinner." He handed her a ham and cheese sandwich wrapped in plastic. She wolfed it down with noisy growls of gratitude. "There's a nice motel not far from here, near the beach," Jeffrey said. "We can stay there a couple of days till we've

163

rounded up some basic furniture and victuals. Then we'll move back here."

"It'll be nicer than ever when I'm finished with it," Vicky said.

He put his arms around her again. "I almost lost you."

She touched her finger to his lips.

"Can we go now?" Daria asked.

"Yes, we can go now," said Jeffrey.

In the car Jeffrey said, "I've been weak." Vicky understood, and said nothing, staring at the unfamiliar road. The clouds had broken and a full moon shone on the choppy sea. The trees glistened from the recent rain. "She's had a power over me; I don't know what it is, but I feel it weakening. Or maybe I'm getting stronger," he continued. "Still, she seems to know exactly where to strike, and when. No matter how strong I get, there's that vulnerable place." He reached across the car seat, taking her hand. "Please be patient."

"It must not go on," Vicky said solemnly.

"What can I do? Tell me, what can I do?"

Vicky looked at the moon's reflection darting over the sea, as if it radiated from the speeding car. "I think you've got to hurt her, Jeffrey."

He received the statement in brooding silence. "I don't know if it's in my nature. And even if it were, I think of Daria. Her respect, her good opinion of me, they're very important. I don't know if I want to risk them by descending to her mother's level." He glanced quickly over his shoulder. Daria was crumpled in the corner of the backseat behind him, singing in a tinkly voice. "Daria's the chink in my armor. She's my blind spot," he said.

"At least you recognize that much," Vicky said. But she knew that wasn't enough.

The motel was clean and tidy, with a sitting room with a couch for Daria and a separate bedroom for them. It had a balcony on the ocean, with wicker furniture and rainproof cushions. There was a tiny kitchenette with a small stove and refrigerator. They checked in, dumped their bags, and drove into East Hampton for seafood. While driving around with Daria during the

164

storm, Jeffrey had picked up some kitchen utensils and supplies. Now, feeling refreshed and well fed, they stopped at a market and picked up some bread and eggs, orange juice and milk, butter and jelly for breakfast. They returned to the motel, and Jeffrey stocked the shelves and refrigerator while Vicky changed Daria into her nightgown and got her ready for bed. Daria was oddly distracted, singing a crazy song, her eyes empty as if her mind had vacated her head. Vicky asked her a question or two about the cottage, but Daria scarcely heard her—or didn't want to. Vicky tucked her in, then stood to one side as Jeffrey kissed her and helped her perform some elaborate bedtime prayer that included dolls, goldfish, school friends, even a book. Everyone was mentioned in her prayer but Vicky. Jeffrey made a point of making the child add it as an after-thought.

When Daria was asleep they made love in their motel bed. It was a soft, saggy bed, but Jeffrey's ardor more than made up for the discomfort. The pain of their separation had brought them closer. They had had a good scare, and they'd survived it. Would they survive the next? Vicky listened to Jeffrey's sibilant breathing and wondered.

The next day dawned magnificently. They ate breakfast on their balcony and walked on the beach. The sun was strong and quickly dried up the final traces of last night's storm. Daria seemed more herself, darting from object to object in the sand, twittering like a shore bird picking at shells. They waded ankle-deep into the surf but it was still bitterly cold from the winter. They dried off in the sun, then Jeffrey said, "Let's hit some furniture and antique stores. If we find some good stuff, maybe we could spend tonight in the cottage."

They trudged back to the motel, dressed for town, and got into the car. They found a furniture store in East Hampton where Jeffrey bought a frame and queen-sized mattress set, paying for it with his American Express card. It was to be delivered late in the afternoon. At an antique store nearby they bought a cheap Formica-topped dining table that Vicky said would look pretty with a tablecloth or bright placemats on it. Four bright green metal bridge chairs on sale completed the kitchen decor. They could now live in the house with this minimal furniture. They'd just have to live out of suitcases instead of clothes chests, and they would not be able to occupy the living room until they could afford a couch.

More for the fun of it than anything else, they hit a few antique stores in East Hampton. They browsed through them, exclaiming to Daria to keep her from getting bored, "Look at these pretty brooches!" "Look at these old-fashioned dolls!" Daria oohed and aahed.

In one shop they found a reupholstered Victorian sofa, but the price tag of eight hundred and fifty dollars discouraged them. "I think this place is a little expensive for us," Vicky whispered as they moved regretfully past it. "Yeah, let's go," Jeffrey said. But then he stopped abruptly, tilting his head in the way he had when something upset him.

"What is it?" Vicky asked. "What's the matter?" He looked as he had when he'd stepped into the denuded cottage the day before.

"There," he said, pointing, finger quivering. "That's the nightstand from my bedroom. My nightstand."

"Are you sure?" asked Vicky. She moved to the place he was pointing to. It was a marble-topped table with two vertical doors. It stood on carved ball-and-claw feet. The drawers were embellished with delicate carving and brass pulls. It was made of some dark fruitwood; Vicky wasn't sure what kind. The top was of a delicately veined, pink-hued marble. "Look," Jeffrey said, pointing to a small discoloration on the marble. "Her cigarette. We couldn't get that mark out. This was my favorite bedroom piece. She sold it. She sold it all, Vicky. She sold all the things I love and I'll never see any of it again." Vicky put her arms around him as he buried his face in his hands.

Daria stood behind an old oak armoire, watching her father cry.

Chapter Seven

IN THE END they were able to salvage their week at the beach. They slept in the new bed, Daria in a sleeping bag. Vicky fixed up the dining table with bright placemats and fresh wildflowers. They spent the mornings and early evenings at work on the house, restoring electrical fixtures, scraping and spackling and painting. The middays were spent on the beach, swimming, playing, picnicking. The nights were spent making love. It had never been better. With Amanda removed by the breadth of an ocean, her influence reduced by the replacement of her things with the new furniture bought by Vicky and Jeffrey, the week in the Hamptons was absolutely tonic. Daria flourished in the sunny warmth and the absence of conflict, and by the end of the week was clinging like a daughter to Vicky.

Vicky wished it could go on forever, but it was not to be. They returned to New York on Sunday night, and the following morning on his way to work Jeffrey dropped Daria off with Amanda. As soon as Daria was out of earshot Jeffrey accused Amanda of having robbed him. She denied it, mocking him with laughter. He went to work in a high dudgeon and spent the better part of the day preparing an inventory of every item Amanda had removed from the Hampton cottage, right down to the last pillow and light bulb. He wrote a letter to his attorney, mentioning the name of the movers and the neighbor who had witnessed the pillage, and enclosed the inventory. He demanded immediate action. There was a flurry of accusations, denials, threats, thrusts, and parries.

In the end, as Vicky had predicted, nothing came of any of it.

They lapsed back into their defensive posture, going about their lives as best they could while bracing for Amanda's next unpredictable move. Vicky turned her attention to the coming months. She was rehired by the day camp, this time as head counselor of all girls' groups. The work occupied her mind, used up unchanneled energy, and brought in some meager but needed extra income. It also brought her the unexpected dividend of inspiration; she had begun making notes for stories again. She carried a clipboard as she made her rounds of the campgrounds, but besides the official records she also kept a scratch pad on which she scribbled hasty sketches of children for the tales that were forming in her mind. Many of the children had divorced parents, and Vicky conceived of a collection of stories unified by that theme. For the first time in a year she was eager to write again.

A whole year! She and Jeffrey had been together almost twelve months. She realized that they now had a history; a large-ish segment of their lives could be recorded and chronicled. And what a year it had been— exhilarating, frightening, terrible, wonderful. Would she go through it again if she had a chance? One part of her said, Never. Another said, Without any doubt whatever.

July was a good month, carefee and relaxed. For one thing, they learned that the landlord of Vicky's building had run into financial difficulties and withdrawn the co-op plan, releasing a dreadful stranglehold on their finances. But the big reason—she could not of course tell this to Jeffrey—was that they didn't have to take care of Daria. Daria went to day camp and on weekends she went away with her mother to a Westport house Amanda had rented for the summer. Although Jeffrey missed the child—and Vicky did too, in her way—there was unquestionably less stress in their lives without her. The sheer logistics of taking care of her put a great strain on them; but on top of that was the perpetual tension she created merely by being Amanda's daughter, the embodiment of the woman whose life seemed bent toward the objective of hurting them, even destroying them.

That was why the month of August loomed so portentously for Vicky.

Jeffrey's separation agreement with Amanda gave him custody of Daria the entire month of August. Because Vicky was working, they arranged for Daria's camp bus to drop her at Jeffrey's office. Daria would stay there playing quietly until Jeffrey finished work, then he'd bring her home for dinner. When camp season ended, they would all go out to the summer house.

These arrangements were a big headache, but would otherwise be tolerable if it were not for the larger question of Daria's behavior. The tension she created by her mere presence was palpable and infectious. In spite of the fact that Daria had loosened up toward the end of the week they spent together in the summer house, Vicky's relief to see the child go back to her mother had been enormous. If that was how Vicky felt after one week, how would she feel after a month?

Shutting the anticipation out of her mind, she resolved to enjoy July with Jeffrey to the fullest, and she planned and executed every day with deep relish. They went to movies, had lingering drinks at sidewalk cafes on balmy evenings, watched the Macy's Fourth of July fireworks display, stuffed themselves at street fairs, and even took a Circle Line boat tour around Manhattan. The last weekend of July they spent at the Hampton summer house.

It was there, as they lay on their bed after making love, that Vicky told him how much she wanted to have his baby. "Not just *a* baby, Jeffrey. *Your* baby."

Lying with her head on his shoulder, she could not see his expression, but she could feel his head nod reflectively. She was not sure what it meant. "The doctor said the miscarriage was a fluke. There's nothing wrong with me, if that's what concerns you."

"That's not what concerns me," he said.

"It's the money, isn't it?"

"Our finances are stretched to the limit as it is."

"I know. But if we think like that we'll never start a family." She rolled over and rested on her elbows gazing down at him. His eyes searched the ceiling dreamily. "I know how much you love children. You can't tell me Daria is enough."

"Sometimes I think she's more than enough."

"Another child would be very good for you," Vicky said. "It would take some of the pain out of missing Daria."

"It would also create more problems with Daria. Jealousy, resentment..."

"Isn't that true of any sibling?"

"I suppose. Why do I feel it would be different for Daria? I mean, more intense?"

"You know why."

"Amanda, you mean?" He turned it over in his mind. "Yes. She would really boil over if we had a child. El shitto would hit el fanno," he chuckled. Vicky held her breath, letting him examine the concept from every angle. Finally, he said, "Fuck her! She's meddled in everything else we've done. She's not going to meddle in this. If we want a baby, by Christ, we're going to have a baby."

"Oh, Jeffrey, that's what I was hoping you would say!" She fell on him, burrowing her head into his neck and hugging him tightly. "We'll have to be married first, of course."

"Of course. If there's going to be a bastard in this family, I want to be him."

"You? A bastard? If only you were a little more of one!"

They sighed in unison and rolled into each other's arms.

August came, and with it Daria and her little suitcase. At Vicky's insistence Jeffrey had helped Daria pack this time, checking items off from a list Vicky gave him.

At first Daria seemed homesick. She spent nearly an hour every evening talking to her mother on the phone, relating everything she did in minutest detail. ("We had fried chicken and I had one wing and part of a leg, mostly the crisp skin but some of the meat, mashed potatoes, string beans which I didn't eat too many of, apple juice, and for dessert I had three Oreos and a glass of milk.") She explained the plots of television programs like "The Muppet Show" to her mother and discussed which cartoon shows she'd be watching on

Saturday morning. A small crisis arose when Vicky put her foot down about the child watching too much television. Daria complained to her mother, and Amanda complained to Jeffrey. Jeffrey told her firmly that as long as he had custody, Daria would do things the way *he* wanted her to do things. Vicky applauded when he hung up the phone. But as the weeks wore on she noticed that Jeffrey allowed Daria to watch more and more television.

In the Sunday *Times* Vicky read an announcement of the New York Philharmonic concerts in Central Park. The one with the fireworks was coming up soon, and she convinced Jeffrey that this would be a splendid thing to do with Daria.

"I think it's a great idea. When is it?" Jeffrey asked.

"Thursday night."

"Won't it be too late for her?"

"Let's see how tired she gets." Vicky said. "She can sleep on the bus to camp."

The program was Brahms, Respighi, and the *1812 Overture*, which was when the fireworks went off. "I'll make a picnic," Vicky said. "We'll have a terrific time. You can bring Daria straight from work."

Jeffrey laughed.

The day before the concert Vicky went shopping in the little deli in her neighborhood. She bought stuffed grape leaves, rare roast beef, sliced Virginia ham and Swiss cheese for sandwiches, cole slaw, pickles, potato salad, and a bag of Wise potato chips for Daria. She decided to bring a thermos of lemonade in addition to a chilled bottle of white wine. Then she went to the Korean market and bought green grapes, oranges, and a pound of fresh peaches. Satisfied that she had enough food for at least ten people, she went home and put her load of goodies into the refrigerator. Then she got out her wicker basket and packed it with paper plates, napkins, forks, paper cups, a bottle opener, and a sharp knife. She would make the sandwiches fresh when she got home from work the next day, then she'd put the entire basket in the refrigerator until she left the apartment, to make sure everything would be as cool as possible.

On Thursday she rushed in from camp and found a

note Jeffrey had left that morning. "Call me," it said. She did. "I may be a little late," he said. They had arranged to meet near the far side of the Great Lawn, away from the chaos in the center of the field where it was more crowded. Vicky was to have a little red banner on a stick raised overhead, so he'd see her.

"What should I do?" Vicky asked.

"There are going to be lots of people there, what with the fireworks and everything, so you'd better go ahead and find us a place. I'll get there as soon as I can. I'll come in a taxi."

"All right, but make sure Daria goes to the bathroom," she reminded him.

She set out for the park, feeling apprehensive. Crowds were not her favorite scene, and it was so hard to find someone in this one, especially after six o'clock, when Jeffrey said he might arrive. She hoped for the best as she made her way to Central Park West and kept pace with the throng heading for the Great Lawn. There seemed to be a lot more people than she recalled from the last concert she'd attended two years ago.

When she arrived near the shell that had been set up for the concert, she was astonished at the size of the audience. She found a space on the very fringe, not far from the trees edging the field, but the space between her blanket and the trees quickly filled with people. She raised her little red homemade banner (an old scarf), pushing the stick into the turf, then she opened the lid of her picnic basket and began to set out her bounty. All around her, groups of people, couples, families were doing the same. There were no arranged paths to walk on, so a steady stream of people swept past, walking on the edge of everyone else's blankets, to a chorus of "Excuse me's" and "I'm sorry's." The feasts laid out ranged from full-course dinners starting with pâté and ending with strawberry mousse served on china with linen napkins to elaborate outdoor barbecues on large grills. People ate Kentucky Fried Chicken, boxed lunches from the Brasserie, or whole meals purchased at Zabar's, delectable cold entrees, cheeses, and beautiful breads. Vicky got hungry and tired as she sat in the stifling August heat waiting for Jeffrey and Daria. She allowed herself one bite of a roast beef sandwich and a sip of cold lemonade. She worried about the wine getting too warm and was glad she'd packed a plastic container of ice to put in the cups. Jeffrey hated wine on ice but he also hated white wine served warm.

She kept craning her neck and finally stood up and looked around, but there was no sign of Jeffrey. There were, however, thousands more people who had arrived after Vicky, filling the field as far as the eye could see. She could see balloons bobbing in the air, elaborate banners raised indicating different groups, block associations, friends, birthday parties, so that latecomers could join the crowd. People stood up and called to each other, smoked grass, got drunk, tossed Frisbees, tried to contain children or dogs. Despite her fear of crowds she reveled in the feeling of the place.

But there was still no sign of Jeffrey. Vicky looked at her watch. Six forty-five. He was really late. He must have had an awful problem at work. Vicky hoped it wasn't anything too serious; his firm had just begun to earn good money again after the winter's slump. She sat down and stared at the blanket she was sitting on. Maybe if she didn't look, she would be rewarded by the sight of Jeffrey when she next raised her head ... Jeffrey coming toward her, wending his way slowly around the blankets, holding Daria's hand and looking wonderfully out of place in his business suit and tie. She had brought a sport shirt for him to change into so he wouldn't feel so sweaty at the end of an August day's work.

But when she scanned the crowd there was still no sign of him, unless—wait! Over there, past the very last group on the fringe of the crowd, wasn't that Jeffrey? She stood up and waved, calling to him. The figure seemed to acknowledge her and started weaving through the obstacle course. But there was no child with him, and as he got closer Vicky realized it wasn't Jeffrey.

Disappointed, she looked toward the band shell, wondering whether they would arrive with enough time to eat before it got really dark. She was about to turn her face back to the western approaches to the park whence she expected Jeffrey to appear, but something else caught her attention—a glimpse of red hair of unmistakable hue and texture. A flash flood of fright swept through her stomach and up into her heart, causing it

173

to trip-hammer like a cornered animal's. At first she said to herself, No, it couldn't be, it makes no sense. Not here, at a Philharmonic concert, not in this ocean of humanity; it has to be someone else. She studied her more closely. She stood about thirty yards away, wearing white pants and a frilled blouse with a red summer scarf tied bandanna-style around her neck, an elegant little red leather bag suspended by a gold chain from her shoulder. She was looking directly at Vicky, and there was no question but that she saw her. Vicky tried to see if anyone was with her, but her vision was blocked by a small army of bobbing heads. Vicky was almost always alert for the appearance of Amanda, but here of all places she'd thought it safe to drop her guard—a foolish assumption. Amanda fixed Vicky in her gaze and began walking toward her. Her pace was unhurried and dignified despite the countless obstacles through which she had to maneuver.

Despite her panic Vicky debated standing her ground. Amanda's intentions might not necessarily be hostile. Perhaps she was merely looking for Daria. Perhaps she had decided to be civil. And what could Amanda do, surrounded by thousands of potential witnesses? Vicky looked around her at the people in her immediate vicinity. They couldn't care less about Vicky, absorbed as they were with opening their picnic hampers, eating and drinking, necking, changing their babies' diapers, reading, waving, dancing—you couldn't find more indifference in a crowd of last-minute Christmas shoppers in Macy's.

Amanda was closing in, and if there was ever a question of Amanda's civility, it was dispelled by the stare of hate and the imprecation that twisted the woman's lips, an oath that Vicky could not hear, but did not need to hear, either. When Amanda touched the clasp of her purse, that was all Vicky needed. She remembered the vial of gin Amanda had thrown in her face at the restaurant and her warning that the next time the vial would contain nothing so innocuous.

Vicky backed away, stepping on something soft. A voice behind her said, "For Christ's sake, lady!" Vicky turned and looked down. She had stepped on a wedge of soft Brie cheese on a paper plate. It stuck to the heel

174

of her shoe. A young couple was scrambling to save a wine bottle spewing its contents on their antique quilt.

"Oh, I'm so sorry," Vicky said. The cheese comically stuck to her foot, and the paper plate flopped as she backed off their blanket. She looked up and saw Amanda only some twenty yards away. Vicky quickly scanned the crowd, hoping to see Jeffrey. No luck. She made her decision. She turned and ran.

In her headlong impulse to get away, Vicky did not realize that if she moved diagonally she would reach the edge of the field sooner; rather, in her blind haste, she chose to move in a zigzagging, arbitrary pattern back down the field, away from the band shell but deeper into the heart of the crowd. As she plunged through the groups of concertgoers, she realized the futility of her flight, for it was impossible to run with any speed when there was no path on the ground, no place to put her feet.

Several times she narrowly avoided hurting people. She tried to leap across the blankets and mats stretched out on the ground. She bumped into people drinking wine or beer; their drinks flew out of their hands, spraying their neighbors and Vicky's legs. She stepped into lavish picnics, her shoes pushing into a mound of potato salad on one picnic blanket, a tabouli salad on the next. In a moment of panic as she pushed forward, she almost stepped on a baby's head; he was lying across the corner of a blanket, playing with a rattle. She adjusted her stride and instead nearly broke her ankle as her foot turned on a freshly made cheesecake.

All around her, cries went up. "Hey, what d'ya think you're doin'?" "Watch where you're going!" Surprisingly, many people did not seem to notice, but went on eating and drinking even after she had run over their dinner, crushing a bag of potato chips or upsetting a bottle of champagne in an ice bucket.

She ran helter-skelter; there was no trail. She zigged, she zagged, she cut corners, she stopped and stared again. Her breath came in agonizing short gasps. She ran smack into a chunky Puerto Rican man grilling meat on sticks for his family.

"Hey," he said as he grabbed her. "You almost knocked hot coals all over my kids!"

175

"Please," she begged. "Let me go. It's an emergency." Her chest heaved with the effort of trying to catch her breath. The man stared at her. His face was damp with sweat. His eyes were narrow and small, very dark. She thought wildly for an instant that he had been put there to stop her, to make sure Amanda would catch her. But then he dropped her arms and she pushed off once more, not bothering to look back, afraid to see that just this once, Amanda was indeed there, right behind her. She had no more strength left. All these thousands and thousands of people and no one bothered to ask if she needed help. All they cared about was if you stepped in their cole slaw.

She could not run very fast now; her legs were cramping. But she could see the perimeter of the field. It was crowded, but at least it was a way out. She was almost there, almost, when she tripped over the outstretched legs of a good-looking young man in shorts and a shirt with ragged sleeves. She fell onto his blanket and into a plate of chili. She heard cruel laughter behind her. She was certain it was Amanda's.

"Are you all right?" the young man asked, lifting her up. Her shirt was covered with the reddish-brown mess.

She stared at him with frightened eyes, knowing she must look deranged. She got to her feet, ignoring the stab of the pain from the ankle she had injured that winter, and hobbled away, blinking back tears.

She reached the path and limped toward the exit at Eighty-first Street. She kept looking for Jeffrey but knew it was too late; he was no doubt already at the blanket wondering where she had gone. Her ankle throbbed, and by the time she reached the park exit she could scarcely walk. People arriving for the concert with their blankets stared at her. She knew she must look awful, her jeans stained with red wine, her shirt covered with clotted chili. She stumbled out to the street looking for a taxi, when she heard someone calling. "Vicky, Vicky! Over here!" She saw Jeffrey standing by a taxi door paying the driver, Daria at his side. He handed some bills to the cabbie, then took Daria by the hand and swung her up onto the sidewalk. He moved quickly toward Vicky.

"Oh, Jeff," she sobbed, collapsing in his arms.

He led her over to a bench, half carrying her as her feet gave way, while Daria followed curiously, dressed in her camp T-shirt and shorts. Passersby stared at the scene with mild interest; Vicky knew she must look like a park crazy.

"What happened? My God, look at you!"

"Amanda," Vicky gasped.

His eyebrows furrowed.

"Amanda was there," she repeated, "waiting for me."

"Waiting for you? In the middle of a quarter of a million people?"

"She knew where I was. She came after me with acid."

Jeffrey looked around, hoping no one was listening. "Vicky, you've got to calm down."

But Vicky was out of control. "Did you tell her?"

"Tell her what?"

"Where I was going to be? Where we were supposed to meet?"

"Why the hell would I do that?"

"Did *she?*"

"Did who?" He followed the line of Vicky's gaze. "Daria? Are you crazy?"

Daria stared at Vicky curiously, studying her stained, torn clothing and unkempt hair with round, candid eyes.

Vicky pulled away from Jeffrey's grasp and confronted Daria, who shrank a couple of steps. "Did you speak to your mother today?"

Daria shook her head.

"Did you tell her where you were going?"

Daria looked at her father like a client in the witness chair glancing at her lawyer. Jeffrey's jaw was clamped in anger, but he hesitated to restrain Vicky, who was puffed up like some fighting bird prepared to battle to the death.

"Did you tell your mother where you were going this evening?" Vicky asked again. Despite her ordeal, she addressed Daria with a calm voice. There was no mistaking her determination, however.

"No, I didn't. Really." Her eyes were huge and innocent.

"Did you tell her where we were supposed to meet?"

"She didn't know," Jeffrey interjected.

Vicky ignored him, glaring at Daria. "Did you know where we were supposed to meet? Did you overhear your daddy and me talking about it on the phone this afternoon?"

"Daddy, she's scaring me," Daria said, running to her father and taking refuge behind his legs.

"Could she have overheard you, Jeffrey?"

"Vicky, this is enough. You're getting hysterical. And you're making Daria hysterial, too. In another minute you're going to make *me* hysterical. Now can we please calm down?"

"You've never believed me, never taken my side," Vicky said, starting to shake and sob. Jeffrey looked helplessly at her. Suddenly her eyes flashed with indignation. "And where were you, anyway? If you'd been on time—"

"Daria locked herself in the bathroom in my office. I had to take the door off the hinges."

"Great, just great. I could have been scarred for life while you're getting her out of the bathroom! I could have crushed somebody's baby or broken my leg running away. Look at me. I'm covered with chili and cheese and macaroni and wine and pâté and God knows what else..."

She continued to fulminate for another minute, Jeffrey standing by futilely as Daria hid behind him with a terrified look in her eyes. At length Vicky wound down and she slumped on the bench.

Jeffrey put his arm around her.

"Everything's spoiled," Vicky sobbed. "She spoils everything, everything we do."

"Who does she mean, Daddy?" Daria asked.

"She doesn't mean you, sweetie," her father reassured her.

"I had such a nice picnic," Vicky said wistfully. "Ham and cheese sandwiches, lemonade, a bottle of wine, some fresh fruit..."

"We'll go right back in there, find our basket, and have our picnic," Jeffrey asserted.

"No, it's ruined. I just want to go home and go to sleep. You can take Daria in there if you want."

"No, we'll go home together."

178

"We're not going to see the fireworks?" Daria asked.

"No, honey, Vicky's upset."

"What's upsetting her?"

"Never mind." Jeffrey looked at Vicky, flashing a warning.

Vicky shook her head in disgust.

They rose and walked toward the intersection as the strains of the Philharmonic filled the evening air over the city.

One day, late in the afternoon, several weeks into the new school term, Vicky heard the lock turn in her door, far too early for it to be Jeffrey. She tensed and a charge of adrenaline shot through her body. She looked around for a weapon but before she could locate anything suitable Jeffrey appeared. He was beaming and his feet shuffled to the rhythm of some unheard jig. He held something behind his back.

"Jeffrey! What are you doing home so early?"

"Close your eyes and hold out your hands."

"What is it?"

"Just close your eyes and hold out your hands."

She did as he instructed. She heard a rattle of paper and felt a cylindrical package laid across both of her hands. Flowers? She opened her eyes. Flowers they were. Taped to the paper wrapper was an envelope, too large to be a note card from a flower shop. She looked at it closely. It bore the seal of the State of New York. "Oh, God, I think I know what this is," she said, fumbling with it. She removed the document from the envelope and opened it, scanning the fine print, her eyes racing past "whereases" and "plantiffs" and stamps and seals, seeking the words that she had endured over a year of suffering and fear to have the satisfaction of reading. Suddenly Jeffrey's index finger tapped a line toward the bottom of the page. Her hands shook violently but she managed to make out the words "granted" and "dissolved." She threw her arms around Jeffrey's neck and began sobbing with joy.

"Hey, they're only roses," he said. Then he started crying, too.

* * *

179

He gave her ten minutes to change, then guided her out of the building to Columbus Avenue. "We've got some serious celebrating to do," he said.

"Where are we going?"

"How about Ruelle's?"

"That's a madhouse."

"Perfect!" he replied.

It was early enough so that the most popular bar and meeting place on Columbus Avenue wasn't yet jammed with postwork drinkers, diners, and the singles crowd. Jeffrey took a table upstairs on the mezzanine level, overlooking the bar and street. The place had wood paneling, brass, bright lights; it was festive—perfect, as Jeffrey had said. He ordered a bottle of champagne. After the first glass he clasped her right hand in both of his and said, "Have I asked you lately to marry me?"

"Not lately, no. I was beginning to wonder. I was certain you'd never be free."

"Well, I am, and I'm asking you to marry me."

"When?"

"Now. We'll ask the waiter to perform the ceremony."

"I don't think he's ordained," Vicky laughed.

"I'll baptize him with champagne."

"Not at thirty dollars a bottle you won't!"

"Well?"

He looked at her with soft eyes.

"Well what?"

"Well, will you marry me?"

"Well, I certainly will marry you, Jeffrey Keating."

He grinned and pulled her toward him, kissing her softly.

He poured more champagne, and they talked about details of wedding and honeymoon. It was to be a simple civil wedding at City Hall. For their honeymoon he would take her to an inn in New England. They chattered on like teenagers, kissing and embracing and entwining fingers. Then the corners of Jeffrey's mouth turned down, and Vicky guessed what had crossed his mind.

"You're wondering about Daria," she said.

He nodded. "What do you think she's going to do?"

"Adjust," said Vicky. "With difficulty, but she'll adjust."

"Why with difficulty? To her there won't be any difference between our living together and our being married."

"To her mother there will be. It'll put you farther out of reach."

He pondered, making paths in the water rings on the table with his index finger. "So you think she's going to work on Daria?"

"Jeffrey, it's hard to say what Amanda's going to do. But I can't believe she's going to be thrilled, and you can be sure she'll impart her emotions to her daughter. And don't forget, getting married is a prelude to having children. That's *really* going to uncork the genie for Daria."

"All kids are jealous of new siblings," Jeffrey said.

"Her mother will see to it that Daria is particularly jealous of ours," Vicky answered.

"What a depressing thought." Jeffrey splashed his palm on the table.

"I said she'd adjust," Vicky repeated.

"Yes, but at what cost?"

She put her head on his shoulder. "I'll help you with her. I'll help you with everything. I'll even help you get out of your pants as soon as we get home."

"That won't be necessary. I'm taking them off in the elevator."

Which is precisely what he did. They were the only ones in it and, incredibly, there was no one in the corridor when they stepped off the elevator. He waddled to their door with his trousers around his ankles, and Vicky squealed as he drunkenly fumbled for his keys. At last he found them, and they'd no sooner stepped inside than he kicked his pants off, took her in his arms, and stripped off her clothes. "Here?" she asked, as he pulled her to the rug.

"Here," he said, removing her panties and lowering himself between her welcoming thighs.

They were married in a simple ceremony at City Hall just before Thanksgiving. Daria was not present; her mother forbade it. Neither did their parents attend.

Jeffrey's father was still recuperating, and Vicky's father still didn't entirely approve. Vicky's brother did drive down from Massachusetts at his sister's insistence; she wanted him there "in case." She was certain Amanda would show up and try to disrupt the ceremony.

But nothing happened. Instead Vicky spent the time in front of the judge constantly glancing over her shoulder, expecting the worst, and ending up as nervous as if Amanda had been there, glaring at them.

They lunched at Windows on the World, toasting each other, and Vicky's brother, a college professor, made a little speech filled with eighteenth-century sexual innuendoes. Their plan was to spend that night in their apartment and then head for an inn in New England for a long weekend. The morning they were to leave, Vicky pulled down her battered old suitcase and prepared to pack their clothes. "I hate this thing," she said. "It's torn, it's falling apart, and it smells of mildew."

"I know," Jeffrey said. "That's why I think you ought to look in the hall closet before putting our things in that disgrace."

Vicky tilted her head, then went into the hall and returned with an enormous gift-wrapped box. She tore the paper off, then opened the cardboard lid of a carton. She reached inside and removed a duffel-sized bag made of supple leather whose fragrance filled the room. Attached to the handle was a name tag; it said, "Mr. and Mrs. Jeffrey Keating." Vicky jumped up and down, clapping her hands. "This is gorgeous. It must have cost a fortune!"

"Mrs. Keating goes in style," he said.

For a second Vicky couldn't make the connection between herself and "Mrs. Keating." Irrationally, she felt there was only one Mrs. Keating, and that was Amanda. She felt as if she were poaching on Amanda's name. It would take awhile for her to get over that, to feel that the name belonged to her, and indeed that it belonged to her only. As a divorced woman, Amanda could call herself "Mrs. Amanda Keating," but formal etiquette prohibited her from calling herself "Mrs. Jeffrey Keating." Vicky stood a little straighter and said

182

to herself, Dammit, I've earned the right to Jeffrey's name and no one can take that away from me now.

"I hope you'll throw in a sexy nightgown or two," Jeffrey said. "But in case you forget, I've thrown one in for you."

He was gone to pick up their rented car before she could open the bag, but the moment the door closed she unzipped the main compartment and removed the most beautiful nightgown she'd ever seen, clinging powder-blue silk with exquisite Belgian lace around a plunging neckline, and only two spaghetti straps to hold it up. She crushed it to her face and felt a throbbing between her legs where Jeffrey had been the night before. She shuddered both in remembrance and anticipation, then hastily packed the rest of their things and sat on the edge of the bed, waiting for the doorman to summon her downstairs.

It was all too good to be true. Perhaps every bride feels that way, but Vicky had particularly good reason to say that to herself. The wedding had gone uneventfully and so far the wedding journey had, too. By "uneventful" Vicky meant only one thing: no Amanda, not a phone call, not a note, not a whisper. And that worried Vicky, worried her so much it threatened to spoil her honeymoon. Was that Amanda's strategy? Did she have Vicky so well conditioned that she could upset her by doing nothing? Never had the phrase "waiting for the other shoe to drop" been so appropriate; you could drive someone crazy by merely dropping one shoe and holding the second suspended for an unendurable time.

Vicky wanted to make this observation to Jeffrey but refrained for fear of jinxing their holiday. He had picked her up in a sporty Dodge Charger, fire-engine red, and as he steered onto the Saw Mill River Parkway heading north for the Berkshires, he had turned on the radio and selected something with a driving rock beat to which he pounded the steering wheel in rhythm. He was like a teenager cruising in a hotrod, and his joy was infectious. She picked up the beat and sang with him, pounding on the dashboard, feeling as if she were exorcising an evil spirit in some primitive ritual. By the time they got to Route 7 in Connecticut, the last leg of their journey to Massachusetts, Amanda seemed as distant and insubstantial as a childhood memory.

The place was called Five Gables, outside Lee, and with its split-oak floors and colonial furniture, pungent fire and complimentary glass of sherry served to them while their luggage was being carried upstairs, it was for Vicky the very place she'd dreamed of for a honeymoon. Their room had a four-poster bed, its own fireplace, and antique furniture with needlepoint upholstery. The view from their room was of a garden with a bowered walk.

The bathroom was spacious, the walls decorated with charming wallpaper. As Vicky stood at the door surveying it, Jeffrey came up behind her and put his arms around her. "How about a bath, a little lovemaking, and a little dinner, Mrs. K.?"

"Nothing could make me happier, Mr. K."

They stripped out of their clothes, and Vicky drew the bath. The tub was a modern one, and big enough for two if they interlocked their legs—which of course they did. They soaked for ten minutes, then soaped each other sensuously. "Tell me," Vicky said, "how did you know about this place? It's divine."

He shrugged. "Uh, someone told me, I believe."

Vicky squinted at him. "I don't believe you."

"Honest." He raised his right hand solemnly.

"Jeffrey Keating, you can't lie very well. You've been here before, haven't you?" she said teasingly. "Did you take a girl here once?"

"Ask me no questions and I'll tell you no lies."

"You did," she said, splashing him playfully. "You brought another girl here, didn't you?"

But Jeffrey's eyes were clouded with distress and guilt. "That's enough, Vicky."

"Oh, come on, I'm not going to bite your head off if you brought someone else here, as long as it wasn't—" Suddenly she froze. Jeffrey was gulping. His eyes were averted. The shock was so great Vicky had difficulty catching her breath. "You came here with *her?*"

"I told you not to ask. But, honey, it was a long time ago."

"How long?" Vicky asked, pushing herself up out of the tub. "Your honeymoon, maybe?"

"No. Hey, sit down, don't do this, not today of all times." He took her by the wrist but she shook loose, clambering out of the tub with a great splash. She grabbed a bath towel, rubbed herself perfunctorily, and stormed into the bedroom. Moments later Jeffrey followed, soaking wet and without a towel, forming a puddle on the braided rug next to the bed where Vicky lay on her stomach, sobbing.

"Vicky, for crying out loud—"

"I *am* crying out loud, you—you bastard!" Jeffrey recoiled in shock. He couldn't remember hearing that word out of Vicky's mouth, referring to him or to anyone else. She turned over and looked at him wrathfully. "I was afraid she was going to spoil it somehow, but I never thought she'd use you as her—her prime minister."

"Vicky, that's a rotten thing to say."

"Taking me here was a rotten thing to do. Is this the room you stayed in? Did you take a bath together in there, too?"

"No, no, it was nothing like—"

"I'm surprised the owner didn't say something. 'Didn't you used to have red hair, Mrs. Keating?' Oh, Jeffrey, how could you have done this to me on my honeymoon?" She buried her face in a pillow. Jeffrey collapsed in an armchair near the fireplace and stared across the room. After a minute or two Vicky lifted her face from the pillow. Her eyes were red and swollen and her hair was damp where tears had wet it. When she spoke, it was with clogged nose. "Don't you understand?"

Jeffrey looked dejectedly at her. "I guess I do."

"No. No, I don't think you do. You think I'm just jealous because you brought Amanda here. Well, that's not it at all. From the very first she's harassed me, threatened me, spied on me, followed me, chased me, interfered with me, tried to hurt me, tried to kill me even, though I'm sure you don't believe that. She's robbed you, impoverished you, tried to alienate you from me and from your daughter, aggravated you until you got sick—I know we're stuck with her forever, but I was hoping that for just a few days, the most important ones of my life, I could feel free of her, completely. And I thought I was. Now I learn her ghost is wandering

185

around this very hotel, maybe this very room. Do you understand a little better?"

Jeffrey hung his head in mute acknowledgment. Then, all at once, he jumped to his feet. "Yes, I do indeed." He tossed their bags on the bed and started throwing their things into it.

"What are you doing?"

"Righting a wrong. I made a big mistake, but it's not too late to correct it."

"I don't understand."

"We're checking out."

"Are you crazy?"

"Stop yakking and get our stuff from the bathroom."

"Where are we going?"

"Someplace neither of us has ever been to."

"But where?"

He looked up from his frenzied activity. "I haven't the faintest idea," he said, "but I'm sure it'll be terrific."

And it was. They lumbered down the inn stairs to the desk and told the astonished owner that Jeffrey had just been called back to New York on a business emergency. Jeffrey paid for the day and apologized, and off they went, heading toward Lenox. They slowly drove past numerous hotels, inns, and bed-and-breakfasts, trying to gauge each place's warmth and hospitality from the outside. At last they came to an old Victorian house set back from the road behind immaculately barbered shrubbery and mowed grass. The sign outside said, "Satisfied Guests for Over 100 Years."

"I vote yes," said Jeffrey.

"Unanimous," Vicky chimed in. "I really need to be satisfied."

"And satisfied you shall be." He pulled the car into the driveway and took Vicky by the hands. "I'm a fool."

"Sometimes you are. But so am I, sometimes. Let's put it behind us and start our honeymoon again."

Jeffrey looked at his watch, raised his other hand, and brought it down like a starter signaling the beginning of a race. "Now."

"Now."

They kissed, got out of the car, and walked up to the front door.

Chapter Eight

"WHEN DO YOU THINK we should tell Daria?" Vicky asked. She sat on the couch, Jeffrey on the floor beside her, his head in her lap. She caressed it dreamily. On the coffee table stood a bottle of Chablis and two almost-empty glasses.

"Well," Jeffrey said, "if we tell her now, she'll have that much more time to adjust to it."

"And worry about it," Vicky added.

"She won't worry about it if we put it to her positively."

"She will when her mother puts it to her negatively."

"Amanda has been blessedly quiet since we got married," Jeffrey observed.

"A dormant volcano. She's getting laid regularly, don't forget."

"How can I forget, with Daria faithfully reporting the comings and goings of Amanda's lovers. What's this latest one's name? Raul? Rah-ooooollll," Jeffrey bayed like a wolf at the moon.

"Raul is our best friend right now. I hope they're divinely happy." Vicky said. "If they break up and Amanda doesn't replace him, you're going to have her around your neck. And God knows where I'm going to have her." She put her hand under his chin and directed his face up to hers. "Jeffrey, I want to tell you something very important."

"You're going to have a baby, right? No, you just told me that."

"Be serious. What I want to tell you is that I'm seriously worried."

"About what?"

"About the baby's safety."

He opened his mouth to make a quip, but swallowed it, intimidated by her solemnity. "How do you mean?"

"I'm afraid Amanda will try to harm it."

He reacted reflexively. "I seriously doubt it. She's done some rotten things in her day, but I don't think child abuse is in her repertoire."

"Darling, listen to me. I'm not sure Amanda *would;* the important thing is that I'm afraid. I want you to respect that, no matter how irrational it sounds to you. I want you to protect me and the baby, even if you don't feel there's a threat. I don't think I have too many eccentricities, so maybe you could indulge just this one and mark it down to hysteria. It's not uncommon among pregnant women, you know."

He looked at her thoughtfully. "What exactly are you afraid Amanda will do?"

"I don't know." That was not true, but how could she tell him about the dreams she'd had, lurid nightmares of being attacked on the street by someone wielding a knife or a club, aiming a blow at her swollen midriff. In other dreams she was pushing a carriage down the street when an assailant leaped out of a shop door and pushed Vicky to the ground, stealing the carriage or striking the baby with a fist or weapon. The nightmares had begun on her wedding night and had come back to her on the average of once a week. Some were vague and unfocused, making her wake up sweating, heart thundering, nails biting into the flesh of her palms. Others were so graphic she could make out the threads on her assailant's sleeve. But not his face. Or was it *her* face? "I don't know," she repeated. "But please protect me."

"I'll do what I can, I promise. But I can't be with you every minute of every day."

"Of course," she said sadly.

He put his arms around her knees and pressed his face to them. "Don't worry so much."

"That's my job. I worry about your other child, too."

"I know. You don't know how much it means to me." He got to his feet and paced for a moment or two. "I think we should tell Daria sooner rather than later. Gives us more time to candy-coat the pill."

"Are you calling our child a pill?" Vicky teased.

"I've never met one who wasn't."

"Ours will be the first. How do you like Justin for a boy, Rosalie if it's a girl?"

He considered. "I like. And you know what?" He sat down beside her and took her hands in his. "I think I'm going to like being a new father. I think I'm going to like it a lot."

She threw her arms around him. "You've made me very happy, saying that. I know what your doubts are, your reservations. But trust me."

He nodded and pressed his lips to her cheek.

And so they told Daria. They told her in a Mc-Donald's on Broadway after treating her to a Big Mac, two orders of french fries, and a Coke. "You're going to have a baby brother or sister!" Jeffrey said, grinning.

She looked at him quizzically. "Which one?"

"Which one what?"

"Which one, a brother or a sister?"

"We don't know yet, sweetie. Which one would you prefer?"

"A sister, definitely."

Jeffrey arched one eyebrow. "What's wrong with kid brothers?"

"All the girls at school hate theirs," she said.

Jeffrey looked at Vicky for help. "Little boys are fun, too. And when they grow up a little, they can protect you."

"From what?"

Vicky looked back to Jeffrey for help. It wasn't going quite the way they'd hoped. "From bad people," Jeffrey said with a feeble shrug.

"I don't care. I definitely don't want a brother."

"Well, we'll talk about it some more," her father said.

"Can I get an ice cream?"

Daria didn't talk about it any more. She ignored the subject, and declined to take any and all bait offered by her father or stepmother to make her talk about her feelings, let alone express enthusiasm. But presently she started manifesting some unsettling symptoms. Something was bothering her.

Throughout the months that followed, Daria became moody, irritable, difficult to control, and at times even

189

threatening. Her "I will not's" and "No's!" expressed more than simple childish waywardness; Vicky discerned a hostility in them that frightened her. Daria demanded all of both Jeffrey's and Vicky's attention, and when she was not present Vicky felt her spirit always there, lurking, hiding, watching from behind closed doors. This problem, combined with Vicky's pervasive fear that Amanda would do something, made her pregnancy a less than blissful time.

She gave notice at school that she would not be returning in the fall. They could not afford a housekeeper if she was to return to work; she planned to take freelance editing jobs, plus some typing. Her class gave her a baby shower; she was touched by their kindness and wondered, sadly, as she opened the girls' lovely gifts, if her own stepdaughter would ever extend her any similar loving favors.

As the time of the birth grew nearer, Daria became even more intractable, particularly on one subject: the baby's sex. The baby had better not be a boy. Daria's opposition was strange; logically, a girl should have been more threatening, but all the while Vicky sensed that Daria knew something they didn't. Was it something her mother had told her?

August passed slowly; Daria's demands continued unabated and even at the summer house she continued to whine and fret. Jeffrey tried to keep the peace but he, too, found his nerves on edge. All in all, the pregnancy had become a nightmare for everyone. They looked forward to some peace when Daria returned to her mother in the fall. Instead, the time bomb they had been sitting on exploded.

Jeffrey brought Daria back to Amanda on Monday evening, Labor Day. He left with Daria and her belongings, and Vicky remembered she needed some orange juice for the morning. She decided to go to the local grocery that was open on Sundays and holidays. She went to the top drawer of the chest where she kept her wallet. She'd started putting it there after discovering Daria looking through her handbag one afternoon. She opened the drawer and lifted a pile of cotton underpants.

The wallet was not there.

Vicky puckered her mouth and stared at the drawer. She groped around it, then closed it and stared into space for a moment, trying to remember where she might have put it. She hadn't taken it with her today when they'd gone for brunch at Teacher's. The last time she'd used it was Sunday, when she'd pulled a dollar out of it to get the Sunday *New York Times*. But she was certain she'd returned the wallet to its hiding place. Nevertheless, she opened her closet and looked in her handbag, hanging over a nail inside the door. She found tissues, checkbook, pen, set of keys, hairbrush, lipstick, mirror, but no wallet.

She was mystified but not yet alarmed. It was entirely possible that Jeffrey had taken it, having run out of money over the long weekend, and had forgotten to tell her he was borrowing hers. But why would he take her wallet—why not just remove the money? Maybe he'd taken the money out and put the wallet someplace else.

She searched everywhere, holding out hope of a logical explanation, prepared to clap herself on the head as soon as she remembered where it was. But it was nowhere, not in the remotest imaginable place like the cabinet under the sink or the silverware drawer in the kitchen. Jeffrey had to have it. Either that or—

She froze, her jaw clamping solemnly.

Or Daria.

At first Vicky smiled and snapped her fingers. Of course! Daria was fascinated with her wallet, had gone through Vicky's drawers as curious children will, had found the wallet, played with it, and put it among her games and toys, which is where Vicky looked. Daria had been given a corner of their bedroom closet, and there she stacked her boxes of playthings, her Tiddly Winks and Old Maid cards and Candy Land and Chutes and Ladders, her crayons and paints and pencils, her doll clothes, and one box filled with the miscellany of childhood, dolls' arms and legs, old keys, a few coins, shoelaces, game pieces and pegs, miniature farm animals, playing cards, souvenir buttons, junk.

Everything but Vicky's wallet.

And that's when Vicky started contemplating the worst. But she held her direst suspicions in check until

Jeffrey could get back, praying that he had the wallet or knew where she'd misplaced it.

When she heard his key in the lock she raced to the door and confronted him. He was totally downcast, his eyes faintly moist. He kissed her perfunctorily, lumbered into the living room, and fell heavily into the armchair. "I don't think I felt this bad even when I walked out on them."

Vicky was anxious to ask him about the wallet but he looked so mournful she held herself back. She put her hands on his neck and massaged it. "You've become more attached to each other," she said.

He turned and put his arms around her, pressing his cheek against her protruding belly. "I'm going to miss her terribly," he said with voice choked with emotion.

"But you'll see her in a few days when the visitation rights go back into effect. Every other weekend, plus one day during the week. It's not as if she's being taken away forever."

"It's not the same. Not the same as having her all the time."

I'll say! Vicky said to herself. Not having Daria all the time was like a vacation in the Bahamas.

Jeffrey looked up at her with red eyes. "Maybe we should sue for custody."

Vicky felt her knees go weak. Given the ordeal she'd just gone through with Daria all summer long, plus the prospect of the baby, Jeffrey's straitened finances, and the dimensions of their one-bedroom apartment, suing for custody of Daria was the most appalling suggestion she had ever heard. It was tempting to say so, too, but she knew Jeffrey was speaking out of frustration of having to return Daria to her mother after spending so much, and such intense, time with the child. Vicky was certain he'd drop the notion after a few days. So she diplomatically said, "It's a very serious step. We'd really have to talk it through quite thoroughly."

"Yes," he nodded. "I can think of half a dozen major obstacles right off."

"So can I," Vicky said, adding *amen* to herself.

She fidgeted during the lugubrious silence that followed. She knew this wasn't a good time to bring up the missing wallet, but she simply had to know. Besides, there were credit cards and other valuable items in it, such as her Social Security card and her driver's license. If someone else had the wallet, there was no end of mischief that person could make with those things.

"Say, darling, you didn't happen to see my wallet around here, did you?" She tried to sound as nonchalant as possible.

"No." Jeffrey's voice was nasal, as if his eyes were still draining silent tears shed over Daria.

"You didn't borrow any money from it over the weekend?"

"No, I went to the bank before Saturday. I still have thirty dollars in my wallet. Why?"

"I seem to have misplaced mine. Would you happen to remember when you saw me with it last?"

He looked at his fingernails. "It wasn't today. I'm sure of that. Yesterday?"

"When yesterday? What did I do with it?"

He shrugged. "I'm sure it's around here someplace."

"It's not. I've looked everywhere."

He became mildly interested. "You looked in your drawers?"

"Yes."

"All your drawers?"

"Yes. And all yours. And all the drawers in the house. Name a place, I've looked there."

He did. He named every possible place it might be, then reconstructed the entire weekend day by day, hoping to remind her. But after confirming that he saw her take a dollar out of it to buy the Sunday paper and then return the wallet to its customary place, he could not think of when he'd seen her holding it, or even an occasion when she needed it between Sunday morning and Monday evening. "I'm going to have to look myself," he said with a loud sigh. "Just what I needed."

She apologized as he got to his feet noisily. He went into the bedroom and thoroughly examined every drawer, every article of clothing (both hers and his), and every piece of furniture. He pulled the bed and chests away from the walls, groped around the closets, examined on, in, and under every item.

She watched him when he came to Daria's corner. "Maybe Daria played with it," he said, but with skepticism and certainly with no sense of outrage that the child might have taken so valuable a piece of personal property without asking permission. Vicky hoped he would come to the conclusion on his own that Daria might well have taken the wallet home with her. But she could see, as he replaced her toys, games, and clothes and proceeded into the bathroom, that that idea was still very remote from his consciousness.

He took apart the bathroom, the living room, the entry hall, the kitchen, and every closet and cabinet, shaking his head in wider and wider arcs, his oaths getting louder and gamier with every room.

"If it's not here we've got to take some prompt action," Vicky said.

"How much money did you have in it?"

"Only about fifteen dollars. But there's my Citicard—someone could get cash out of my bank account with it."

"Only if they know the code number. What else?"

"My Master Charge card, my Gimbel's card, my Bloomingdale's card."

"You'll have to stop them all, first thing tomorrow morning."

"Oh God, oh God, oh God." She pounded her fist against her palm. "What about my driver's license?"

"You'll have to report it missing tomorrow, too. What a drag." He comforted her with an arm around her shoulder as she sat at the desk chair, head drooping. Then she looked up at him, uncertain and hesitant, took a deep breath, and said, "Now Jeffrey, don't take this the wrong way, but...do you think it's possible the wallet could have...um...fallen into Daria's suitcase when you packed it?"

She silently rebuked herself. The question was phrased too feebly. As if the wallet might somehow have flown out of her drawer by itself and landed in Daria's suitcase! She was not surprised, therefore, when Jeffrey answered unhesitatingly.

"No, and besides, you inspected it yourself when I finished."

"But we did leave it open in case there were last-minute things we'd forgotten."

"Sure. But there weren't any, and when I closed it I

194

didn't see—" He bit off the rest of the sentence as he understood, at long last, what Vicky had been steering him toward. He raised his eyes to hers, and there was an unnerving hostility in their narrow focus. "You think she took it," he said with no upward inflection, a statement and not a question.

The air suddenly felt charged, as if an electricity-laden storm cloud had descended on the room. Confronted so directly by him, she could not find the courage to answer yes. She shrugged plaintively, as if to say, "That's where the evidence points," but she could not utter the words.

"I can't believe you even think such a thing," he said.

She still held her tongue, hoping that as he reasoned it out for himself he would indeed believe she could think such a thing, and perhaps he could even think such a thing himself. But what he said was "Daria is not a thief."

"I'm not saying she is," Vicky said. "It could have been an accident. She might have found it, played with it, and—"

"And put it accidentally at the bottom of her clothes and forgotten it was in there? Come on, Vicky, that's not what you think at all." His voice had risen in pitch and volume as he mocked her. She could feel it winding like a steel band of unknown tensile strength. When it snapped, it would snap explosively. "You and she have been at each other's throats all summer long. In fact, since we got married."

"She hates our being married. She's seething with jealousy. I've tried to make you see that, but you've refused."

"Of course I've seen it. I'm not stupid. But it takes two to tango."

The remark, however quietly spoken, was like a thunderclap. Vicky stared at him dumbly, wondering if she understood correctly. "Do you mean you think I've provoked her?"

"It takes two to tango, that's all I'm going to say."

"No, that's not all you're going to say. You're going to say you think I've provoked her jealousy. That I haven't bent over backward to make her feel welcome and loved here. That I haven't given you two every opportunity to be together so she knows you love her as much as ever. That I haven't suffered her slighting me and ignoring me and wounding me, her ingratitude and hostility, hoping that just once you'd intervene and say something to her."

"Say what?"

"Say 'This is my wife, your stepmother. I love her and I expect you to respect her.' Instead, you've pampered and indulged her and reinforced her hostility to me, and whenever I've tried to say something to you about it, all you've said to me is 'Have pity on this poor innocent victim of a tragic divorce.' Well, what about *this* victim?" Vicky pounded her breastbone. Jeffrey stood wavering on his heels, uncertainty filling his eyes. Vicky knew she had scored important points, but she had a head of steam and couldn't, didn't want to, hold back. "As a matter of fact, Jeffrey, I *do* believe she took it. I found her playing with it once and hid it in my drawer. I've found my drawers messed up a few times and I know she goes through them. Yes, I believe she took my wallet. If I'm wrong, I'll spend the rest of my life apologizing to you."

"I don't care about apologies. I care how you feel about my daughter. If you dislike her, if you suspect her, if you think she's a thief or a—God knows what else you think of her, how the hell are you and I going to live together in peace? How are we supposed to live together at all?"

"I don't know, and right now I don't care. I feel her behavior is your responsibility. She doesn't listen to me and she won't as long as you continue turning a blind eye to her."

He stood in frozen indecision for a moment, then went to the phone. "I'm going to call her."

Vicky stared. "What are you going to say?"

"I'm going to ask her about the wallet," he said, pushing the buttons on his phone.

Vicky laughed. "What do you think she's going to say?"

He cleared his throat and puffed out his chest. "It's Jeffrey, let me speak to Daria," he said into the phone. His voice was stern and authoritative, sparking Vicky's hope that he would at last speak to her the way he should have been speaking to her all along. But then his voice turned to treacle. The change was so astonishing Vicky's mouth dropped in shock. "Hi, honey," he purred. "It's Daddy."

"Oh, shit," said Vicky, pushing out of the armchair and leaving the room. She really didn't want to hear the conversation and didn't really need to. As the strains of Jeffrey's lilting, half apologetic voice drifted into the bedroom, Vicky reached for the writing pad on her night table and unhappily started making a list of the phone calls she would have to make the next morning.

Chapter Nine

THE NEXT MORNING was one of the most horrible Vicky could remember. Low pearl-gray clouds scudded across the city, clipping the tops of buildings and wreathing them in fog and drizzle. Just the right weather for a first-class depression, and Vicky had a first-class depression.

Her quarrel with Jeffrey had not only continued long into the night but had escalated as resentments that had been stewing for over a year boiled over, filling their home with acrimony. They had finally fallen asleep after two in the morning, rolling as far from each other as the limits of the bed would permit.

Despite the honeyed delivery of Jeffrey's interrogation, Daria had gotten hysterical on the telephone when Jeffrey asked her whether the wallet had "turned up" in her suitcase. Then Amanda took the phone out of Daria's hands and remonstrated her ex-husband for daring to so much as think that his own daughter was a common thief. From the bedroom Vicky could hear Jeffrey's responses weakening as Amanda's wrath soared to heights of righteousness. In the end he apologized. Vicky was speechless with anger.

She heard him open a cabinet door, and from the clinking of bottles she knew he was making himself a drink. He remained in the living room a half hour, then came into the bedroom. There was a quiet fury in his eyes.

"The wallet wasn't there, of course."

"Of course."

"Daria was shattered that I accused her."

"I heard you talking to her," Vicky said. "You didn't

198

accuse her. If she feels accused, it's because she feels guilty about something."

Jeffrey gazed at her with something close to hatred in his eyes, and Vicky drew her knees protectively closer to her belly, wondering if he was going to get violent. He stepped into the room and approached her. She shrank back against the headboard. He hovered over her for a moment, trembling, then yanked open the top drawer of her night table and pulled everything out, throwing it on the floor. "What are you doing?"

"I'm going to find that fucking wallet, and when I do I'm going to stuff it down your throat!" He ransacked every drawer, then went to the closet and pulled every garment off the hangers, turning pockets inside out, shaking pants and jackets and sweaters and blouses and leaving them in a mound in the middle of the bedroom floor. Vicky began to cry.

"You're acting crazy."

"It's here somewhere, I'm certain," he said, proceeding to his own wardrobe but carefully replacing the clothes after searching his pockets. Vicky made no attempt to stop him; it would have done no good anyway. He was on a furious tear, and it was better for him to vent his rage on her clothing than on her person. She pressed her palms and fingertips to her swollen stomach, massaging it to keep herself calm, remembering the cramps she had felt when she'd lost the first baby and determined not to let her emotions get out of hand.

He did not, of course, produce the wallet. When he collapsed on the edge of the bed, panting, Vicky got up and methodically began picking up her things, folding them, and replacing them in her drawers. The air was poisoned with animosity.

Finally Jeffrey said, "I won't live with somebody who hates my daughter."

"I don't hate her at all. She's troubled and you refuse to face it."

"You don't understand her."

"You don't understand yourself. Maybe you're jealous of the baby, too, and that's why you can't understand Daria's jealousy. She's afraid it's going to take you away from her, and you're afraid it's going to take me away from you."

"That's bullshit," he snapped, but Vicky could see him reflecting on it as he fumed. "I can't live like this anymore."

"What do you propose? You want to return to Amanda? *She* loves Daria! *She* understands you. Oh, does she ever understand you!"

"I sometimes think I should never—"

"Please don't say it," Vicky cried, pressing her hands harder to her tummy. "I'll never forgive you if you finish that sentence."

He seemed to hover over a brink, debating with himself about leaping into the abyss. Her penetrating stare informed him in no certain terms that if he leaped he took the marriage with him. He held his tongue, except for a kind of groaning sigh, and began going around the room picking up the scattered articles and putting them back.

But the damage had been done by his merely uttering the thought, and as she went through the agonizing tedium of calling the credit card company and department stores, her bank and the Motor Vehicle Bureau the next morning, she fought back tears so bitter that had she let them go she might never have stopped crying. After all they had been through together, to think that Jeffrey regretted everything left her unutterably depressed.

But wait—didn't she have regrets of her own? Hadn't she had trepidations about getting involved with a married man? And hadn't she wished at least a dozen times that she'd listened to her conscience and spurned him? She was more in love with Jeffrey than ever before, but at times like this, when Amanda's hand reached across the city and clutched her marriage by the throat, didn't Vicky, too, think it might have been better if Jeffrey had never left his first wife?

These reflections lifted Vicky's spirits somewhat. She was equally responsible for the state of her relationship with Jeffrey; she could by no means blame him entirely. And that meant she was equally responsible with him for restoring injured feelings. She phoned him at the office.

"How are you?"

"Depressed," he said.

"Me too. Darling, I'm sorry."

"Me too. I didn't mean—"

"It's all right," she murmured.

"No, it's not. We're expecting a baby. We can't tear each other up like we did last night."

"I know."

"I've been thinking about Daria, and, well, maybe you're right. It's very hard to face, but maybe you're right. About her and about me, the way I coddle her. I'm willing to admit she might have taken your wallet."

Vicky bit her lip. "Oh Jeffrey, I don't know whether to laugh or cry. It must be terribly painful for you."

"I'm all right. Have you made your calls?"

"Yes. It's the biggest drag of all time." She hesitated, then spoke the little lie she had prepared. "You know, when I got the *Times* Sunday morning, maybe I did bring my wallet. It's possible I could have left it at the newsstand.

Now there was a pause at the other end of the line. "Thank you. Now I know how much you love me."

Vicky's mood was lightened for the rest of the day, but one dark cloud continued to hover over her. If Daria had indeed taken her wallet, it would come into Amanda's possession. There was nothing that Amanda could do with the canceled cards, but the idea that Amanda even had them filled Vicky with unspeakable revulsion and fear, as if a witch had been given a hank of her hair with which to invoke a spell or curse. Who knew what mischief Amanda could make with those things?

Jeffrey brought her a new wallet as a peace offering that evening. Then they made love. It was getting harder and harder to find a comfortable postion. They ended up on their sides in what Jeffrey called their V formation. The larger the tummy got, the wider the angle of the V would have to be, until it reached ninety degrees, he joked. Afterward Jeffrey fell asleep, and Vicky was just drifting off herself when she sat up with a start. She remembered another item in the wallet, one that could be put to devastating use in Amanda's hands.

In one of the compartments was her obstetrician's card. It had, of course, his name, address, and phone number. With it, Amanda could learn at which hospital

201

Vicky was going to have her baby, and even approximately when.

She got out of bed and paced the living room, thinking through the implications. What was to stop Amanda from gaining access to the obstetrical floor while Vicky was in labor? Or from posing as a relative and visiting the maternity wing—even the baby nursery itself? Cold fear took hold of Vicky as she thought of Amanda prowling those corridors, looking at the cards on the bassinets, searching for the one that said "Keating." Perhaps she could don a uniform or an orderly's gown and find a way to get to the baby?

Vicky had had many paranoid fantasies since Amanda came into her life, but now that she was pregnant the fantasies had doubled in intensity. Tonight they redoubled, driving her into a frenzy of worry and wild thoughts. Should she switch hospitals? Change doctors? Find a midwife and have the baby at home? The sense of violation she felt knowing that Amanda might be able to prey on her or her baby at their moment of utmost vulnerability left Vicky quivering with outrage and loathing. How desperately she wanted to waken Jeffrey and tell him, but after the awful convulsion of their fight she didn't dare provoke another quarrel. This was one problem she was going to have to solve strictly on her own.

She leafed through a magazine just to distract her attention and calm herself so that she could go back to the bedroom and get some sleep. It had the desired effect, as she realized that there was no genuine evidence that Daria had taken the wallet, or, if she had, that she'd given it to her mother, or, if Amanda had it, that she would do anything with its contents. Vicky decided it would avail her nothing to fret herself sick, so she would simply watch and wait to see whether Amanda sent her some sort of signal, tried to buy something with one of the credit cards or to pose as Vicky.

It was not long before Vicky got the signal.

Her regular appointment with her obstetrician was the following Tuesday. In the third trimester of her pregnancy he'd suggested she visit him every other week. A little before two-thirty she arrived, waving familiarly at Andrea, the nurse at the desk. Andrea looked at her peculiarly, ran her finger down her appointment calendar, looked up again and said, "Are you sure you're supposed to be here, Mrs. Keating?"

"Of course. I have an appointment. Every other Tuesday at two-thirty."

"I know, but you changed your appointment to Friday, remember? I have it written down here. You called yesterday morning."

"I did? No, I don't think I did." Vicky walked to the desk and looked over Andrea's shoulder at the calendar. Her name was crossed out for today and penned in on the line for Friday at four P.M. "It must be an error," Vicky said. "I never called."

"Well, then, somebody must have telephoned in your name," the nurse said, not wanting to contradict Vicky but not prepared to back down, either.

"Yes," Vicky said, "somebody must have." She felt a charge of cold fear in the pit of her stomach. "I'll come back Friday."

"I feel terrible," Andrea said. "I can squeeze you in now if you want to wait a half hour."

"No, I'll come back." She went to the door, dazed. Then she turned around. "Don't let anybody change my appointment except me, okay?"

"Sure. How will I know it's you?"

"Uh, I'll give you a code word. I'll say my middle name, Sarah."

"A code word, Sarah," Andrea said, looking strangely at Vicky.

"Someone's been playing practical jokes on me lately," Vicky explained.

"Weird," said Andrea.

When Vicky got home she went directly to the kitchen, opened a drawer, removed a small sharp paring knife, and put it in her handbag, first wrapping the blade in a piece of paper towel so that it wouldn't damage the bag or cut her accidentally when she reached into it. She practiced removing the knife quickly and brandishing it. She did not feel foolish.

The last six weeks of Vicky's pregnancy mingled anticipation and fear in a combination she thought must be unique. Physically she felt fine. Her weight gain had followed the prescribed graph perfectly, and both her own and the baby's functions were normal. She had no worries about the delivery itself. She'd taken an exercise class and felt strong and ready for the test.

All this was counterbalanced by an irrational nervousness bordering on panic. The dreams that had begun soon after she became pregnant had gotten worse, more sharply focused, except for the face of her assailant, who always was shrouded in haze or wore a mask or scarf. But the locale, the actual street on which Vicky was assaulted, was always the same one, and each time she dreamed about it she noticed another detail, wares in the windows, gold-leaf printing on the doors, birdlime on the awnings, cracks in the sidewalk. When she shopped or strolled she studied the surroundings carefully, expecting one day to find a perfect match between the template of her nightmares and the reality of the street. Awaking from such dreams, trembling and sweating profusely and panting, she rehearsed in her mind how she would fend off an attacker, and in the morning she would open her purse and check the knife she kept at the ready there.

And then there were Daria's visits. In the weeks following the theft of her wallet Daria was a model child during her midweek and weekend visits, open and affectionate, cooperative and polite. Vicky hoped against hope that Daria had turned the corner, that perhaps the act of taking Vicky's property and Jeffrey's phone call that night had chastened her and forced her to come to terms with her hostility to Vicky, to her father's remarriage, to the forthcoming baby. But something about Daria's behavior didn't ring true to Vicky, and with each visit she became more convinced that it was a performance—a first-rate performance, but a performance nevertheless. She knew that Jeffrey did not see it, but she knew better than to express her suspicion to him. He spoke glowingly on several occasions about the change in Daria and how it indicated that she had made an important adjustment. Only Vicky observed the subtle telltale signs, the cold glint in Daria's eyes, the faint patronizing tone in her voice, the ambiguous smile that played on her lips when she thought no one noticed. Vicky concluded that Daria had not changed;

she'd merely gone deeper underground because she'd almost been caught red-handed.

Just what the child could or might do Vicky didn't know, but Vicky always kept her ears cocked at night on the occasions of Daria's visits, and her constant vigilance, combined with the exhaustion from poor sleep, made Vicky apprehensive and irritable. As the weeks progressed her paranoia grew, extending beyond Amanda and Daria to Jeffrey himself. Not that she thought of him as an active conspirator; rather, by his passivity and good-natured skepticism, he was an element that could not be relied on to take action in Vicky's defense if something did happen. Whereas ordinarily she might have been able to share her obsessive fantasies with him and get his reassurances, she bottled them up, and that only intensified them and added to her nervousness and frustration. She began to dread the possibility that she would not be in control during delivery, and something awful would happen while she was helpless.

She tried to daydream like an ordinary mother-to-be but could never get past the labor room, could never imagine herself in the picture of the mother on whose breast the newborn is being laid. Then, one cool afternoon early in November as she stopped in front of a park to watch the children, she understood why she was blocked. It was because Daria had said she didn't want a brother, and deep down Vicky wanted a little boy. Every time she tried to fantasize having that boy child, the memory of Daria's vow of implacable hatred intruded, obliterating the pleasure of anticipation and leaving a void.

The delivery of her baby became an obsessive challenge, a high wall which, once scaled, would afford a vista of boundless joy. But first the wall had to be scaled.

It happened on Thanksgiving.

For some weeks she'd been experiencing the practice contractions known as Braxton-Hicks, a hardening of the uterus that lasted for half a minute or so, like the clenching and relaxing of a fist. She'd been waiting for them to regularize, and on the Wednesday night before Thanksgiving they did. Not intensely, not grindingly, but regularly, and with growing force. It was two weeks before Vicky's due date.

They had decided against traveling up to Connecticut to spend the holiday with her parents, and Vicky had overruled dinner at a restaurant. In the end she roasted a pullet at home; if she couldn't eat dinner, at least Jeffrey would. She remembered Thanksgiving of the previous year when Jeffrey took her to that quaint inn on their honeymoon, which they shared with Amanda's ghost. Now, as Jeffrey ate his chicken and she swallowed a mouthful of cherry Jell-O as they waited for the next contraction, Vicky wondered whether Amanda would preside over the birth of this child as she'd presided somehow over every other important event in Vicky's life since meeting Jeffrey.

A contraction took place and Jeffrey looked at his watch. "Twenty-five minutes."

"Did you call the doctor?"

"Uh-huh. He's having Thanksgiving dinner in Westchester, but he's ready to hop in the car as soon as we send up the flare."

He refilled his plate, taking another leg and some rice and gravy. He ate with more zest than she'd seen in months. Worry had kept him lean; supporting two households, fretting about Daria, providing for a new baby, keeping his business running, had taken a toll. His hair had wisps of gray at the sideburns and his eyes had lost some of the prankish sparkle that had so endeared him to her at the beginning. But this evening he was relaxed, happy, more jovial than she'd seen him in a long time. "I'm glad to see you eating so well," she said.

"I'm not the one having the baby," he grinned as he gnawed on the drumstick.

"I can't believe I am. I can't relate this incredibly awkward lump in my tummy to anything human."

"That's not uncommon."

She looked up at him. "I forgot you've been through it before."

He shrugged. "It's in all the pregnancy books."

Vicky's mood darkened. "I've been meaning to ask you. What hospital was Daria delivered in?"

Jeffrey opened his mouth to answer, then hesitated,

206

squinting at her. "This is going to be one of those trap questions."

"What do you mean?"

"You know what I mean."

"No, honest. I was just curious."

He looked distrustfully at her. "Lenox Hill."

She prodded his wrist with her spoon. "You're lying," she laughed. "I can always tell when you're lying."

He reddened.

"Was it Mount Sinai?"

He buried his mouth in his chicken leg and made a muffled sound.

"It was Mount Sinai, wasn't it?"

He swallowed his food. "What are you going to do, cancel your delivery just because it's taking place at the same hospital as Amanda's was?"

"Don't be..." She gritted her teeth as the next contraction swelled like a large wave that never seemed to break. "...silly." She panted. "Time?"

"Ten minutes."

"Ten? You're sure?"

He tapped his watch. "The big hand is on the three. Last time it was on the one." He looked up at her and frowned. "What's that look in your eyes?"

"Nothing."

"It's not nothing. I've seen that look in your eyes. You're thinking about Amanda. Goddammit, I *knew* that question was a trap! Didn't I tell you folks that question was a trap? You certainly did tell us, Jeffrey." He looked at her: "Tell me what's upsetting you."

"You're not just going to make fun of it?"

"No, I'm not. I'm not going to make fun of it because I'm going to get too pissed off to make fun of it."

"You don't even know what I'm thinking."

"Yes, I do. You're thinking the experience is going to be spoiled because Amanda was there before you. Which is about the most childish thing I've ever heard."

"That's not what I'm thinking."

"Well, you better tell me what it is."

She pushed away from the table and slowly, unsteadily, got to her feet. Jeffrey jumped up and steadied her, helping her to the couch. "I'd better call the doctor. Do you have your things packed?"

207

She looked up at him, puffing from the exertion. "I'm not going."

He tilted his head as if she'd just addressed him in Swahili. "You're not going where?"

"I'm not going to the hospital," Vicky declared.

"I see," he said ironically. "You've decided you're not going to have a baby after all. You realized just in time that we can't afford it and there'll be no place to put it."

"No. I've simply decided to have the baby here."

He gaped. "I know I'm dreaming and I'm going to wake up any second. You're going to have the baby here. In this sterile, fully equipped, up-to-date medical environment staffed with the finest obstetrical personnel money can buy. Come on, Vicky, don't go lunatic on me. Having a baby is hard enough without a straitjacket."

"I don't want to go to the hospital. I want to have my baby here." She tensed and her jaw went rigid as another contraction knotted her insides. She fixed her eyes on a focal point across the room, a copy of a volume of Pushkin's poems, and breathed steadily and deliberately as she'd been taught. The wave subsided and she looked at Jeffrey, who looked at his watch. "Ten minutes," he said. He sat down beside her. "Please tell me, explain it to me so I can help you. If there's really a good reason we'll have the baby here, okay? I'll boil water and send our charwoman on the cow to fetch the midwife, is that a deal?"

"Don't make fun of me. You're supposed to be supportive at a time like this."

"I'm not going to support behavior that jeopardizes your health, my baby's safety, or my own sanity, so you'd better start talking, honey, because if I don't have a good answer by the next contraction I'm slinging you over my shoulder, all hundred forty pounds of you—"

"A hundred thirty-eight," she corrected.

"—and hauling you bodily to Mount Sinai." He looked at his watch. "I figure you have eight and a half minutes."

"All right, I'll tell you," she said. "I've decided I will not expose myself or the baby to any danger."

"Danger? From what? From the finest obstetrical

unit in the city? From a doctor so well reputed he can get away with charging eighteen hundred and fifty dollars for a delivery? From—ah, from Amanda, right? You're afraid she's going to do something. You're afraid she's going to come to the hospital, isn't that it?"

Hearing it articulated by someone else made it sound so foolish she reddened.

Jeffrey's jaw tightened in anger, but after wrestling with it for a few moments he gained control over himself. He spoke quietly. "Tell me exactly what you're afraid of. First of all, unless she's clairvoyant she can't even know you're in labor."

"Sometimes she *is* clairvoyant. You've said so yourself." She regarded him stonily. "Admit it."

"All right, even granting she is, or has bribed the admitting office to phone her when you show up at the hospital, or has bugged your underpants and is monitoring your contractions, how do you think she's going to gain admittance to the obstetrical floor?"

"They have piles of gowns in the fathers' waiting room. She could put one on and sneak in."

"You've really thought this one through, haven't you?" Jeffrey said. He was laughing, but Victoria braced herself for sarcasm. "I mean, this is no impromptu fantasy, this is one elaborate, exquisitely detailed, major league paranoid delusion. This is the Moby Dick of anxiety attacks. You've been working on this one for a long time. Okay, she's on the obstetrical floor, now what happens? She goes into the labor room, where I'm sitting with you, and picks the one minute when I chance to doze off?"

"No, she waits till I'm in the delivery room—"

"Where her head of flaming red hair goes totally unnoticed."

"It's under a cap," Vicky explained. "And she's wearing a mask." She laughed involuntarily. "It sounds stupid when I say it aloud."

"Do you really think so? Gee, I'm beginning to enjoy it. Don't leave me hanging—what happens next?"

"She has a sharp instrument, a scalpel..." Vicky shuddered. "Don't tease me anymore, Jeffrey. It's really horrible."

209

"I'm just trying to get the fantasy out on the table where you can see how foolish it is."

Vicky's face transformed into a mask of volcanic anger. "Don't tell me how foolish it is. You don't know the half of what's been going on with that woman—what it was like in the department store or the restaurant or when she chased me at the concert. I haven't even told you about Willa. You wouldn't call me foolish if you knew about that!"

"Willa? What has Willa got to do with Amanda?"

"She...they..." Vicky swallowed hard and decided not to tell him about her suspicion that Amanda had willed Willa's death. She could see he thought Vicky was on the edge of a breakdown. If she had told him about Willa it would be the last straw, and God only knew what he would do. Maybe he *would* have her put in a straitjacket. And listening to herself talk, she wondered if she deserved to be placed in one. "Never mind."

Jeffrey looked at his watch. A contraction was due any moment now. "Look," he said, with the calm of a policeman reasoning with a potential suicide, "we know Amanda is out of town for Thanksgiving. So even if there was some magical way she could find out you're in labor, she could hardly be expected to fly into town on her broomstick to preside over your delivery."

"How do you know she's out of town?"

"Because she told me she was going to be, remember? I asked to take Daria to the Macy's parade and Amanda said they were going out of town. Suppose I call there? Will that satisfy you?"

"It would help."

Jeffrey went to the telephone, picked up the receiver, and punched seven numbers with a carefree smile on his face. He carried the phone to the couch and handed the receiver to Vicky. "Here. Listen."

Vicky listened to the comforting signal of a ringing telephone. Though she might not be absolutely reassured if no one picked it up, she would certainly breathe much easier. She heard it ring twice, three times, and was about to hang up when there was a voice at the other end of the line. Vicky felt the blood draining out of her face. She handed the phone to Jeffrey, who had overheard Amanda's honeyed "Hello." His mouth had dropped open.

"Uh, hello," he croaked. "Amanda? What are you doing home?"

Vicky felt the next contraction coming on. She tried to do her breathing but she was so shocked she lost the rhythm and doubled up in wracking pain as Jeffrey stammered into the telephone. "Oh no," he was saying, "I just took a chance you might be home. I wanted to, uh, wish Daria a happy Thanksgiving. Put her on, please?"

The contraction was so intense Vicky thought she would pass out. She knew that the wave of terror that had swept over her when Amanda answered had added to the pain. What was worse, she knew that this was going to be a night of fear, just as she'd predicted. The fear was going to make her 'abor infinitely harder than it would have been. She started to cry, muffling her sobs with a pillow as Jeffrey, as nonchalantly as he could, spoke to Daria.

He hung up at last. "She says her plans fell through at the last moment," he said. He looked genuinely shaken.

"You tipped her off."

"Huh?"

"Your call tipped her off. She knew you had no valid reason to phone there. She's figured out you called to see if she was in town or not. She's figured out I'd be nervous about her when I went into labor, and I'd want to know if she was in town. She's figured out I'm in labor, Jeffrey." Vicky started to shake wildly. Jeffrey threw a comforter around her shoulders and held her.

"That's preposterous, Vicky; this has gone too far. Either you get hold of yourself or I'm going to call Bellevue Hospital and you'll have the baby in the goddam psychiatric ward."

Vicky shivered uncontrollably as Jeffrey continued. "Are you listening to me? We're going to call the doctor, and we're going to meet him at Mount Sinai, and I'm going to stick by your side every moment. I'll even ask them to let me in the delivery room. You said they let fathers in, didn't you?"

"Only if they've taken Lamaze classes," Vicky said through clenched teeth.

"I'll ask for special dispensation," he said.

"If you could that would be great. Please try." She started to rise from the couch. Suddenly she was aware of something warm and wet trickling down her legs. "Oh my God. My water's broken," she cried.

Jeffrey ran back to the phone to call the doctor as Vicky shuffled miserably into the bedroom. Her suitcase was packed except for her toothbrush and a few other toilet articles, which she now assembled, interrupted by another contraction which she managed to handle better than the last. She looked at the clock on her night table. Only five minutes had passed since the convulsive contraction she'd had on the couch. She finished packing, closed the suitcase, and waddled to the bedroom door. Jeffrey was still on the phone. Vicky held up five fingers. Jeffrey nodded and said, "Five minutes apart. Right. Me panic? Doctor, you're talking to Mr. Cool himself. See you in a half hour."

Jeffrey put down the phone, stared at Vicky, and said, "Mr. Cool is going to faint."

"You'd better not. I'm going to need you tonight like I've never needed you before."

"I'll be there."

"Every minute. You promised."

"Every minute." He went to the intercom and called down to the doorman to get a cab.

"You have the gown on backwards, Mr. Keating," the nurse said. "It opens at the back, not the front." She pulled the drab green gown off Jeffrey by the sleeves, turned it around, put it on him and tied it at the back.

He modeled it for Vicky, pirouetting like a mannequin at a fashion show. "Now all I need to be a real doctor is the Mercedes."

Vicky smiled feebly through the pain of the latest contraction. They'd been coming three minutes apart for two hours, but they'd intensified the last fifteen minutes. The doctor had examined her and found her fully effaced and dilated, and declared they were ready. Jeffrey had asked to be allowed in the delivery room.

The doctor said, "I think the regulations here require you to have passed the Lamaze course."

"Oh, uh, I did, I did. I just left my certificate at home in all the excitement."

The doctor looked at Jeffrey with penetrating eyes. "Just stay out of everybody's way and coach Victoria to do her breathing."

"Absolutely," Jeffrey grinned.

Vicky sighed with relief to know Jeffrey would be with her for the delivery, but even as they wheeled her down the corridor from the labor room to the delivery room, she studied the faces of nurses and orderlies, certain that Amanda would materialize. Jeffrey, knowing what was running through his wife's mind, kept up a running patter of humorous remarks. "This one is definitely her," he said, indicating an old, fat, gray-haired nurse in a tight blue uniform. "Note how cunningly Amanda has stuffed pillows into her purloined size eighteen uniform and dyed her hair." As they turned a corner he gestured at a doctor lounging outside the nurses' station. "Amazing what a good makeup artist can do to make a thirty-five-year-old redheaded woman look like a sixty-year-old bald man."

"Jeffrey, kindly shut up." Vicky moaned. But his banter had done the trick. As the gurney passed through the doors of the delivery room, Vicky had relaxed and finally decided she was out of danger.

That's when she saw the figure in the delivery room, a tall woman in nurse's uniform and cap, standing at a table with her back turned to them. She was preparing a variety of gleaming instruments, holding a scalpel up to the light. A fugitive wisp of hair trailed down her neck. It was auburn. Jeffrey had noticed her, too, and had stepped in front of the gurney, stationing himself at Vicky's feet.

The figure turned suddenly. Vicky screamed and Jeffrey braced himself.

Then he laughed.

The Puerto Rican nurse with the auburn hair looked at both of them as though they were crazy.

Vicky gave birth to a boy at four minutes after two Friday morning. He weighed seven pounds five ounces and was twenty-one inches long. He had thin, dark hair, flat ears, and a pretty mouth. They named him Justin Dwight Keating, for his two grandfathers. He had a nice disposition, easy and undemanding. Jeffrey was ecstatic, phoning friends and family and business associates to boast about his little boy. Vicky had elected to breast-feed her child, and tired and sore as she was from her ordeal, she longed for the nurses to bring her baby out to her and place it on her breast, and when they did she rhapsodized to Jeffrey over every finger and toe, every contour and wrinkle, every gesture. Flowers, plants, cards, and telegrams arrived at her bedside in a seemingly endless parade, evoking the realization for both of them that they had more well-wishing friends and acquaintances than they'd thought. It helped to place in perspective the one element marring the perfection of these days.

"Have you told Daria?" Vicky asked him late Saturday afternoon after the baby had been taken back to the nursery.

"Uh, no." Jeffrey fluttered around her bed, straightening up the covers and table littered with gift wrap, cards, telegrams, paper cups, flower petals, hospital literature, and newspapers.

"Don't you think you should?"

"I'll get around to it."

She laid a hand on his arm. "Why don't you call her now?"

He shrugged, reaching into his pocket for some change.

"The phone's right here, dummy," she said, gesturing at the bedside telephone. She shared a large room with three other new mothers, separated by curtains. "You don't want to speak to her, do you?"

He shrugged again. The gesture represented anything but indifference. He looked away from her.

"What are you afraid of?" After a pause she answered her own question. "Same thing I'm afraid of."

"She said she didn't want a brother."

"Children say all sorts of things, most of which should be ignored. I guarantee, three hours after she lays eyes on him she'll be as much in love with him as we are."

Vicky gestured at the telephone again, and Jeffrey

picked it up and dialed. Vicky wished she truly felt as confident as she tried to convey to Jeffrey, but from the moment the doctor had announced the baby's sex in the delivery room she had experienced pangs of apprehension and regret, strictly because of Daria's avowed enmity against a boy. It had spoiled what should have been one of the sublime moments in her life, and it continued to spoil things every time she looked at the baby and anticipated the struggle she was going to have with Daria's feelings. And with Jeffrey's—for now he would be divided.

"It's Jeffrey. Let me speak to Daria," he said into the phone. "What do you mean, she doesn't want to talk to me?" Vicky saw his face darken as he listened. She pushed herself up in bed, leaning forward, straining to hear. "Well," he finally said, "your spy system is as effective as ever." He cupped the phone and said to Vicky, "She knows everything, the size, the weight, the sex, the time."

Vicky bit her fingers and started worrying about her milk. If she got unduly upset her milk might not come in. She understood why Jeffrey would have preferred to call from a pay phone; he wanted to spare her this. Now it was too late, and her uneasiness mounted as she gleaned snatches of conversation. "You did? When? Well, it's the last time you'll ever see him.... Screw you. Let me speak to Daria.... I don't give a shit, she's got to speak to me. What have you said to her?... Don't play innocent with me, you bitch." His fingers were white from gripping the phone. His jaw muscles were taut and strained, his eyes narrowed with smoldering anger. Vicky tugged frantically on his sleeve, begging for an explanation, but he stared into space waiting for Daria to be brought to the telephone. At last he tilted his head; someone was talking to him. "I'll get you for this, Amanda," he said between clenched teeth, slamming the phone back on its cradle.

He sat down on the edge of the bed, staring out the window overlooking the almost barren trees of Central Park silhouetted in the November dusk. His body trembled. He panted so hard Vicky thought he was going to start sobbing. "I don't believe her," Jeffrey said. "She's making it all up."

215

"What did she say?"

"She said Daria doesn't want to visit us anymore. God knows what she's told the child. 'Your daddy and Vicky have a baby of their own; they don't need you anymore.' I've got to speak to her. I'll go to school Monday morning. Amanda's gone too far this time. I won't allow this."

"What did you mean when you said, 'It's the last time you'll ever see him'?"

When he looked at Vicky there were tears in his eyes. "She says she—"

"Came here? Oh God! Of all the things I feared, this was the worst."

"She's lying, Vicky. She just said it to upset you. I've been here almost every minute of every visiting hour."

"Almost every one. But not every one."

"She knew you were due around now. We may even have tipped her off that you were in labor when we phoned Thursday evening. She called the hospital, found out all the details. Anyone can. Then she made up the story about coming here, just because she knew how much it would upset us."

The explanation made sense, but just enough sense, as all explanations of Amanda's behavior did, for which reason Vicky breathed only a little easier. But deep inside she did not trust logical explanations.

She put up a brave front for Jeffrey. "If she lied about that, then she's lying about Daria, too. Daria loves you and she's going to love the baby. Go to see her at school Monday, you'll find out for yourself," she said to Jeffrey. But she was no more convinced about that than she was about anything else. Vicky had observed Daria's hostility. No doubt her mother was exploiting and aggravating it, but its source was Daria's own heart. There were rough times ahead. "I told you I'd help you, and I will," she said, pulling Jeffrey close and kissing him. "We won't let her do this to us."

But when Jeffrey visited the hospital Monday he had the stunned look of a disaster victim. He had learned the truth. Daria didn't want to come to their house, wanted nothing to do with the baby. They were plunged into a turmoil of mixed emotions that lasted weeks,

216

ranging from the joy of bringing the baby home from the hospital to the strain of adjusting to him, to the anger and despair over Daria. In one way it was fortunate Daria was not visiting with them in her present emotional state, as it might well have rent their household asunder. But her sullen absence caused almost as much upset, with Jeffrey perpetually fretting about her, visiting her several mornings a week before school began for hasty and frustrating attempts at reconciliation, and spending hours on phone calls with friends and even a child psychologist, trying to find a way to break through his daughter's armor.

That's when Amanda, with her superb timing, emerged from the curtain of lofty indifference behind which she'd been hiding, and attacked. She began to call nightly, complaining that Jeffrey was not living up to his agreement to take Daria every other weekend and one day midweek every week. This was severely inconveniencing Amanda, who looked forward to relief from parental cares on those days but was now saddled with the child, and a sulky child at that. Jeffrey was outraged. How was he supposed to take Daria if Daria didn't want to come? And what was Amanda doing to *make* Daria come? Was Amanda making it any easier? Was she helping the child cope with her fears, or was she inflaming them instead? Amanda said it was his problem; no one asked him to leave his wife and daughter for another woman, marry her, and have a baby with her. Amanda's bitterness over the divorce, which had been quiescent during Vicky's pregnancy, now flared higher and brighter than ever. She insisted Jeffrey send Daria to a psychotherapist. She called Vicky, too, snapping off cruel taunts before Vicky could hang up the phone.

Finally, after two harrowing weeks, Daria herself called, saying, "Mommy says you should take me for the weekend."

"Only if you want to come," he replied with a show of indifference.

"I'll come," she said.

"Don't do me any favors," Jeffrey replied. Vicky, sitting beside him as he talked on the phone, silently applauded.

"No, I'll come," she repeated.

"Small triumphs," he said to Vicky. "Her mother's probably got a hot date lined up for the weekend and wants to get rid of Daria anyway. But I'll take what I can get."

"It's a start," Vicky said. "Now, play with the baby. He hasn't seen you smile in two weeks."

Small triumphs indeed. Daria spent the entire weekend with them pretending the baby did not exist. This was no small accomplishment considering the modest dimensions of the apartment, made even smaller by the presence of a bassinet, a small chest of drawers, and a changing table in the bedroom, requiring anyone wishing to traverse the room to clamber over the bed; and considering the constant activity attending the feeding, changing, pampering, playing with, and caring for the newborn. But ignore it all she did, scarcely glancing at the baby from Saturday morning to Sunday evening.

Jeffrey and Vicky had decided to play it cool, going about their business, paying neither more nor less attention to Daria than before, and not asking her to so much as acknowledge the existence of the baby. Daria played with her own baby, the babushka doll she had had for as long as Vicky could remember. The doll, with its hollow skirt and empty, unpleasant eyes, had become somewhat threadbare and greasy, but although the child had many other dolls, Sasha was the only one with which she seemed to have an emotional relationship. Sometimes Vicky overheard Daria talking to it, and over the next few months as Daria conducted what Jeffrey termed her "cold war" against her father and stepmother, Vicky was to observe remarkable parallels between Justin's development and Sasha's; Sasha's, that is, as played by Daria babbling in a corner with her doll and toys. When Justin was constipated, Sasha was constipated, when Justin began to smile, Sasha began to smile; when Justin spat up, Sasha spat up.

To Vicky it was a fascinating process; for Jeffrey it was frustrating to see his older child reject his younger one so thoroughly. Vicky said, "She isn't rejecting him, just rejecting her attachment to him."

"What makes you think she's attached to him?"

"She shows it through the doll."

218

"Why can't she show it directly?"

"Because she's afraid her mother will punish her."

"For what? For liking a two-month-old baby?"

"This two-month-old baby represents everything Amanda hates and fears, and Daria knows it. But there's something else at work in your daughter's mixed-up head that makes me hopeful."

"And what's that?" Jeffrey asked.

"It's that Daria needs your love and approval. That's threatened by her rotten behavior. To win you back, sooner or later she has to salute this flag," she said, holding Justin up. "Are you Mommy's little flag?" She gave him a gentle shake and he made a gurgling coo.

"And when do you think that blessed event will happen?"

"Be patient, darling. Her mother is feeding her the party propaganda line with a ladle. Daria must know it can't all be true, but she's frightened. Just love her. Take her to lunch and a movie the next weekend we have her."

"Won't that just reinforce her belief that she's still my only child?"

"It might. But it might also help her realize that she's still very special to you. Sooner or later she'll send us a sign that she's ready to surrender."

"When do you think that will be?"

Vicky had the answer ready at hand. "When Justin and that hideous doll come together in her mind."

One snowy Sunday afternoon in February they were all at home. Jeffrey was in the bedroom watching a hockey game on television. Justin lolled in the small portable crib which had replaced the bassinet he'd been in. Daria sat Indian-style on the floor beside the bed, drawing with a box of forty-eight colored pens she'd gotten for Christmas. Vicky sat in the living room reading the Sunday *Times*.

Jeffrey got up during a commercial break and joined Vicky in the living room. Vicky had circled ads for some two-bedroom apartments they ought to look at, and Jeffrey glanced at them over her shoulder. The rents were impossible—they started around two thousand dollars a month for anything in a decent building. At those

219

prices, there was no point in even looking. It was all very depressing.

Suddenly Vicky put her hand on Jeffrey's arm. "Listen."

Jeffrey cocked his ear and heard Daria twittering in the voice she used to pretend she was her doll Sasha. That was not unusual. But what was, was the hiccuping giggle of Justin. It sounded as if they were talking to each other. Jeffrey pulled Vicky to her feet and they tiptoed to the bedroom and looked in. Daria held her doll over the crib, and Sasha was introducing herself to Justin. "I'm in the third grade," the doll said. "My homeroom teacher is Mrs. Platt, and she's very strict." Justin looked wide-eyed at the doll, his arms and legs pumping in the air in an expression of excitement. He uttered squeals of delight.

Vicky backed away and led Jeffrey back into the living room. "You were right," Jeffrey said. The relief on his face was almost euphoric.

After a half hour Justin's attention flagged and he began to get whiny. Jeffrey and Vicky went back into the bedroom, where Daria stood at the foot of the crib holding her doll up as before. "I see you've been speaking to your brother," Jeffrey said.

"No, I haven't. Sasha has, and I'm very upset with her," she said, giving the doll a hard shake. "And he's not my brother, he's my half-brother."

Jeffrey's smile froze on his face. "Who told you that?"

"My mommy."

"Well, young lady, in this household you'll call him your brother."

"I won't call him anything at all," she said, stamping her feet and returning to her pens.

This strange behavior continued for several months. Whenever she visited them she would conduct a warm, loving relationship with Justin—but only through her surrogate, the doll. Daria herself still denied Justin's existence totally. Apparently this phenomenon carried over to Daria's other home and her school. At a parent-teacher meeting, Daria's teacher, Mrs. Platt, told Jeffrey that Daria had said on several occasions that she didn't have a brother. Amanda called constantly, throwing "schizophrenic" and other psychiatric jargon at Jeffrey and pressing him to send the child to a psychiatrist, even threatening to hire lawyers to compel him. Jeffrey argued that it was Amanda who was forcing Daria to deny Justin's existence, and as soon as she herself accepted the baby's existence, Daria's dividedness would quickly heal. Scarcely a night went by that Jeffrey and Amanda did not fight about Daria, and Amanda stepped up her campaign by mailing them clippings from magazines, photocopies of articles from medical journals, and even whole books. Amanda even called Jeffrey's parents in California to complain about their son's treatment of their granddaughter and the damage it was causing. The subject had begun to consume all of Amanda's energies, it seemed. After one ugly fight, when Amanda screamed into the telephone so loudly that Jeffrey had to take the phone away from his ear, and Vicky could hear the woman's shrieking rants halfway across the living room, Jeffrey hung up and said, "I think she's gone off the deep end."

Then Vicky's phone rang. She picked it up and listened. "Your child is going to die," Amanda said. Her voice was icy calm, in astonishing contrast to the insane shrieking of a moment earlier. Vicky hung up at once, but she stood stunned. She had never heard such menace in Amanda's voice in all the time she'd known her. Vicky started to quake and rushed to the crib to hoist her little boy into her arms and clutch him tightly to her breast. "Never," she whispered into the tiny ear. "Never."

Vicky now went uneasily into the streets with the carriage or stroller, permitting herself not a moment's relaxation. Her recurring dream had returned after a few months' hiatus, only this time the assassin's face was more distinct than ever before; it mingled Amanda, Daria, and sometimes even Sasha the doll. The figure would jump out at her as she strolled on some recognizable avenue with Justin, window-shopping and reveling in the spring sunshine.

Spring was in the air, but all of the joy she associated with it was dampened by Amanda's continual harassment and Daria's continued hostility, which had forced Jeffrey to contemplate psychotherapy for the child. Even

221

Vicky, who'd been opposed to it, now wondered if it might not be the best thing. She couldn't live this way much longer.

She looked forward to the spring school vacation, when Amanda was to take Daria to Palm Beach to visit some friends. Almost three weeks without the two of them—it was unbearably sweet to contemplate.

On the Sunday evening before they were to go, Daria came into the bedroom where Vicky and Jeffrey were packing her things for the return trip to her mother's house. Daria spied the Russian doll on the bed beside her suitcase. "Sasha wants to stay with Justin while I'm gone," she announced.

Vicky and Jeffrey exchanged glances.

"She wants to make sure he's all right while I'm away," Daria explained.

"Certainly," Vicky said, picking up the doll and placing it on top of the dresser adjacent to the baby's crib, so that it looked protectively down on him. "How's this?"

"Fine," said Daria. She looked very grown-up in a plaid jumper and blouse, her auburn tresses tricked out in green ribbons. She was going to be a beauty, Vicky observed. She was also, she added silently, going to be a very screwed-up kid if she didn't break her mother's grip. As Daria gazed at the doll perched over Justin's crib, a strange expression came over her face. Vicky recalled where she'd seen it; it was the smile she'd seen on Daria's face in the yearbook—dark and frightening, disturbing.

The smile fled as quickly as it had come. Daria dutifully kissed her stepmother, then left with her father for the return trip to her mother's house. Vicky turned the baby onto his stomach for his early evening catnap, then lay down on the couch to read. She dozed for a while, then woke with a start. Suddenly she sensed something was very wrong. It was past the time when Justin was supposed to waken. Usually he announced his waking with a bleat, or she could hear the rattles suspended over his crib as he stirred or batted them with his hands and feet. But this time she heard nothing. All at once a cold fear settled into her stomach. He wasn't breathing anymore. He wasn't moving anymore. She ran into the bedroom, and as she entered she heard a muffled sound coming from the crib, very faint. She felt reassured.

But then when she reached the side of the crib and peered in she felt the whole world fall away. She cried out; her voice was loud and terrfied to her own ears.

Then she bent down and grabbed the thing off Justin's head. He was on his back, his head wedged in a corner of his crib, both his arms caught under the plastic bumpers that were supposed to protect the baby from hitting his head on the wood of the crib, and over his face the thing was smothering him. His skin had turned red from the effort of breathing. She scooped him into her arms and clutched him tightly, crying with gladness and relief, then stared down at the floor at the thing she had tossed away, the thing that had been robbing her child of the air he breathed. It was Daria's Russian doll, its red lips grinning maniacally, its skirts pulled up and its empty bottom gaping at her.

Chapter Ten

VICKY THREW THE DOLL down the incinerator. And with the destruction of that disturbing effigy she felt cleansed. The house had been purged of one more sign of Amanda's influence. And now, oddly, Daria began to come around.

The change did not happen overnight. In fact, at first it was barely perceptible. Jeffrey, furious over the doll incident, became less tolerant and indulgent of his daughter. Daria seemed to benefit from his strictness and became more responsive, shyly but definitely indicating she might want to be part of the family after all.

With no doll to intercede for her anymore in her dealings with the baby, Daria began to talk to Justin directly. Encouraged by his smiles, she would play with him for increasingly longer periods of time. They did not leave her alone with the baby, for they were still spooked by what had happened. And so they observed how she had begun to interact with her brother. It gave them hope. It was a slow start but it was better than what they had before.

It also became apparent that Daria was not getting along with her mother. Possibly because she enjoyed her visits to her father's home more, possibly because of the baby, Daria reported increasingly often that her mother yelled at her, bullied her, and picked quarrels with her. They were soon to find out that Daria's reports of her mother's problems were all true, and worse than they knew. One evening, as Jeffrey was returning Daria to her mother's house, Amanda called Vicky on the phone and poured out a torrent of disgusting abuse that bordered on the ravings of a maniac. Fifteen minutes later Jeffrey returned, shaking his head. "I saw her," he said. "I hadn't seen her when I picked up Daria yesterday, but I saw her now. I need a drink."

"What is it? What's happened?"

"She's become...old. She didn't have any makeup on and I could see the lines on her face. Her hair wasn't brushed and she smelled like she'd been drinking. Her eyes were red and she looked like a witch." He stared, stunned, then plopped into his armchair. "Daria was afraid to go home. I was afraid to leave her there. Amanda looks like she's falling apart. I'm really worried."

"About Amanda?"

"About Daria. I don't care what happens to Amanda, but Daria living in that house...I don't know."

Vicky stood over him, holding Justin. "She phoned me while you were gone. She was vile."

"I can believe it." He twisted in his chair and looked at her. "If she touches a hair on my daughter's head I'm going to sue for custody."

"Yes," Vicky said, remembering the sad look in Daria's eyes when they'd said good-bye. "I'll help you."

An important change had come over Jeffrey, too. The birth of his son had made him fiercely protective of Vicky, Justin, and Daria. He had at last broken the spell that Amanda seemed to have had over him, and though he fell far short of sharing Vicky's conviction that Amanda had supernatural powers, he was able to deal much more objectively with Amanda than ever before. He recognized her as his enemy, and was prepared to do whatever he had to do to fend her off.

And fend her off he did. She called him at both home and office shrieking hysterically about anything and everything, ranging from the appearance of cockroaches on her kitchen floor to Daria's betrayal in daring to speak of her baby brother in her mother's presence. Jeffrey handled her coolly, calmly, and even with humor, as if realizing that she was losing her potency. It was this loss that only seemed to raise her hysteria to even higher pitches.

"I think she's going to blow," Jeffrey said after one such fulmination.

"What can we do?" Vicky asked.

"I've spoken to a lawyer. He's developing a strategy for a custody suit."

"That would really make her blow," Vicky said, laughing nervously.

"I have to rescue Daria; that's all I know or care about."

"Yes," said Vicky. But it was not all she knew or cared about. She was concerned about Amanda's death threat. She hadn't told Jeffrey about it because it would worry him sick, and because she feared that repeating it would make it seem even more real and powerful. And what could he do about it? He couldn't stay home with Vicky and Justin to watch over them every minute of every day. But every minute of every day Vicky listened for sounds outside her apartment, answered telephone calls with an arm cocked to slam the receiver down, went on shopping errands with the intense alertness of a mother bear, her arms and legs tensed for ambush, her eyes scanning buildings and corners for the glimpse of something out of place, of someone watching and waiting to spring. In her purse she still carried the paring knife wrapped in paper towels.

It was a crazy way to live, like a commando with a baby carriage, and she realized she must look slightly ridiculous crouched on the edge of a park bench ready to spring like a tiger for the throat of any suspected aggressor. But she preferred that to the alternative of being caught unaware. Amanda's threats over the last few weeks had grown wilder and crazier, and, like a balloon, seemed to become emptier the more they swelled. But how could anyone be sure?

Spring ripened into a glorious May, and with Justin approaching his sixth month Vicky felt she could range further and freer with him on the random carriage trips they took around their neighborhood. On one particularly beautiful afternoon she settled him inside his carriage, tucking into his arms his favorite stuffed toy, a small dog, that he liked to hug and babble to. Dressed in a blue knit sweater with a hood, he looked, Vicky observed, like one of the cute Seven Dwarfs. She beamed with pride at what she had produced. Jeffrey had accused her of being "infernally smug" about Justin, but hastened to add she had every right to be. Justin was a glorious baby, with a ready, if gummy, smile for everybody.

She checked the canvas bag in which she carried all his things—his spare diapers and disposable wipes, his tube of ointment, his bottle of apple juice, a few rattles, and a few first-aid items. She placed the bag on the rack under the carriage. Then she checked her own handbag—the wallet, the keys, the tissues, the sunglasses, the writing pad and pen, and the knife were all there.

As she propelled the carriage toward Columbus Avenue she was greeted by the familiar faces of elderly men and women who waggled their fingers at Justin and remarked on his good looks and how much he'd grown. Vicky swelled with pride, and felt a deep kinship with humanity, wondering how anybody could know anything about life who did not have a child.

The neighborhood seemed to be improving every spring. There were so many new shops on Broadway that enhanced the respectability of the avenue. In fact, some of the stores carried surprisingly fashionable and expensive merchandise, far beyond her means. She had to settle for longing, lingering looks into shop windows that proved frustrating, both because she could never afford the clothes and because she was no longer sure what looked good on her. Her breasts were still large from feeding and would remain so until Justin was completely weaned. Her waist was almost the same dimension as it had been before she'd gotten pregnant, but her tummy was soft and needed firming up. There was a layer of flesh on her hips that she was told would disappear when she discontinued breast-feeding but was unsightly now, at least to Vicky. Jeffrey liked the hour-glass touches that postpregnancy had bestowed on his wife's body. But bathing suit time was coming and Vicky fretted. She sighed and pushed on, informing Justin that she was going to start a rigorous exercise program tomorrow morning absolutely.

She crossed Broadway, heading east, and found herself on Columbus Avenue before a row of shops that looked irresistibly inviting—a big airy flower store, a housewares shop, a chic shoe store, a Korean fruit market, a bakery, a chocolate and sweets shop, and...a new place she had not seen before but which seemed to have replaced a leather goods store that had been there last fall. Vicky strolled closer. It was a children's clothing store, and in the window were displayed some of the most enchanting imported things she had ever seen—knit sweaters and pants in a rainbow of colors, bright quilts, mohair carriage blankets, handmade wooden toys—a veritable treasure trove right in her neighborhood. She searched the window for something she could get for Justin and noted a few items, particularly a pair of overalls with bunny appliques on them. She raised her eyes from the wicker carriage displayed in the center of the window, filled with tiny hats and bathing suits, to look for the shop name.

Her heart thudded, and her gorge rose in her throat.

The shop's awning, closed flat against the top of the window, was black. Painted on it was the store's name: "Rosemary's Baby."

She stared in disbelief, her eyes starting to swim with dizziness. This was the store of her dreams. The new shop, the black awning, the half-perceived name, and in her dreams death was supposed to strike on this very spot. She tensed and pulled the carriage around, wanting to get as far from the store as she could in order to regain her composure. But her way was blocked.

Planted before the carriage, eyes red and insane, was Amanda. Jeffrey had described her as old, and now Vicky could see for herself what he'd meant. There were creases in her face and throat and crow's feet in the corners of her eyes. Her hair had lost its luster, and rouge had been applied heavily to her cheeks. Her lips were cracked, and those eyes...

Vicky felt faint, but she fought back the weakness and looked around the avenue for someone to help. There was a couple across the street, and a girl jogged past, wearing headphones.

"So this is Daria's little baby brother," Amanda said.

"Go away. Don't you touch him," Vicky said, pulling the carriage back.

"But I wouldn't hurt him. I love babies. I had one myself, remember, until you took her away from me. First you took my husband, now you take my daughter."

"I haven't taken anybody away from you. Get out of here." Vicky remembered the knife in her purse, but she hadn't counted on the fact that she would need to keep both hands on the handle of the carriage. She let go for a second with her right hand to swipe at Amanda, who was leaning over the carriage. She was dressed, as usual, exquisitely, in plum-colored silk pants with matching tunic and jacket. On her feet were gold sandals with flat heels. On her wrists were gold bangles and an expensive-looking watch. But the face! The juices seemed to have been drained from it.

Amanda threw her head back and laughed. Vicky was chilled to the bone—that terrible laugh. She looked down at Justin. His eyes were closed, fluttering in the first stage of sleep. As fast as lightning she calculated her options. Should she push Amanda out of the way with the carriage? Or pull the carriage back and run? Should she scream? Oh, that would be just what Amanda wanted; she'd play innocent and Vicky would make an utter fool of herself. Perhaps she could quickly lift Justin out of the carriage and run into the shop, or some other shop. But she had *always* run away, and the time had come to stop running and confront Amanda squarely and bravely.

"I only want to look," Amanda said, closing in again.

"No," Vicky answered with a backhand swipe that just grazed Amanda's chin.

"But you see *my* child, and now you're taking her away from me. Why can't I see yours?"

"What are you talking about?"

"My lawyer told me. Jeffrey is going to sue me for custody of Daria."

"Daria doesn't want to live with you anymore. She's afraid of you."

"You made her afraid of me."

"You're crazy." Vicky tightened her grip on the carriage as Amanda grasped the front end and pulled.

"Your baby for mine," Amanda said, eyes now blazing with torment.

"You'll never take my baby, never!" Vicky pulled the carriage back, then shoved it hard, straight into Amanda's stomach. Vicky heard her breath go out with a gasp. Amanda staggered backward, clutching her groin, but recovered and closed in again with remarkable agility and speed. She shoved Vicky and grasped the handle of the carriage.

"Help," Vicky cried, "someone help me, please!"

But no one came forward. The sidewalk seemed empty of people, just as it did in the dreams she had had. It was Vicky and Amanda, wrestling for control of the carriage.

Amanda fought with superhuman strength. Vicky never knew a woman could be so strong. Amanda pried at Vicky's fingers while Vicky clutched the handle with all her might. She kicked Amanda, hitting her ankles again and again, but Amanda in her fury seemed impervious to pain.

Suddenly she chopped Vicky's hands and struck her with an elbow in the solar plexus. Vicky felt the air rushing out of her lungs and her fingers loosening on the carriage. Her knees buckled and Amanda struck her in the face. Vicky felt blackness falling like a heavy drape over her face, heard herself groaning, helplessly watched her fingers releasing the carriage handle. She crumpled to the sidewalk on her bad ankle.

Amanda gained control of the carriage and started to push it up the avenue. "My baby!" Vicky screamed, fighting the pain and darkness back and staggering to her feet. She noticed people across the avenue watching, but no one came forward; everyone seemed frozen in a tableau of wonder or indifference. She managed to grab Amanda's jacket. Amanda jerked to a halt, whirled, and struck Vicky in the face with her hand and wrist. The sharp edges of Amanda's jewelry gashed Vicky's cheek and lip, and she tasted blood in her mouth. She reeled with the force of the blow, her skull ringing and her vision blurring. But she came to again, determined to protect her baby if she had to die in the act.

She could hear Amanda shrieking madly, like some cackling witch out of a children's play, and watched with sickening horror as Amanda swiveled the carriage toward the avenue and pushed it with all her strength straight out over the curb and directly into the oncoming traffic rushing down Columbus Avenue.

Vicky screamed, and it was as if there were a thousand screams echoing among the buildings.

Morty Stein had just dropped his fare off at Seventy-seventh and Columbus Avenue, a well-dressed guy meeting someone for a drink at one of the numerous restaurants that had sprung up on Columbus. Not a bad tip—a dollar over the three seventy-five on the meter for an easy ride out of midtown. Stein reached for the volume knob of the radio he kept on the seat beside him and turned it up louder so he could hear the Mets game in progress, three-one Phillies in the eighth. He looked at his watch when he pulled up to the light at Seventy-second. Almost four and time to go back to the garage; he wondered if he should look for one more fare and risk getting taken out of his way home to Queens, or just be content with what he'd earned and flip the "Off Duty" switch and call it a day. As the light changed he accelerated, timing his speed to coordinate with the stoplights staggered at twenty three miles an hour on the southbound one-way avenue. His eyes darted from side to side, more from habit than from genuine interest in picking up customers. Jeannie had said his eyes darted even when they went for a ride in the country; at a Bar Mitzvah recently she told the table his eyes darted when they were in bed together.

About two blocks down Columbus on the right side he saw a woman loaded with shopping bags waving at him. Ordinarily he'd have kept within the speed limit, but this clown in a Checker next to him honked his horn acknowledging her signal. Stein cursed; the son-ofabitch was going to steal his customer. He glanced to see the complexion of the driver. It wouldn't be a white guy, he was sure, unless it was one of those college kids who hadn't learned the ethics and manners of the cab-driving fraternity. He accelerated to keep himself between the marauding taxi and his customer, cursing the blacks, the Puerto Ricans, the Greeks, and even, God forgive him, the Israelis who had muscled in on what had used to be the exclusive province of the old guard with manners and principles.

It all happened so fast.

On his right, on the curb side, he saw two women fighting over a baby carriage, a redhead and a dark-haired woman. On top of everything else, the ball game

(Mookie Wilson had just hit a double with one man on) and the race to the customer, Stein still had time to try to figure out who the women were and why they were fighting. The older one, the redhead, might be the other one's mother and they were quarreling over who was going to push the carriage, maybe?

What he had not calculated was that the redhead would push the carriage into Columbus Avenue.

Morty Stein had seen a lot of things in his day. He had seen a girl go down on a man in broad daylight in the back of his taxi; he had seen a three-hundred-fifty-pound black woman hold a BB gun to his head and demand his money; he had seen a lot of other things you just wouldn't believe. But this he had never seen before, and he had no time to reflect on a course of action. He just acted, and only later on, as he related the story again and again, first to the police and doctors, then to his wife, then to his buddies at the garage and at the cafeteria where all the cabbies met for lunch, was he able to rationalize the decisions he had made instinctively, his muscles responding to impulses dispatched by a brain computing faster than he could articulate.

The carriage bounded off the curb and rolled in front of his taxi, maybe ten yards in front of him. He had no room to maneuver to his left because that sonofabitchin' fare-stealing foreigner was blocking him. So it was either hit the carriage or swerve to his right; hitting the brakes would not do it, that was easy to see. For that split second he wondered if there was actually a baby in the carriage; no woman in her right mind would do that to a baby. Maybe the carriage was empty, or just had a doll or groceries in it, in which case he wouldn't mind running into it, doing a little damage to his grille.

But if he swerved right? Someone was going to get hurt, maybe killed, and it might be himself. One of the women had started to run after the carriage, and both she and the other one were in his path. Behind them was a storefront. By aiming for the gap between the parked car where these two women were, he might hit one or both and rack up the cab and the store but at least he'd save the baby. He swerved right, closing his eyes, not wanting to see. He felt the front wheels jolt

232

over the curb. His head struck the roof of the cab and he felt himself losing consciousness. He still had the presence of mind to hit his brake pedal, but it wouldn't stop him from colliding with the store. Just before he did he felt the whump of his grille striking something soft and yielding, and an instant before he rammed through the window of Rosemary's Baby, he knew that one of the women had not gotten out of his way in time. The last thing he remembered was the shattering of glass and wondering whether the sonofabitch in that other taxi had seen the baby carriage in time...

Fifteen minutes later another taxi sped uptown, occupied by Jeffrey Keating. Tears streaming down from his eyes, he sat huddled miserably in the backseat, trembling uncontrollably and hyperventilating with panic. The world seemed unreal to him, as in a dream, and even the words of the driver trying to be helpful were muffled and seemed to be slowed down.

The phone call that had precipitated the cab ride had come only a minute or two earlier. "Uh, Mr. Keating, this is Detective Sergeant Antonelli of the Twentieth Precinct. Uh, there's been an accident involving, um, your...w—wife..."

Jeffrey jumped to his feet, eyes wide, the phone pressed desperately to his ear. "An accident? What kind of accident?"

"A vehicular accident sir. A taxi ran up on the curb and, uh, struck your wife; at least we have tentative I.D. it was your wife. Victoria Keating?"

"This is a joke," Jeffrey shouted, knowing it was not but needing to deny what he had just heard.

"No joke, Mr. Keating. I wish it were."

"What...what happened to her? Is she all right?"

"She was taken to Roosevelt Hospital; she's in surgery now. Mr. Keating, I'd be lying if I told you it looked good for her."

"Oh God. Where should I go?" Jeffrey had felt a wall of fear fall on him. He felt his knees buckle and it was all he could do to remain conscious.

"You'd better come to the hospital, emergency entrance. Ask for me, Detective Sergeant Antonelli."

"But my wife—"

"There's nothing you can do about her, Mr. Keating. It's in the hands of the surgeons. I want to talk to you about some aspects...your child..."

"My child? My son?"

"Yes, he's all right, we're pretty sure. Doctors are checking him now, but there doesn't seem—"

"I'll be right there." Jeffrey hung up, grabbed his jacket from the coat closet in the reception room, blurted an explanation to his secretary, and raced on wobbly legs out of his building and into the street, looking for a taxi.

The ride seemed to take forever, and when they encountered heavy crosstown traffic Jeffrey wanted to jump out of the cab and run the rest of the way, but his driver restrained him. "What's the point, mister? In your condition you'll just exhaust or hurt yourself and you'll be no good for anything. See, we're almost to Sixth Avenue. Once we clear it we're home free."

Two minutes later the cab burst out of the traffic jam and raced the rest of the way. Jeffrey threw a ten-dollar bill at the driver and charged out of the taxi, leaving the door open. His legs were like rubber as he burst into the emergency entrance. "Detective Sergeant Antonelli," he said to the nurse inside the admitting office window, "where can I find him?"

"I think he's in the waiting room. It's through there," she pointed.

He took one step then turned back. "My wife..."

"Who's your wife!"

"Mrs. Keating?"

"Which Mrs. Keating?"

"Which...why, Victoria Keating."

"Which Victoria Keating?" The nurse was serious. "We got two Victoria Keatings."

"Huh? What?" Jeffrey leaned so far through the window that half his torso was inside the admitting office.

"Mister, there's a lot of confusion; you better talk to the detective."

Jeffrey shook his head, trying to clear it. He was certain this was a nightmare from which he would soon awaken, his arms around Vicky's back, holding her tightly to him in the warmth of their bed, while Justin slept placidly in his crib. But until then he had to abide

234

by the nightmare's scenario, and so he rushed through the swinging doors indicated by the nurse's index finger. There was a gloomy waiting room on the other side, with rows of plastic seats populated by people with bandages, crutches, and canes, surrounded by their families, children irreverently playing tag until their parents' names were called. Jeffrey scanned the room, picking out the stocky man with a plaid sports jacket and porkpie hat standing with his back to Jeffrey talking to a woman. Jeffrey picked his way through the crowd and tapped the man on the back. "Detective Antonelli?"

He turned, and when he did the face of the woman he'd been talking to was revealed to Jeffrey.

"Vicky!"

She was in his arms in moments, sobs quaking her entire body, her nails digging deep into Jeffrey's back. He held her tightly, comforting her with endearments while the detective launched a long, apologetic explanation of which Jeffrey managed to catch only every third word "... wallet identified her as Victoria Keating ... didn't connect the baby with your wife ... called you back but you were gone ... can't tell you how sorry ..."

Jeffrey gently released Vicky so he could examine her. Her left cheek had a purple bruise that would undoubtedly turn darker, and her lip was cut. There were scrapes on her elbows and hands and knees, some of which had been bandaged, the superficial ones merely dabbed with a tincture. Her dress was torn in several places.

"The baby ... ?" Jeffrey asked.

"Pediatrician's examining him," the detective eagerly volunteered, "but he doesn't appear to have been injured."

Jeffrey took a deep breath. "Okay, now would someone please tell me what the hell happened?"

"Amanda," Vicky said, tears springing into her eyes again.

"Amanda? What has Amanda got to do with this?"

Vicky collapsed into a chair, crying as she relived her experience. Detective Antonelli stepped forward in her place and said, "Your ex-wife apparently accosted

235

your current, uh, your second wife while she was strolling with her baby. Uh, your baby. A quarrel ensued, and according to your wife, your ex-wife wrested the carriage from your wife's hands and pushed it into oncoming traffic on Columbus Avenue."

"Jesus. Amanda!"

"A taxi bearing down on the carriage swerved to avoid it and ran up on the curb. It narrowly missed your wife, who had started to run into the street to rescue the carriage. But it struck your ex-wife and carried her through the plate-glass window of a shop."

Jeffrey buried his face in his hands. "God."

"The driver suffered a concussion and broken ribs," the detective explained, looking at his feet.

"And my—my ex-wife?"

He shook his head. "We were told just before you got here. She, uh, didn't make it. The broken glass cut her almost completely in half."

Jeffrey sat down heavily in the seat beside Vicky. "I never thought she would go that far," he said.

"I couldn't make you believe me," Vicky said. "She was deranged, Jeffrey. Homicidal. But you didn't want to see it."

Jeffrey sat silently, head hung. Then he looked up with a start. "Daria!"

"We've ascertained she's with a housekeeper, Mr. Keating. She doesn't know about Mrs. Keating; that is, the other Mrs. Keating."

"I'll have to go there. Oh God, when I think of having to tell her!"

Jeffrey sat silently, absorbing the myriad changes in his life that this event portended. Then his head snapped up and he glared at the detective. "You told me on the phone it was my wife."

"I know," the detective answered sheepishly. "By the time we got the whole thing untangled you'd already left your office. You see, Mr. Keating, your ex-wife was carrying your wife's—uh, this lady's here—identification in her purse. When the police officer reaching the scene opened your ex-wife's purse, he found your wife's wallet. He went through the papers and there was a card saying to notify you in case of—"

"The *wallet!*" Jeffrey gasped.

"We don't know why she was carrying it, Mr. Keating. Like your wife says, the woman sounds like she may have been deranged. We're going to have to investigate this matter further, I'm afraid."

"Certainly."

"See, we didn't know that your wife, *this* wife, was the mother of the child. She was hysterical when we arrived, and the police officer on the scene thought she was a baby-sitter or something. I'm really sorrier'n hell to have alarmed you, Mr. Keating."

"It's all right. I—"

Before he could say anything more, Vicky had jumped to her feet and raced over to a young woman in a white gown carrying Justin, who was grinning and cooing. "My baby," she cried as she took him into her arms. Jeffrey was not far behind her. Together they embraced their son and said a silent prayer to God that he was all right, that they were, all of them, all right.

"I have to get Daria," Jeffrey said after the paperwork was finished and there were no more questions from the detectives. Vicky held Justin tightly. He was fussing hungrily now, completely oblivious to the events that his existence had unleashed that day. "I'll send you home with Justin if you like," Jeffrey said.

"No," Vicky said. "I'll go with you. We'll do this as a family."

"As a family," Jeffrey said. "Right, Justin?"

Justin reached up and wrapped his fingers around Jeffrey's index finger as Jeffrey hailed a cab and instructed the driver to take them to the home of his late ex-wife.

A FAREWELL TO FRANCE
Noel Barber

"Exciting...suspenseful...Masterful Storytelling"
Washington Post

As war gathered to destroy their world, they
promised to love each other forever, though
their families were forced to become enemies.
He was the French-American heir to the famous
champagne vineyards of Chateau Douzy. She
was the breathtakingly sensuous daughter of
Italian aristocracy. Caught in the onslaught
of war's intrigues and horrors, they were
separated by the sacrifices demanded of them
by family and nation. Yet they were bound
across time and tragedy by a pledge sworn in
the passion of young love, when a beautiful
world seemed theirs forever.

"Involving and realistic...A journey to which
it's hard to say farewell...The backdrop of
World War II adds excitement and suspense."
Detroit News

An **AVON** Paperback   68064-5/$3.95

Three Novels from the
New York Times Bestselling Author

NEAL TRAVIS

CASTLES
79913-8/$3.50

A woman reaches for her dream when she joins Castles, a prestigious international real estate firm, and follows her driving passion for life from the playgrounds of Bel Air to the boardrooms of New York. On her way to the top, there would be men who tried to keep her down, but one man would make her see the beautiful, extraordinary woman she was.

PALACES
84517-2/$3.95

The dazzling, sexy novel of a woman's struggle to the heights in Hollywood. Caught up in the fast international scene that burns up talent and dreams, fighting against power moguls who have the leverage to crush, she achieves fame and fortune at Palace Productions. Yet amid all the glamour and excitement in the celluloid world of illusions, she almost loses the one man whose love is real.

And now...

MANSIONS
88419-4/$3.95

Her first success—as Washington's top TV news personality—was ruined by a lover's betrayal. As wife to the young scion of the Mansion media empire, she was expected to sacrifice herself and her dreams. But if the world gave her a woman's choice between love and success, she gave the world a woman's triumph. And when real success was hers, she was ready for the man who offered her love.

AVON PAPERBACKS